YOUNG ROCHESTER
A Novel Based on his Life During the Years
1664–1667

YOUNG ROCHESTER

*A Novel Based on his Life
During the Years 1664–1667*

Joan Ruddle

The Book Guild Ltd
Sussex, England

Although based on historical fact, this is a fictionalised
biography of John Wilmot, Earl of Rochester

The Book Guild Ltd.
25 High Street,
Lewes, Sussex

First published 1996
© Joan Ruddle, 1996
Set in Times
Typesetting by Poole Typesetting (Wessex) Ltd.
Bournemouth, Dorset.
Printed in Great Britain by
Bookcraft (Bath) Ltd.

A catalogue record for this book is
available from the British Library

ISBN 1 85776 077 8

CONTENTS

An imaginative reconstruction of his first years at court, and of his service at sea, during the years 1664–1667.

To Pamela, and all my friends in the Royal Borough of Kingston Upon Thames, and the London Borough of Richmond.

ACKNOWLEDGEMENTS

My thanks are due to the staff of the British Library, the Public Record Office, the National Maritime Museum and the County Record Offices of Buckinghamshire, Somerset, Surrey and Greater London for their advice and assistance in tracing seventeenth century records and correspondence, and to my tutors at the City Literary Institute and at Adult Education Centres in Buckinghamshire, Oxfordshire and Greater London, for their help and encouragement over a period of many years.

Joan Ruddle

1

Abduction and Imprisonment

A coach swung out of Whitehall Gate and travelled in the direction of Charing Cross. It had gone scarcely three hundred yards when four horsemen galloped into the road.

'Hold, or I'll blow out your brains!'

Lord Hawley's coachman brought the horses to a shuddering halt. In the twilight of the May evening he saw that the men were masked and armed. Two of the assailants stationed themselves on either side of the coach shafts, pointing their pistols towards him, whilst a third went to the rear. The leader of the group swung lightly down from his saddle and wrenched open the coach door.

Lord Hawley, his face suffused with anger, glared at the intruder.

'God's wounds, are we to be challenged by rogues at the very entrance to the Palace? What are the times coming to? Well, scoundrel, is it my purse you are wanting?'

'No, my Lord, the fair jewel beside you.'

Lord Hawley frowned; the fellow's voice was cultivated. This was no common thief. He turned to his grand-daughter.

'Wench, do you know this fine fellow?'

'His voice is familiar.' Elizabeth looked closely at the masked man. Half-pleased, half-irritated, she recognised a large ruby ring on his left hand. 'What foolery is this, my Lord? Have you not business enough with the Maids of Honour, that you must come disturbing me upon my way home?'

The masked figure laughed, showing strong white teeth.

'Cool and unperturbed – as ever. I had entertained hope you might swoon when a masked man attempted rape.'

'Rape – ?' choked Elizabeth indignantly. 'You stupid play-acting fool!'

'Who is this damned fellow?' interrupted Lord Hawley impatiently.

''Tis my Lord Rochester, engaged upon another of his japes,' said Elizabeth scornfully, as a strong slender hand grasped her arm. The young man levelled his pistol at her grandfather.

'Lord Hawley, your charge is coming with me. Do not attempt to stop us, or I shall let this damned thing off – and perhaps send us all to kingdom come.'

He tightened his grasp upon Elizabeth's wrist. 'Come sweet Bess, we must away.'

'You must be out of your wits Sir,' said Elizabeth as she struggled to free herself from his hold.

'Neither mad, nor fooling.' He pulled her roughly towards him. 'I shall kill us all if you will not come with me.'

Elizabeth, astonished at the desperation of his tone, froze into immobility, unsure of how far the dangerous farce might go.

'Here, Will,' called Rochester to a burly figure who had appeared out of the shadows. Will seized Elizabeth, who offered no further resistance. She was carried swiftly across the road towards a waiting coach and unceremoniously deposited inside. Will slammed the door and climbed up next to the driver. Six horses were whipped up and the coach set off in the direction of Charing Cross.

Rochester bowed to Lord Hawley. 'I must apologise for my lack of ceremony. Do not fear for your grand-daughter, Sir. I have appointed two women to attend her.'

'You cursed young puppy...' spluttered the old man as the young Earl swung onto his horse and galloped off. 'You'll rue this day,' he roared as the other masked figures spurred after their leader. The hoof-beats died away, and all was silence again in the warm May night.

Ordering his coachman to turn back into the Palace, Lord Hawley made emphatic complaint to the King. Following the issue of a Proclamation, the processes of law were swiftly set in

2

motion. It called upon *all Sheriffs, Mayors, Officers of the Reeve, and other His Majesty's men and loving subjects to search for all persons who shall appear guilty of the high misdemeanour of abducting Mistress Elizabeth Mallet from the care of her guardians, and having found, to apprehend and detain them in safe custody until further order.*

* * *

John Wilmot, Earl of Rochester, looked around his sparsely furnished room in the Tower of London, and gloomily reflected upon the events of the past few days. He was in a damnable fix. Never, in all his eighteen years, had he succeeded in displeasing so many people at one time. He looked up at the small window, but it was set too high in the wall to afford him a view. He was lodged in the Bell Tower, and was enjoying accommodation reserved for prisoners of high rank. However, the appointments were far from luxurious. The adjoining room contained only a bed and a small cupboard, and the Tower, even at the end of May, was chillingly cold. He flung himself upon the only chair, and had no alternative but to ponder his folly.

The King was greatly angered. The heiress's relations were furious – breathing fire and brimstone, his Majesty had said – and his own were icily disapproving. God knows what Elizabeth thought, he mused.

John rose from his chair and paced restlessly about the room. A successful abduction would have made a dramatic beginning to their life together, but Elizabeth had been snatched from him in front of a crowd of grinning yokels before the adventure had even started. She had made it clear that he had placed her in a situation she found both farcical and humiliating.

'Fool,' she had hissed as he had surrendered his sword to Bevil Skelton, the Captain of the Guard, 'cannot you be consistent – even in villainy?'

But what could he have done? Skelton was a friend of his, and she wouldn't have wished him killed, would she? So now he was in the Tower – under the King's extreme displeasure. Would he ever see her, or the world, again?

He doubted whether he would ever unravel the mystery of her feelings. In spite of her scornful air, he was convinced that she loved him. Had he not, upon many an occasion, caught her observing him from beneath the thick fringe of her eyelashes? Her eyes were fascinating – brown with flecks of gold, and a hint of mischief in their depths...

He threw himself down into the chair again. Surely, he asked himself, she had found his company enjoyable? She had once told him that she preferred his conversation to that of any other man at court. Her rejection of his marriage proposal, a month ago, had amazed him. Had he been mistaken in thinking that he was favoured?

To be sure, her family had not welcomed his overtures. He had no estate, and no prospect of one, but he was sure that this objection would have weighed little with her. She had little respect for the opinion of her step-father, Sir John Warr, and her fortune was not in his control. Did she suspect the young earl of wanting her money, then? Her fortune was a great advantage, but it was her person which had attracted him.

He had discussed his courtship with three friends, Henry Sidney, Harry Savile and Harry Killigrew. They had all considered him justified in believing that the heiress loved him...

'She's never content but when she is talking of you, and then finds all the faults in you she can.' The sleepy blue eyes of Henry Sidney glinted with amusement. 'She reminds me of a lady who would always quarrel with me when I came to see her, but cried if I stayed away.'

'Buckhurst says women say "no" only to save their modesty,' put in Harry Killigrew, 'and despise us if we press them not further...'

'Or they think we lack vigour, or determination, or both,' added John. Suddenly a brilliant idea flashed in his mind: he would teach the jilt a lesson! He turned to his friends. 'Would you help me abduct her?'

The three had stared at him in amazement. Then Harry Savile declared that he, for one, would assist him with all the resources in his power. The others agreed it would be a capital jest, and plans were made for its speedy execution.

4

·The escapade had led to his present plight in the Tower, but luckily nothing was known of his friends' part in the affair: he had steadfastly refused to give the names of the other assailants of Lord Hawley's coach.

The King had promised that irate nobleman that all the rogues, rapists, and impertinent young puppies involved in the abduction would be brought to justice. His Majesty had therefore been considerably embarrassed by John's refusal to reveal the names of his associates. It was fortunate that they had dispersed at Knightsbridge. He and Will had been the only ones to be arrested later, at Uxbridge. Gill and Doll had been allowed to attend on Elizabeth until her friends arrived. Poor Will, what the devil had happened to him?

A cold draught blew under the cell door. John's feet were turning to lead. Their frozen state brought to mind his return from France a bare five months ago. He had ridden from Rye during a freezing night to deliver Madame's letter to the King. Fine powdery snow had scurried about him as he rode into Whitehall in the early hours of Christmas Day 1664. When he contrasted the warmth of his reception then with the reversal of his fortunes now, the memory seemed like a dream.

'The King rose at five,' Lord Manchester had told him. 'He is working in his laboratory, but he has consented to see you now.' Manchester, the elderly Court Chamberlain, was married to a woman in John's family, and felt it incumbent upon himself to promote the interest of his wife's younger relatives. Besides, one never knew when ambitious young men, who had the favour of Madame, the King's sister, might prove useful...

He escorted John through a seemingly endless succession of corridors, galleries, and reception rooms. Eventually they arrived at a small room on the park side of the palace.

Manchester knocked upon the door with his staff, and spoke in subdued tones to the servant who admitted them.

'Chiffinch, my Lord Rochester has a letter from the Duchess of Orleans which must be delivered into the King's own hands.'

Chiffinch turned an equivocal gaze in John's direction, shrugged, and disappeared into the adjoining chamber. John, a little puzzled at his cavalier reception, turned to Manchester in surprise, but the Court Chamberlain seemed unruffled by Chiffinch's lack of respect. John recalled, with some amusement, the affability of Manchester's address to the fellow. The plainly dressed servant was evidently a person of some importance.

Within a few minutes John was admitted to the King's laboratory. The book-lined room was crowded with benches, jars, tubs and chemical apparatus, but the apartment itself appeared empty.

A deep voice suddenly pierced the silence. 'I hear you come post haste from Paris, young man. What do their astronomers think of the new star?'

John, startled, jumped about him. His Majesty was raising himself from a telescope placed before a window within a curtained alcove. John fell to his knees as the King extended his hand.

'Faith, Johnny, enough of ceremony. Stand and let me look at you.'

John raised his eyes and found himself disconcerted at the depth of the King's gaze. Shrewd eyes took in every detail of his appearance, and a humorous smile played about Charles's mouth as he listened to the young man's replies.

'You arrive with the comet,' declared the King. An extraordinary long tailed star had appeared in the sky that December, and had set all London agog with speculation. The superstitious considered it a herald of great events, battles at sea, disasters on land – even, some opined, the appearance of Beelzebub himself.

'But it could not presage a more pleasant event than the arrival of the son of my old friend,' smiled Charles. 'Odsfish, child, but you have grown – and your conversation is greatly improved!' The King laughed, 'Faith, Johnny, when I first laid eyes upon you, you were suffering from a plethora of schoolmen, and an excess of petticoat government at home. You were a most accomplished young pedant, and could produce a Latin tag for every occasion.'

A little discomfited by the King's ironic teasing, John nevertheless managed to summon a diplomatic smile. 'God save your Majesty for delivering me from such a fate.'

Charles put an arm across John's shoulders. 'The dire fore-casts of your lady mother, concerning those "vile debauches" in Oxford, have not materialised, have they?'

'No,' laughed John, 'but the debauches amounted to no more than an occasional drink with the fellows after dark, and an experimental visit to Oxford Kate's.' He wrinkled his nose. 'Faugh, how she stank! I could no more have touched her than laid down in the kennel.'

Charles gave a slow smile. 'Young gallants like yourself have the pick of delicacies, and have no need of desperate remedies.'

John's colour heightened. He suspected he was being laughed at. 'Those who do must indeed deserve our compassion.'

The King laughed. 'Compassion is a quality well befitting Christian princes.'

John seized a good opening and ventured a request. 'Your Majesty has been most compassionate and generous – at least to me. May I hope that your generosity will afford me some employment in your service?'

Charles looked thoughtful. 'You are as yet too young for a post of importance, and you have no estate. You must marry with advantage. Will you leave this to my arrangement?'

John, aware that he had little fortune to look to in life, save that which came by the King's favour, nevertheless muttered that he could not marry without loving the lady in question.

Charles, noticing his hesitation, smiled kindly. 'There are many ladies at court, both rich and fair.'

'Wit and good nature are necessary too, Sir.'

Charles raised a brow. 'Wit and good nature together? One must not ask for too much in this world – but I have no doubt that one of our court beauties will persuade you to settle for something a little less than perfection.'

John grinned. 'I must indeed sound an ungrateful dog, but I am in no great hurry to assume the responsibilities of a married man.'

'Time and a woman will no doubt change your mind,' Charles replied. 'And I will make it my business to see that she is rich.'

Lost in these reminiscences, John was aroused abruptly from

his reverie by the sound of the postern gate being opened. The door creaked unmercifully, and he could hear the tramp of the guard's feet. There were shouts of salutation, but nothing could be seen from the high window of his room, even when he climbed onto his chair. Soon, however, the commotion died down; he was left again to silence – and the demon of regret.

Why had his hopes come to nothing? He had first seen Elizabeth in Charles's company. After supper one evening Charles had risen, saying, 'Come, Johnny, let us see if your bright eyes can persuade Mistress Stewart to show kindness to her unfortunate King.' Laughter had greeted the suggestion. Harry Savile, a great favourite with Charles in his times of relaxation, adopted a stolid stance and pompous expression. 'Your Majesty considers then that my Lord of Rochester is a fit and proper person for election to our Committee?'

'Aye,' quipped Charles, 'and I am relying upon you to instruct him in his duties.'

As they made their way along the Stone Gallery, John enquired of Savile, 'What is this Committee?'

'Why, the Committee of Getting Mrs Stewart for the King.'

John blinked. 'A committee of pandars?'

Harry laughed. 'The highest in the land are members: his Grace of Buckingham, my Lord Arlington, presbyterian Lord Ashley, and of course myself – the witty, the lively, the talented Mr Savile.'

Charles turned and addressed John. 'As that worthy has agreed to give of his services, it would be churlish of you to refuse yours.'

John nodded. 'I shall endeavour to outshine all previous members. What is to be my title? Pandar Extraordinary?'

The King frowned. 'Pandar? A cruel word, Johnny.'

'Ambassador to the Diet then? Your Majesty was pleased to appoint my father to the post, and he obtained £10,000 for his King's use from the stolid Germans!'

The King laughed as they entered Frances Stewart's apartments. They found her seated at a small table watching the magnificently dressed Duke of Buckingham build her a castle of cards. She was indeed a dazzling creature, brilliantly fair, with large blue eyes; but John's gaze was immediately taken by the girl at her side. A perfect foil for the looks of Frances, her dark brown hair curled luxuriantly around a vivid, intelligent face. The young man's gaze travelled over the rich curve of lace at her bodice. Her shape, full-formed and rounded, would have tempted St Anthony out of his cell.

Charles kissed the hand of Frances, retaining it as he gazed into the clear blue eyes.

Frances smiled. 'Your Majesty has not introduced me to his new companion.'

Charles, remembering John, effected a brief introduction, and then turned to the dark-haired girl. 'I see, Mistress Mallet, that you have your guitar. May we hear you sing?'

'Sire, your wish is my command.' She curtsied gracefully. The soft voice betrayed a hint of the west country in its tone. 'Shall I sing Lord Buckhurst's song?'

'Aye,' said the King. 'It suits well with your philosophy and with that of your friend here.' Charles turned to Frances, taking both her hands into his own.

Elizabeth exchanged a knowing glance with Frances and struck a few chords upon her guitar.

> *Oh my Saccharissa tell,*
> *How could nature take delight*
> *That a heart so hard should dwell*
> *In a frame so soft and white.*

The song, artfully rendered, told the sad tale of a shepherd aflame with passion for a nymph who bid him quench it in a brook. John admired Elizabeth's interpretation, but wondered idly how long it had taken Buckhurst to compose such an effete example of pastoral verse. There were middens and pig sties in the country, as well trees and purling streams.

The performance over, the King leaned forward and said to Elizabeth, 'I am relying on you to rid this young man of his objection to marriage.'

'Your Majesty should know better than to bring him to me,' Elizabeth replied, 'for you know I have no mind to marry and let an idle good-for-nothing fellow spend my money for me.'

'Ah,' said the King, 'my Lord Rochester is not idle; he is very studious and well-read. Also, he has travelled far, and is very entertaining. It is my wish you should become better acquainted.'

John bent over the young woman he found so disturbingly attractive. 'You are disinclined to relieve me of my objection to marriage, but you have freed me of at least one error.'

'Oh, what is that, I pray you?'

'That good voices and ill faces had been inseparable. I thought it but the privilege of angels to look fair and sing well.'

'How many more of these fine things can you say?'

'Very few, for you look so killingly that I am mute with wonder.'

Elizabeth looked at him coolly, although her heart beat faster. A magnificent young gallant stood before her, a fortune in French lace at his neck and wrists. His brilliant eyes regarded her with undisguised admiration, but they were a trifle too bold, and she bridled at the hint of mockery she detected in their depths.

'This will not give you the reputation of a wit with me. You travelling fellows live upon the stock you have got abroad, and to repeat with a good memory all that you have heard before is all the wit you have.'

The bold eyes had not wavered in their stare. 'You speak truly lady, but I crave your indulgence to be heard.'

Elizabeth warmed to her theme. 'It serves you for the first day or two, but like cormorants, when you have regorged what you have taken in, you are the leanest things in nature.'

John laughed, bending his head nearer. 'Then, Madam, make use of me but two or three days together and I will impart all that I have learned extraordinary in foreign climes.'

'La, Sir, all?'

'Yes, and of the one thing which I never saw till I came home.'

'And what is that?'

'That I never saw a lady of better voice, or better wit in the whole of the countries of France or Italy, and that if I should not declare myself passionately in love with you, I should have less wit than you think I have.'

10

Elizabeth smiled serenely. 'A very plain and pithy declaration, Sir. I imagine you have been travelling in Spain or some of the hot countries where men come to the point immediately.'

John, feeling at a loss, nevertheless contrived to arrange his face with a superior smile. He took a deep breath and rejoined, 'I fear you have been reared in the cold countries where they swear, promise, contract, but never enjoy, and where...' his face lit up, 'pretty women know how to keep men talking, thus deferring greater intimacies.'

Elizabeth looked at him severely, then caught the mischief in his eye and laughed unaffectedly. 'Now that we have proved what clever creatures we are, could we not talk sensibly?'

'What conversation would you consider sensible? Perhaps you would be good enough to provide me with an example?'

Tiring of his verbal fencing, Elizabeth murmured, 'Talk of something which interests you. If I know nothing of it, I may learn from your conversation.'

John fell silent, trying to gauge her sincerity. 'I fear you might find it tedious.'

'Perhaps, but I should come to know you better. We might even like each other in the end...' Elizabeth's voice tailed off. She dropped her eyes. John bent closer, enjoying a feeling of greater intimacy, when a cry from Frances Stewart distracted them. The Duke of Buckingham's castle of cards had come fluttering to the ground.

'Oh, Georgie, build it up again, please,' cooed Frances, flinging her arms around Buckingham's neck.

'What will you give me if I do' teased the Duke.

'I will give you an excessively kind ... kiss,' she ended lamely.

Laughter, squeals, horseplay and witticisms followed. John leaned over Elizabeth, murmuring, 'Would it be sensible to ask why a monarch, shrewd, experienced, sagacious, should be enslaved by a silly chit of a girl?'

Elizabeth shrugged. 'Who can account for the vagaries of love?' She turned grave eyes up to him. 'But you underestimate Frances. Beneath that childishness there is canny Scots good sense. She knows what she seeks from life, a good marriage, and she is not to be tricked into an undesirable situation.'

11

'And what is that undesirable situation?'

'She has no ambition to be the King's whore.'

John raised a brow. 'How original. Most of the impecunious maids about court would count their honour well lost in the King's bed.' He bent his head closer. 'But I know of an even greater miracle.'

'What is that, I beseech you?'

'A woman who speaks well of her female friends.' John smiled into the brown eyes before him. 'Would you be as good a friend to a man?'

'Did he deserve it, yes. But men are conceited, impatient creatures and care not to squander time upon tame pleasures.'

'I must confess to my share of male conceit, but claim I have patience when working for something I value.' Catching hold of her hand, he held it firmly. 'Will you try my patience – and my friendship?'

'Perhaps both.' She smiled as she raised her gold-brown eyes to his glittering grey ones and they laughed together.

Surely, John mused, those eyes had regarded him with genuine liking at that time? He strode restlessly about the cell. Of course, she was an accomplished flirt. What woman in Charles's court was not? But she had more wit and good sense than was usually found in young women of seventeen...

Recollection of past happiness became too painful, and John was relieved when he heard the sound of a key being turned in the lock. He turned towards the door.

'Sir Walter St John to see you, my Lord.' The jailer admitted a soberly dressed man of some forty years of age. John, on seeing his visitor, dropped to his knees. It was his mother's much-respected brother.

'I hope, nephew, that I find you in a suitably contrite frame of mind.'

'Who could fail to be contrite, kicking one's heels in the Tower, and with hunger gnawing at one's belly. I have had no food for twenty-four hours.'

Sir Walter looked concerned but disapproving. John braced himself for a pious, though well-meant lecture.

'I fear John, that you are unaware of the extent of your

disgrace. Your family have been put to great disadvantage by your headstrong, your licentious behaviour.'

'My family disgraced?' John was genuinely astonished. 'But they have had nothing to do with it.'

'It is said in town that covetousness inspired us to encourage your folly, and the King looks greatly askance upon us all.'

John's feelings were a welter of resentment and exasperation. His indignation at the town's ill-natured surmise jostled with annoyance at the King's supposition that he was incapable of an independent action. Attempting the abduction with the supposed encouragement of his respectable relations? The idea was laughable!

'What am I to do?'

'You must write an apology to Lord Hawley and Sir John Warr, and a humble petition to the King. Explain your actions as well as you can, and remember...' Sir Walter lowered his rheumaticky bones into the only available chair. 'You must express the utmost contrition.'

John flung away impatiently. 'Will that get me out of here?'

Sir Walter looked grave. 'I do not think, John, that you are aware of the strength and importance of the people you have offended. The Mallets of Enmore are rich and powerful in their own county, and their blood is better than yours.'

John curled his lip. 'Better than mine?' The old fool was on his favourite tack of blood and lineage. A bantering tone entered the young man's voice. 'How can this be, when I am related to you?'

Sir Walter, exuding self-satisfaction, warmed to his theme. 'It is true that through your mother you have St John blood, but remember that the Mallets have held Enmore since the days of the Conqueror. Your Wilmot forbears were naught but thrusting yeomen in the time of old Queen Bess.'

'I am well aware that the Wilmot fortunes were founded by a needy Elizabethan adventurer,' snapped John, 'but I have not forgotten that my present lack of money is due to the loyalty of those forebears to the Crown during the Civil Wars. I hope his Majesty remembers that, together with the fact that many a blue-blooded family preferred to hide their gold.' He paused,

13

noting his uncle's discomfiture, before adding maliciously, 'Sir John St John was a notable example, I believe.'

Sir Walter rallied to the defence. 'My father sought to provide for his family in troubled times, and I think, nephew, that you forget three of my brothers died fighting for the King.'

'That may be, but neither do I forget that your uncle, the Lord Chief Justice, opposed the King from the start.'

'I believe,' said Sir Walter stiffly, 'that we had best avoid all mention of the late troubles, and apply our minds to the problem in hand.'

'The problem of a disgraced nephew in the Tower, and the shame on the family name.' Placing his hands in a prayerful attitude, John rolled his eyes heavenwards. He was fond of his uncle, but enjoyed roasting him.

Sir Walter gave him a straight look. 'You are in great trouble nephew, and make an ill exercise of your carping tongue. You would do well to take the advice of the honest pious family you so affect to despise.'

John swallowed an oath, and struggled to keep his voice low. 'I do not despise you, uncle. I have the greatest admiration for your worthy qualities.' Sir Walter's expression did not change.

John took a turn about the room. What did the old fool want from him? He turned. 'I am truly sorry, uncle, for the trouble I have caused. How has my mother taken the news?'

'With great concern. She is sadly pained by your imprudent behaviour. But as you well know, her great indulgence leads her to interpret all your actions in a favourable light.'

John raised a brow. 'This is news to me. Whenever we meet she takes me to task for my frivolity, my extravagance, and my wilful headstrong behaviour.'

'Your mother well knows her duty toward an obdurate child.'

'I am no child, uncle!' John nearly choked with vexation, and walked rapidly towards the other side of the room. 'God's Wounds! At my age my father was fighting in wars upon the Continent.'

He clenched his hands, and felt the fine ruby ring loose upon his finger. He straightened his hand and gazed at its glittering fire. The King had given it to his father, after the Battle of Worcester. It had been presented to Henry Wilmot in appreciation of his loyalty. John valued the ring highly, and yearned to prove himself his father's son.

'If I could do the King some service, perhaps fighting against the Dutch, you might believe that I am now a man.'

The expressive eyes were genuinely serious, and Sir Walter succumbed to their enchantment. His sister's youngest child was his favourite nephew, and he had needed to fight an inclination to grant a premature forgiveness. The lad lacked balance, and the fatal Wilmot charm had allowed him to get his own way far too often. But Anne's good sense and independence were there too! Perhaps some war service would yet bring out the responsible St John strain.

'Would you volunteer for service with the Fleet? It might aid you in regaining his Majesty's favour.'

'Yes, of course.' Excitement invaded every fibre of the young man's being. To prove oneself an effective fighter in a worthy cause was the aim of every true servant of the King.

'Will you make it known? How do I set about it?' The grey eyes were sparkling, all thoughts of gloom or contrition – gone. Sir Walter allowed himself to smile.

'We must first obtain your release.' He looked at John searchingly. 'We are all exerting ourselves on your behalf. Your mother has been pleading your cause with the Duchess of York, and her Highness has agreed to speak to the Duke on your behalf. Your step-grandmother, my Lady Manchester, and your kinsman Sir Allen Apsley have spoken for you as well. We are not neglecting your interests.'

A humbling feeling of gratitude overwhelmed John's self-possession. Saying gruffly that he was much obliged to Sir Walter for the trouble he was taking, he knelt before his uncle.

Sir Walter, mollified by this gesture of submission, raised his nephew, patting him on the shoulder.

'If you follow my advice, I think we shall accomplish your release. But you must forget all thought of marriage for the present. I fear you are greatly out of Mistress Mallet's favour.'

15

2

Setting Sail

On a bright sunny morning in July, John walked gaily through the gardens of St James's Palace. He had attended the King's levée at Whitehall, and had been received with favour. Charles had given him a letter of introduction to Lord Sandwich, Admiral of the Fleet, and he was to start for Yarmouth at first light next morning. John looked up at the blue sky, and thought it augured well for his new life at sea.

Entering the palace through the garden door, John made his way to his mother's apartments. Lady Rochester, through the influence of her old friend Lord Clarendon, had been appointed Groom of the Stole to the latter's daughter, the Duchess of York. Her rooms, furnished with austere elegance, perfectly expressed the personality of their owner. A finely bound Bible, a book of sermons, and a copy of Quarles's *Divine Emblemes* lay upon the polished table. John smiled wryly: his mother's choice of reading matter had not changed with the years. 'Never neglect your prayers, my son,' she had told him as a child. Piety had gone by the board when he commenced his studies at Oxford, but he still admired her high principles and her endeavour to live her religion.

He dropped to one knee as she entered the room. Kissing her hand, he felt as he had done some twelve or fourteen years ago, when she had appeared to him a goddess, infinitely beautiful, infinitely wise. Her features were now imposing rather than beautiful. Since his return from the Continent, John had viewed his mother with new eyes. The goddess was a formidable matriarch, fond of her opinions, and convinced of the rightness of her judgement in all matters.

'You are fortunate, my son, in having regained the King's favour. If you act with valour in his service you have every hope of regaining your former position in his affections. Whatever induced you to act in such headstrong, violent fashion? When your letter reached me at Harwich I was distracted with worry. Sir Allen was at sea with the Duke, and I had no one to turn to for advice.'

'I am surprised, Mother, to hear that you needed advice.'

'I needed advice as to how I should best approach the King,' she snapped, fully aware of the deliberate ambiguity behind his remark. 'You know how reserved he can be with members of my family. It is solely owing to his affection for your father that he has shown you such favour.'

'I know the King loved him dearly.' John laughed. 'He has told me often enough of their adventures after Worcester, when my father was one of his closest companions.'

Lady Rochester's eyes softened as she looked at her son. How like his father he was! He had all his winning ways – and his extravagance in dress. John was wearing a superb plum-coloured velvet, and it recalled to her mind a costume of his father's – such a one as he had worn at St Albans that brief mad summer when he had won her heart. How gay and demanding he had been in his wooing! She had held him off, in spite of her attraction to him. 'I am a woman of principle and honour,' she had said, 'and lie with no man but a husband.'

'Faith, that can soon be remedied,' Harry had laughed. 'Let us find a clown-in-orders so that we may bed legally without delay.' They were married by the house chaplain, but the very next morning had had to part. How little she had seen of him during those troubled days of the Civil War. She realised, with a jolt, how very little she had seen of him at all.

'Do you remember your father?' she said to John. 'You saw him once.'

'Yes, a great laughing fellow – magnificently dressed. He tossed me up to the ceiling – and called me a girl.'

'Ah yes. He insisted that I should take you out of petticoats

17

although you were not of an age for breaching.' She smiled. 'How passionate you were, demanding that your father's orders be complied with – though usually so docile and sweet-tempered a child.' The trouble they had had with him the following day! He swore he would not be dressed, but in his elder brother's suit. In the end she had indulged him, the nursemaid saying, 'You would do well, my Lady, to meet his wishes. These tractable lads are often the most obstinate when something touches them nearly.'

How he had prinked himself in Frank's suit, turning about in front of the glass, and liking what he saw! Frank and Harry had teased him unmercifully about his girlish looks, reducing him to tears, but it had curbed his vanity, and taught him to laugh at himself. Perhaps it had all been for the good. One needed a thick skin at this court, addicted as it was to malicious practical joking. Everything had been so different at the court of the King's father. The troubles had changed all.

Lady Rochester was well launched in recollection. John paced about the room as his mother continued. 'I saw very little of your father after we were married. He went to France with young Prince Charles, and returned to England upon only two occasions. I wondered if you remembered his visit. You were only four years old.'

John flicked a speck of dust from his ruffles. Seeing that she had lost his interest his mother resumed coldly.

'Your father had the folly to visit me, at my father's house in Wiltshire, whilst the King rode to Bristol with Mistress Lane. They had a price on their heads. Like you, he had no thought for danger, or for the harm he might bring upon his family.'

John fixed her with speculative eyes. 'Were you not pleased to see him?'

She detected criticism in his gaze, and declared indignantly, 'We were in great peril had it been known that we were harbouring a malignant.' Shaking an imaginary crease from the thick silk of her skirt, she paused. 'God knows it was hard enough to stay in good odour with the Protector, as it was.'

My mother is in an unusually expansive mood, thought John. What is she driving at?

18

'Now John,' she began sternly. 'you must learn to act responsibly and soberly. You have all your father's better qualities, but must eschew his faults. You must amend your frivolous attitude towards young women. How else are you to be married to advantage – to a chaste, modest maid?'

'I am in no hurry to be married, mother, except to the woman of my choice.'

'The woman of your choice would seem to have no mind for you.'

John raised a brow. 'Does that displease you? I sensed you did not care for Elizabeth.'

'Mistress Mallet seemed to me a highly indulged young woman. Her mother is foolishly fond, and allows her too much licence. The young woman is mighty free with her tongue.'

'But not with her favours.'

'Of course not! A young woman of good family should be courted with some ceremony.'

John grinned. 'How did my father court you – soberly and ceremoniously? How did you meet him?'

Lady Rochester was taken aback. 'Why ... I met him at the house of my mother-in-law. I was then the widow of Sir Henry Lee, and was staying at her house at St Albans.'

'Why did you marry him?'

'Why?' What questions the boy asked! Her son's brusque inquisitorial manner was strangely removed from that of the dutiful child she had once known. Such behaviour resulted from a lack of ceremony allowed between parents and children. She had been talking far too freely. ''Tis no concern of yours, my son,' she said briskly. 'Now, as to your sea voyage – I hope you have sufficient warm clothing?'

'Yes, mother. Will has packed my trunk. We leave for Yarmouth tomorrow.'

A silence fell between them. At last she said, 'God bless you, my child. May heaven keep you from harm. When you return from sea, I shall have several marriage alliances to discuss with you.'

John laughed. His mother meant well, but at times could be most obtuse. 'I have said already that I have no wish to marry.'

19

'Then you should have. It would perhaps bring a stop to your unseemly dalliance with waiting women and other low women of the town.'

'Low women of the town?' John was exasperated. How his mother nagged! Would she never forget that foolish escapade at Oxford? She deserved to be baited, he decided.

'Low women of the town offer better sport than chaste modest wives.'

'Better sport indeed. Your consorting with such whores has spoilt you for the company of honest women. Have you no sense of shame?'

She prosed on... After a stifling hour of dull advice, to which John paid scant attention, he took a thankful leave of his mother, saying that dinner was kept for him elsewhere.

* * *

Leaving St James's at midday, John walked through the palace garden towards the door into the Mall. On his way he heard the sound of sobbing. Looking behind a bush, he saw a young maid seated upon the ground, crying into a basket of washing.

'What is the matter?'

The girl looked up and John saw that it was Sarah, niece of Mrs Cooke, the 'mother' of the Maids of Honour.

'It's that beastly she-cat Temple,' said Sarah. 'She pulled my hair for not arranging her gown to her satisfaction, and then spat in my face – the nasty sandy-haired, freckle-faced bitch!'

'You called her a cat just now.'

Sarah bit her lip, and then smiled through her tears. Her eyes were like wet periwinkles. 'You don't like her, do you?'

John smiled. 'No.'

He remembered Anne Temple, one of the Duchess's Maids. She had a very fine shape, but her face was a smooth mask of stupidity and conceit. Sidney talked to her occasionally and had once told John, 'I left the depths of her ignorance unplumbed.' So she had a nasty temper too? He was not surprised.

Trying to comfort poor little Sarah, he gave her his handkerchief to dry her eyes. Reassured, she returned to her

20

grievance.

'She called me "the kag-handed offspring of a country clod"! My father was an honest yeoman, husbanding the land and making a good living from it, whilst hers spent all his time whoring and drinking in taverns, for all that he said he spent his patrimony in the late King's service.' Sarah's eyes sparkled with indignation. John was amused at her vehemence, but admired her spirit and temper.

'Did you tell her that?'

'Yes, that was why she pulled my hair.'

John noticed her small face, delicate nose, and pointed chin. The lips were red and pouting.

'Forget that disagreeable young woman. Come to Spring Gardens and eat strawberries and cream with me.'

Sarah looked at him in surprise. A Lord to take her to Fox Hall? But then folks often said that this young man was mad. Sarah looked at him speculatively. What strange eyes he had ... but he was certainly very attractive – and amazingly, looked as if he meant what he said.

'Well, are you coming?'

Her eyes lit up. 'Do you think I dare? My aunt has bidden me to take this laundry to my Aunt Joyner in St Martin's Lane.' She pointed to the large basket.

'We will have it delivered by a porter and send some excuse for your non-appearance. Come, let us go.' He swung the basket up onto his shoulder and, taking her by the hand, led her out into the Mall. As they went through the gate they passed Goditha Price, who regarded John with some amusement.

'A porter for maidservants now, my Lord?'

'Yes, when they are as pretty as this one.'

They entered the public thoroughfare and John hailed a burly fellow from the porter's stand. 'Take this to Mistress Joyner of St Martin's Lane,' he said 'and tell her that her niece has been unavoidably delayed.' On sight of the large silver coin in John's hand, the man took up the basket with alacrity and was soon upon his way.

John turned to Sarah. 'Now we will make our way to Westminster Stairs. Have you been to Fox Hall before?'

21

'No, t'will be prodigious fine to see it. All the fine ladies and gentlemen go there.'

John laughed. 'You will be a fine lady this afternoon.'

In King Street he bought her a fringed shawl and a fan, and considered himself well rewarded by the look of delight in her eyes. As they walked towards Westminster Stairs they noticed a cross chalked on the door of one of the houses. "May the Lord have mercy upon us" was written underneath.

Sarah gasped. 'The Plague! Is it in Westminster then?'

'It would appear so. No wonder the King and the Duke of York are arranging for the removal of their households to Hampton Court.'

'Is that why everyone is packing, and wanting their washing done?'

'I should imagine so.'

'Are you going to Hampton Court?'

'No, tomorrow I am going to sea. I am to join the Fleet at Yarmouth.'

'To fight the Dutch?'

'I hope so.'

'How brave' said Sarah, her eyes shining. 'I hate the beastly Hogen-Mogen.'

'Why what have the Dutch done to you?'

Sarah looked a little puzzled. 'Why nothing, but they are the King's enemies and they are taking our trade, and it is right to fight them.'

'They are the King's enemies and it is right to fight them, but I believe it is we who are taking their trade,' said John teasingly.

'Well, I am sure I don't know,' said Sarah, bored with the subject. 'Being a Lord, you must know much more about it than I do.'

John smiled. 'I think that all this Lord knows is that he is damned short of money, but hopes to get some fine prizes from the Dutch to repair his fortune.'

'If you help capture the East India Fleet your fortune will be made.'

'And then I shall buy you a fine silk gown and a box at the

22

King's Theatre every day.'

'And I shall be very proud and haughty and loll my head against the box, and all the town gallants will be in love with me.'

'But you will favour none but me?'

Sarah looked at him mischievously. ''Tis not my intention to favour any. A whore's life is too short and uncertain. I shall be a player-woman, like Mistress Nell Gwynne.'

John's eyes widened. 'But what do you know of acting?'

'Only what I have seen from the Gallery, when the Duchess goes to the theatre.'

'One day I will take you, and we shall sit in the Pit. Would you like that?'

'Do cats mislike cream?'

'Do pretty maids too?' Her vivacious little face was tantalisingly near. It promised to be a very enjoyable afternoon...

* * *

July 1665

'I must apologise, my Lord, for lack of accommodation suitable to your quality,' said Captain Grove brusquely. 'This is all we can provide.'

Looking around at the spartan arrangements, John anticipated an uncomfortable night: a curtain of sailcloth had been hung across a corner of the deck, and a hammock slung between two guns.

'I hear you will be with us only until we reach my Lord Admiral, so perhaps you will make shift to make do.'

John nodded his assent. Reaching Yarmouth, John had reported to Sir Thomas Allen who had assigned him to temporary quarters aboard *Success* until they reached the main fleet, said to be at anchor off the Yorkshire coast.

John stared about the ship. It was a veritable hive of activity: casks, boxes and bundles were being swung on board, and barrels rolled in at portholes from gangways on the quay. He could appreciate that from the captain's point of view he was something of a nuisance.

'I fear you are unconscionably busy.'

The captain nodded curtly. 'Frank Jones here will see to your needs. He will take down your hammock in the morning and will erect a table when you wish to take your meals. I regret the lack of convenience, but before we sail we expect three more volunteers, and will be even more short of space.'

John felt a little indignant at the cavalier treatment afforded him, but was nevertheless of a temperament which adapts quickly to changing conditions. He bowed his acknowledgements to the captain, who then hurried off, leaving him to the attentions of Frank Jones. The old sailor put down his trunk, and John viewed the choppy sea. He shivered despite his cloak. The sweet warm weather had ended the night before he had set out for Yarmouth. He remembered wrapping Sarah in his cloak as they made their way back over the river. A cold wind had sprung up as they left Fox Hall, and it had blown ever since. He turned to Frank Jones.

'Have you seen much service at sea?'

'Aye, nigh on forty years, man and boy.'

Having fought against the Dutch in Oliver's day, the old sailor had much advice to impart. He escorted John around the ship, telling him it was a fifth rate, carrying thirty guns and one hundred and fifty-five men. 'Had we been going on a peaceful expedition,' he said, 'we could have knocked up a cabin for you, but we expect to meet the Dutch, and must have room to work the guns.'

'Of course,' murmured John. 'I appreciate the position.'

The engaging grin which spread across the young man's face drew Frank Jones to regard his charge with more interest than he was used to expend upon young Volunteers. An odd young fellow, he thought, but very civil, which is more than you can expect from most of the Quality.

'Do we sail tomorrow?' John asked.

'Aye, if the wind be fair.'

'Have you served under Lord Sandwich before?'

'Aye, a good commander – concerns himself for his men, which is more than you can say for most of the bastards.'

Frank spat upon the deck. 'We be woefully short of men and supplies. A'miral would not give leave for any ship to sail until they had received their full quota.'

'It would seem that the lack of supplies is being remedied now,' commented John as he looked over the side of the vessel and watched the sailors carrying stores into the hold. Like ants at an anthill, he thought, all seizing an egg as big as themselves and scurrying off below.

'Aye, and men too,' Jones growled as a party of military drew up on the quay. The ship's boatswain was attempting to get order into the motley collection in his charge. The riff-raff lined up before him were the sweepings of the seaport town, and a number of persistent burdens on the poor rate from adjacent country parishes.

'They look a sorry bunch of rascals,' said John. Several of the men seemed ill, and two of the party were decidedly drunk. Another, a fresh-faced young boy, wore an expression of despair.

'Huh, pressed men, every one,' Jones growled. 'Cap'n Grove'll discharge those too sick to stand, but Bosun'll lick t'others into shape,' he chuckled, 'even if 'tis at the rope's end.'

John laughed too, but could not help an uneasy feeling of sympathy as he looked at the face of the troubled young man. He looked ready to drop with fatigue. The party was marched aboard and taken below. John shrugged his shoulders; the methods taken to recruit men for his Majesty's service in time of war were no concern of his. He now had his own duty to do.

* * *

The next morning further Volunteers arrived. 'Mr John Wyndham, Mr Charles Harbord, and Mr Walter Stewart, my Lord,' announced Captain Grove briefly, before hurrying away.

John knew Stewart and Harbord already. Stewart was brother to Frances, the King's favourite, and Harbord kinsman to Lord Sandwich. Greeting Wyndham in his usual easy manner, John learned that he was a younger son of Sir William Wyndham of Williton in Somerset, and a near neighbour of Sir

John Warr.

'I hear you are courting Bess Mallet,' said Wyndham, at which the other two new arrivals laughed heartily.

'Aye, and got a spell of imprisonment for his pains,' added Harbord. 'Has it cooled your ardour, my Lord?'

'No,' said John, 'I will marry the jilt yet.'

'There'll be the Devil to pay if you do,' joked Wyndham. 'She's spoiled and sulky...'

'And haughty and malicious too,' put in Walter Stewart. 'She had the whole of my sister's supper party laughing at her impersonations. His Majesty was most amused with her mimicry of his Lordship here.'

John felt a stab of pain, but his voice remained even. 'What trait of mine did she find particularly amusing?'

'Why, your slow bow, and the way in which you stare at a handsome woman.' Stewart laughed. 'My God, she had you to the life! I had to laugh myself – although I don't like the wench,' he added hastily, seeing the cold glint in John's eye. 'You are well out of that alliance my Lord, in spite of the loss of her money.'

John bowed. 'I am vastly obliged for the good advice, Mr Stewart.' He kept his voice calm, hoping he had sufficiently hidden the feelings of hurt and dread stealing along the fibres of his body, and was thankful for the interruption of Captain Grove.

'Gentlemen, we sail this evening. I must explain that while you will be victualled on board, any wine and other provisions you require over and above the ship's fare must be obtained by yourselves today.'

The Volunteers held a conference and concluded it would be best to take only a small quantity of provisions, as they were short of room to stow them away. It was decided to purchase cheese, some butter and a cask of wine. John, charged with making the purchase in Yarmouth, had difficulty in obtaining wine to his satisfaction. However, when the young gentlemen sampled of it freely that evening, they expressed themselves well satisfied with his choice.

The squadron to which *Success* belonged sailed north with

the tide. It was hoped to meet with Lord Sandwich off Well Bank. As night fell, dark clouds gathered, and the wind rose rapidly. Sir Thomas Allen, the squadron commander, signalled the fleet to scatter, so that each vessel would have more sea room and the chance of a collision be avoided. By midnight the wind had increased to gale force, and the ships were labouring heavily. John did indeed experience a most uncomfortable night. Sleep was impossible, he and his companions were seasick, and the tarpaulin which was supposed to shelter them blew up and down unceasingly. It gave a great bang at every gust, and the rain blew in between the tie ropes. At last the Officer of the Watch took pity upon them and suggested that the Volunteers should rest in his cabin until he had need of it. Thankful to be out of the wind, if only for a few hours, they huddled together on the deck of the cabin. John had never felt more ill in his life. The ship lunged and plunged, and whether his stomach was at his head or his heels he knew not.

When dawn came it was sullen and cold, revealing a choppy sea, but such was the thankfulness of the four young men to be released from their den, that the breaking light seemed to them the fairest sight in the world. The Officer of the Watch, having glanced with some disfavour at the state of his cabin, told them that the wind had lessened in the night and suggested that they should take a turn about the deck.

About an hour later John was supping a tot of brandy in hot water (said by Frank Jones to be a sovereign remedy against chills and a queasy stomach). He charged the young gentlemen the equivalent of his day's wage for each hot drink, but such was their state that they were glad to pay his fee.

John warmed his hands around the battered pewter mug. Lifting his eyes to the grey sky he saw two seamen swinging along the rigging. He admired their skill and their apparent unconcern for danger. One needed the agility of a monkey, and the nerve of an acrobat to be a seaman, he mused. How could one climb so high without being crippled by the thought of falling headlong onto the deck below? A lack of imagination was needed ... or an unquenchable sense of confidence.

Who but that blund'ring blockhead Phaethon
Could e're have thought to drive about the Sun?

He remembered the lines he had written to Elizabeth in the early days of their acquaintance. The recollection was painful. Had she been amusing herself all along, merely playing with his affection and admiration? Surely she knew that he loved her to distraction?

'How now, my Lord, lost in thought over a female friend, or are you solving one of Euclid's propositions?'

Jarred roughly from his reverie, John looked up. Walter Stewart was standing over him.

'Neither, as it happens,' he replied coldly. 'I do have other diversions.' He had, on the previous evening, declared his ability to divert his thoughts from a teasing woman by writing a set of verses, or solving a geometrical problem, and knew that he was now fair game for banter.

Stewart was looking for mischief, and his eye fell upon John's open trunk.

'Good Lord, Harbord, look at this. Books!'

Harbord grinned. 'Books also serve to divert the mind, young fellow. How many has he brought?'

'Two.' Stewart grabbed them and danced away out of reach. ''S wounds, Charles, listen to this: *The Vanity of Dogmatising* – and, what in heaven's name is this?' He threw one of the books over to Harbord.

'*De Veritate* – hell and high water!' gasped Harbord as he rolled about the deck laughing. 'Damme if I'd call 'em diverting.'

'No,' said John, 'absorbing, which is much better.'

Wyndham, standing by during these exchanges, now ventured an enquiry.

'Have you a great interest in the next world, my Lord?'

John looked up suspiciously, but seeing his questioner's friendly demeanour, replied evenly, 'No, I am too busy enjoying the pleasures of this, but I find one of its greatest satisfactions lies in discussion – which is why I am reading *De Veritate*. I hear Lord Herbert's volume postulates a reasonable foundation for religion.'

28

'A reasonable foundation for religion!' sneered Stewart. 'I had thought you the court's leading Hobbist, my Lord.'

'Fear of death at sea has lead him to doubt a philosophy of materialism,' ventured Harbord.

'No,' said John, struggling to keep his temper. 'I greatly admire Hobbes. He has great powers of mind, and is a superb dialectician.'

'What's a dialectician?' piped Stewart, in mock innocence.

'Run along child,' said John 'before I give you a box on the ear.'

Wyndham pursued the subject of Hobbes. 'Have you read *Leviathan*?'

'Read it?' said Harbord. 'It is his Bible! He can explain its meaning, even to Hobbes himself.'

'Indeed,' added Stewart, 'whenever that formidable old bore appears at court his Majesty declares, "Here comes the bear to be baited!"'

'The King sets my Lord and his Grace of Buckingham upon him and announces, "My mastiffs will exercise him."' Harbord looked at John mockingly. 'My Lord is chief dog.'

'Aye,' said John, 'but he beats us off. He has always an answer.'

'I think he is too doctrinaire,' ventured Wyndham tentatively.

John agreed. 'I am gathering arguments against his theories. I hear Glanvill has made some glancing attacks in his direction in *The Vanity of Dogmatising*.'

'So,' said Wyndham, 'your devotional reading amounts to no more than gathering further ammunition for your arguments with Hobbes?'

John grinned. 'You could say that. Have you a more orthodox interest in the subject?'

'I cannot claim to be devout,' confessed Wyndham, 'but I often speculate upon the state after death.'

'Then we shall agree capitally,' said John. 'Have you read the arguments of Lucretius?'

'I am no classical scholar' Wyndham replied, 'but I find the Greek theory of the transmigration of souls most interesting.'

The two of them were soon deep in discussion. Stewart and

29

Harbord exchanged pitying glances, and departed for a turn about the deck.

Frank Jones appeared and called the young men to a scanty ship's breakfast. No one had much appetite, but he advised them to eat a biscuit so that they would have something to vomit with later.

'God, what abominable fare!' grimaced Harbord. 'The water tastes foul.'

'It smells so, too,' complained Stewart.

'Add a little wine to your water,' suggested Frank Jones. 'A small quantity will disguise the stinking.' He cast a wistful eye towards the Volunteers' cask of wine. 'We call such a mixture "beverage wine" aboard, Sir.'

John was about to offer him a tot when the old fellow beat a hasty retreat. Captain Grove had appeared.

'The fleet is to anchor here at Well Bank until we receive further instructions. Sir Thomas Allen has sent a message that we are to attend a meeting aboard the flagship this afternoon. Please be ready, gentlemen.'

Aboard the flagship it was decided that the weather at Well Bank was proving too bad for safe anchorage. Sir Thomas intended taking the fleet to Flamborough Head; Captain Grove was to seek out the admiral and advise him of the change of rendezvous. 'I have no doubt,' said Sir Thomas to the Volunteers, 'that you will be afforded more comfortable accommodation aboard *The Prince*. The Admiral will be pleased to welcome four such promising young men into the King's service.'

Returning to *Success*, they set sail directly, and sighted Lord Sandwich's fleet about noon the next day. *The Prince*, an awe-inspiring sight, reared above them like a castle out of the sea. A first-rater, with ninety guns and a complement of 700 men, she was one of the largest ships in the King's service. The great lanterns, large enough for five men to climb inside, hung on either side of the poop. The whole of the woodwork was superbly carved and gilded. The ship's upper works, painted dark blue with gilt decorations around the port, colourfully balanced the lower part in yellow. Aloft, the flag of St George and Lord Sandwich's silken standard waved in the breeze.

Once the Volunteers were aboard, Lord Sandwich greeted them with formal courtesy and introduced them to Sir Roger Cuttance, the commander of the ship. 'He will assign one of his officers to provide you with a cabin. I look forward to your company at dinner, after which I will acquaint you with your duties.'

John was assigned a small cabin in the stern, near the admiral's stateroom. The others were further along the gallery. John went to see them. 'The quarters are very cramped,' he complained. 'There is scarcely room to hang my hammock, and I shall have to sit on my trunk.'

'Och, ye puir wee laddie,' mocked Stewart. 'The only one of us to have a cabin to himself, and you moan it is not big enough!' He and John engaged in a desultory, half-hearted scuffle until parted by the peaceable Wyndham. He told them that he had been assigned an even smaller cabin which he would have to share with another Volunteer who had not yet arrived.

At dinner the Volunteers were introduced to Sir Thomas Clifford, the Commissioner for Prizes. He was a west-country gentleman of some thirty-five years. He had caught the King's attention by his dedication to business, and was pleased to have been appointed to such an influential post. John thought him a pleasant enough fellow, for a politician, though like all such men he was possessed of a restless ambition. It also appeared from his conversation that he had a consuming hatred of the Dutch. Clifford had fought at Lowestoft, and had also been appointed Commissioner for the Sick and Wounded. He was conscientious and was well acquainted with the administrative problems of the fleet.

Clifford addressed the Admiral. 'I hear we have great want of signal-flags, Sir. Is that correct?'

Sandwich nodded in assent.

John plunged into the conversation. 'I hear that at Lowestoft great confusion arose because of a lack of communication between commanders and the captains of ships. Did this arise from a shortage of colours?'

The silence which settled about Lord Sandwich's table convinced John that he had spoken out of turn.

At last Sandwich replied. 'May I ask the source of your information?' he enquired.

'Why, my uncle – Sir Allen Apsley,' said John. 'He was with the Duke at the time of the Battle, and was greatly shocked to see a fireship of ours bear down upon a Dutchman who had already struck for quarter.' He looked around the faces at the table. Were they all made of wood? 'He said it was pitiful to see so many poor fellows leaping from the fire into the sea, and swimming there as thick as ears of corn together.'

His story elicited no response. Indignantly, he continued. 'The inhuman knave who ran in amongst them burned or drowned five hundred men quite unnecessarily. When questioned why he had failed to decipher the Duke's message, which had been to desist, he said that the correct colours had not been used.'

'Ah ... yes, very likely. That sounds like Holmes,' mused Lord Sandwich. 'His enthusiasm for burning Dutchmen knows no bounds... It was an unfortunate occurrence, the needless massacre of a brave enemy, but such accidents happen in the heat of war.'

His cool tone annoyed John. 'Especially when one is short of colours,' he threw out.

'Exactly,' purred Sir Edward Spragge, commander of the *Lion*. 'I hear that one of our vessels, finding herself in difficulties, and not having the colour necessary to request assistance, ran up the red coat of one of her Volunteers.'

General laughter greeted his sally. He continued, 'No-one knew what the damned fellow wanted! Have a care, my Lord, or we might put your coat to similar use.'

John made a mental note for the future: it would be wiser to keep his mouth shut at the Admiral's dinners.

* * *

Next morning John and Harbord were watching *Swiftsure* come in from Southwold Bay.

'S'blood, look who is arriving!' remarked Harbord. 'I haven't seen Ned Montagu since he was dismissed the court last year, for squeezing the Queen's hand.'

John nearly choked with laughter. 'The hand of squat Catherine?'

'Aye,' grinned Harbord. 'The Queen, having had no admirer before, asked Charles what people meant by squeezing one's hand. "Love," said the King. "Then," said she, "Mr Montagu loves me mightily" – upon which he was turned out of court!'

John raised a brow. 'Charles feared a cuckolding?'

'Great heavens, no! The mischief lay not so much in what Montagu did, as the gossip his behaviour attracted. He is a damned quarrelsome fellow, y'know – always falling out with Manchester on matters of precedence.' Harbord laughed. 'He caused a hellish rumpus about who had the right to hand the Queen into her carriage, and got himself thoroughly disliked for his pains.'

'If he had squeezed her hand with discretion, it would not have mattered so much?'

'Exactly. I hear he has been in the country since his dismissal from court, also that he owes my Lord Sandwich a great deal of money.'

'Then the poor fellow has problems enough!' They laughed together unfeelingly.

Curious to meet the tempter of queens, John paid a visit to Wyndham's cabin. 'Good day t'ye,' said John, giving his friend but a cursory glance as he stared at the new arrival. 'I hear there is a newcomer aboard.'

Wyndham bowed to Montagu. 'This is my Lord Rochester. He is my very good friend.'

John bowed. Montagu nodded, but continued unpacking. A man of some thirty-five years, he was embittered by his experiences at court, and resented having to share a cabin with two young sparks. In any case he was not a man for idle compliment. He had come to sea hoping to redeem himself with his kinsman, Lord Sandwich, but the admiral's greeting had lacked warmth. If the East India Fleet were to be captured, his share of the prize money might allow him to pay his debt, and perhaps put things right between them. Montagu considered it scandalous that a man of his knowledge and experience should be treated in so offhand a fashion.

'I believe, Sir,' said John, 'that like myself, you hope to forget a woman in the heat of war.'

Montagu looked up, suspecting the dazzling smile which accompanied this remark. 'You are misinformed, my Lord,' came the cold reply.

John grinned. 'Come Sir, we are all friends here, and must be merry in our misfortunes, especially when they arise from similar causes. We have, I hear, both aspired to the love of ladies claiming the Royal protection.'

Montagu's taut nerves snapped. He spun and grasped John by the throat. 'I'll not be mocked by a young whelp, scarce dry behind the ears!' His grip tightened around John's neck. 'Keep a civil tongue in your head, and name no ladies to me.'

John gasped for breath, but managed to wrench himself free. 'Faith, Sir, I named none, nor am I like to if you strangle me!'

Montagu released his grip, sending John spinning back against the bulwark. Wyndham ran to his assistance.

'Shall we belabour this bear, my Lord?'

John, still struggling for breath, and dazed with surprise, shook his head. 'He thinks I meant him some discourtesy.' He put his fingers to his throat, and looked at Montagu with indignation. 'I trust, though, that he will not deal with me so hastily in future. 'Twill be an unpleasant voyage if he is to be so touchy.'

Montagu, seeing that John's amazement was genuine, regretted his hasty action. 'Your Lordship has a reputation for raillery. No man taunts me with impunity.'

'Likewise no man mishandles me without chastisement.' John's eyes flashed dangerously. 'Let us tread warily with each other in future.'

Montagu bowed. 'And trust that there will be no further misunderstanding?'

John nodded, and Wyndham, profoundly relieved that a fight had been avoided, hurried his friend out of the door.

'Damned fire-eater. We shall have trouble with him,' he said, when they were out of earshot.

John shrugged. 'Oh, I am not so sure. He is not a ruffling

bully who seeks a quarrel. I must have touched him in a sore place.'

They mounted the companionway in silence. After a while John laughed, his grey eyes glittering with mischief. 'Consider, Jack, what wormwood and gall! To be ruined, not as Anthony, for the sake of great beauty, but for a plain-looking woman with scarce an ounce of charm in her composition! And furthermore, one dull enough to betray his devotion into the bargain!'

* * *

The next day *The Prince* arrived at Flamborough Head and joined with Sir Thomas Allen's squadron. Lord Sandwich held a council of war: he had received intelligence that the Dutch East India Fleet was sheltering in Bergen harbour, under the protection of the King of Denmark. Charles had already informed Sandwich that a secret agreement had been reached in Copenhagen allowing the English to make an attack upon the Dutch in Norwegian waters. The King of Denmark's entry into the war would not be long delayed.

The Volunteers thought the East India Fleet as good as captured. 'They'll be at our mercy, like sitting ducks,' exulted Harbord. John and his friends amused themselves by apportioning the prizes according to their needs. Stewart wanted diamonds; Harbord said he would take spices (having a merchant cousin in the City who would give a good price for them), while John wanted shirts of Indian cotton, and gold.

The fleet set sail and the Volunteers sighted the coast of Norway on the evening of Sunday the twenty-third of July, as a red and gold sunset poured its glories over the sea. Anchored in a desolate fjord, *The Prince* was dwarfed by the great cliffs towering above her sails. John leant over the bulwark and watched reflections in the dark waters below. The weather had been pleasant since they set sail for Norway, and the sea calm all day. His sickness on *Success* seemed only a bad dream. The last two weeks had flown, and he had not thought of Elizabeth for an age; there had been so much to learn, and to discuss, of life at sea.

35

Every morning for the past week, one of the Lieutenants of *The Prince* had instructed the Volunteers in navigation. Lord Sandwich had been insistent that they should acquire some knowledge of the working of a ship, so that their usefulness in times of emergency would be increased.

Stewart had been a little vexed. 'Does he forget we are gentlemen, come to fight? We are not the sons of damned tarpaulins!'

'We lose nothing by learning the skills of those we may be called upon to lead,' said John. He enjoyed hearing of the use of charts and globes, spherical and plane trigonometry, the applications of Gunter's scale, and the use of Briggs's logarithms.

'Tis well enough for you,' groaned Wyndham. 'You study Euclid for pleasure, but we poor mortals prefer to employ ourselves in easier ways.' However, even Stewart came to admit that it would be useful to know how to tack in an adverse wind, and what sail to furl in rough weather.

John quoted from a recommended volume of *Naval Tracts*. '"And in such weather when a landsman hears the seamen cry starbord or port, or bide aloft, or flat a sheet, or haul home a cluling, he thinks he hears a barbarous speech, which he conceives not the meaning of."'

Wyndham laughed. 'That well describes our first night at sea. We were of less use than the idiot cabin boy.'

Later in the day, when the young gentlemen were left to their own devices, they caught cod and ling from the side of a jolly boat, coming back to the fo'csle to cook the fish over a brazier of hot charcoals, and then to eat them with their fingers, trying not to burn their hands in the process.

The days at sea had been great fun, but John derived the keenest pleasure from his growing friendship with young Wyndham. Pacing the great decks of *The Prince*, arms about each other's shoulders, they had discussed everything imaginable, from their tastes in horses and women to their thoughts upon the immortality of the soul. As another day of perfect contentment drew to its close, John watched the rays of the setting sun, and had no inkling that it would be the last time he would feel its warmth upon this northern voyage.

3

Aboard Revenge

Lord Sandwich heard that de Ruyter, the Dutch commander,
was on his way to protect the East India Fleet and escort it to
Holland. He therefore decided to prepare a fleet of small ships
to attack the Indiamen in Bergen before they were rescued by
their countryman.

It was known that the entrance to the harbour was too
narrow to admit the passage of great ships of war. Thus
the main Fleet would await de Ruyter's arrival in the North
Sea. At a council of war Sandwich appointed Sir Thomas
Teddiman, commander of *Revenge* to organise an attack upon
Bergen. Teddiman, a dark-haired, ruddy faced seaman, had no
knowledge of languages or of the diplomatic niceties, so Sir
Thomas Clifford was appointed to advise him in "the discre-
tionary part" of the expedition.

John was watching the bluff Teddiman, and could see that
he was relieved to hear of Clifford's appointment. Several
Volunteers were assigned to Teddiman's flagship, and John
pressed to be allowed to join them. In company with Wyndham
and the rest of his friends, he took up new quarters in *Revenge*.
The fleet of twenty-two ships set sail the same afternoon. By
evening the ships reached Buck ap Ra, a wild and rocky place
eight leagues from their destination.

Teddiman, finding the channel to Bergen constricted and
perilous, adjudged that local assistance would be required if a

speedy passage were to be effected. He and Clifford decided to inform the Danish Governor of their arrival in the hope that he would provide a pilot. Hearing that Charles Harbord spoke both French and Dutch, Clifford decided to send him as a messenger. Harbord left early the next morning, being guided overland by a local peasant, to the fort at Bergen. They expected him back by midday, but it was evening before a weary and dispirited Harbord climbed aboard *Revenge*.

'Well, gentlemen,' said Teddiman, looking up from the despatch Harbord had handed him, 'Governor Ahlfeldt's letter is full of compliment, but he commits himself to nothing and refuses to answer my questions about the disposition of the Dutch in his port. We shall have to shift for ourselves.'

The company looked at each other in dismay. 'Does he not know that Denmark is soon to enter the war, and that he should afford us every assistance?' queried Montagu.

'Apparently not. He prefers to remain neutral. Our orders are to capture or to sink the East India Fleet. We shall do so without his help.' Teddiman looked around the table at the eager faces of the young Volunteers.

'I want you to understand that from the moment the first gun fires you are soldiers under my orders. Learn your stations, and remain there until I call upon you for action. I desire you to stand near the forward rail of the poop, so that you can either run down the ladder to the waist and aid in repelling boarders, or spring onto a Dutch ship if I grapple one alongside. Once our sides grind together, it will be your task to lead the soldiers aboard her. Once there, kill as many Dutchmen as you can. Until we board, arm yourselves with muskets from the racks and fire at men on the enemy ships as we pass. Aim especially at officers, and at men in the rigging. The whole of my attention must be given to the conduct of the battle, so remain at your station until I give the word.'

Sir Thomas rose. 'I bid you good evening, gentlemen.' He nodded to Clifford to follow him, leaving the Volunteers to talk amongst themselves. Harbord was peppered with questions about his visit to Bergen. The commander of the castle had afforded him no formal reception until his letters had been translated. After a wait of two hours Harbord had been taken to see the Governor of the District, General Ahlfeldt. The Governor paid the English many compliments, but refused to be drawn upon the subject of pilots or assistance. The only remark he could be induced to make was 'I write *all* in my letter to your commander, the excellent, the brave, the honoured Sir Thomas Teddiman.'

Harbord said he felt the Danes were not pleased to hear of the English fleet's arrival in their territorial waters. In spite of Ahlfeldt's flowery compliments, the castle commander, Colonel John Caspar de Cicignon, had not warmed towards the English envoy. Harbord had looked about him as much as possible and said that he did not see how the Dutch could be attacked in such a small harbour without the Danes' connivance. 'If their forts opened fire on us, to protect the Dutch, we should be shot to pieces.'

Montagu shifted impatiently in his chair. 'Surely you could have drawn Ahlfeldt to make some revealing remark about his attitude towards us?'

'Considering the circumstances, subtlety was beyond me.'

'And what were those circumstances?' sneered Montagu.

'I did not speak his damned outlandish tongue,' returned Harbord heatedly, 'and his French was not good. We had enough to do, to make each other understand the simplest things.'

'Latin?' insisted Montagu maddeningly, 'Did you not try Latin?'

Harbord was about to respond angrily when Clifford entered the room. Montagu tackled him immediately. In the days of his favour at court, Montagu had been to Copenhagen on a minor diplomatic mission. He considered that he should have been sent to the castle in place of Harbord, who was obviously an untried young cub who had bungled a matter of considerable importance. Montagu told Clifford his thoughts in no uncertain terms. Harbord took umbrage at the doubt of his diplomatic abilities, and it required all Sir Thomas Clifford's patience to pacify both gentlemen.

'I am well persuaded that Mr Harbord was a tactful and efficient messenger. It was not thought that diplomatic abilities or an intimate knowledge of the native language would be necessary at this time. However, as it now seems otherwise, we shall be glad to make use of Mr Montagu's knowledge and experience upon reaching Bergen.'

Montagu, mollified, and unaware that Harbord was grimacing at John behind his back, drew himself up and made a declaration.

'I shall be glad to be of service to his Majesty before I die.'

'Is the sad event imminent?' queried John.

Montagu continued unperturbed. 'I have a premonition that I shall not return from this expedition alive.'

John spluttered over his wine, whilst the rest of the company hooted.

'Heaven preserve us!' cried John. 'Has the Angel of Death appeared to you in a vision?'

Montagu smiled wryly. 'No, my Lord. I leave the contemplation of ghostly appearances to you.'

John blushed and bit his lip. He remembered how Montagu had overheard his conversation with young Wyndham the previous night, when they had spoken of apparitions. He wished their discussion to be kept from the knowledge of Harbord, who would bait him unmercifully if he knew. Luckily, a diversion arose.

'I feel that I too shall not return from Bergen alive.'

John stared at Wyndham in some surprise. Such a thought could be expected from Montagu, a man soured with life's disappointments, but Wyndham was young, only seventeen, and filled with the zest for living.

'What has given you this thought?'

'I cannot say precisely ... merely that I cannot imagine what I shall be doing after this voyage.'

'Spending your prize money, I should hope,' said Harbord, trying to lift the tone of gloom.

But John, his interest aroused, refused to be shifted. 'I wonder,' he put in abruptly, 'what it is in your consciousness which has produced such a feeling. If, as Hobbes says, imagination is merely decaying sense impression, and you have had as yet no experience of death, where does this feeling come from? Is it, as the ancients would say, seated in the soul?'

Wyndham was about to reply, but the others started cat-calling and pelting them with ships biscuits.

'Spare us Hobbes, for tonight at least, my Lord!' begged Harbord, kneeling in mock supplication.

John hurled some of the biscuits at him, endeavouring to hide his irritation. He thought them all unthinking blockheads. *Doesn't he know that we shall all come to it in the end?* Then he saw Wyndham's serious face.

He took a deep breath. 'Oh, to hell with it! Let us be cheerful. We shall trounce the Dutch – and live to be rich!'

* * *

Later that evening John took a turn about the deck with Wyndham. The great cliffs loomed above the ship's masts in the darkness. Wyndham shivered. 'I have grave misgivings about our meeting with the Dutch in Bergen.'

'Why do you think they will beat us – "the lusty, fat, two-legged cheese worms"?'

They laughed edgily, remembering the poorly printed tract sold to John as a ballad when he had been shopping for the wine in Yarmouth: '*The Dutch Boare Dissected, Or a Description of Hogg-Land*'.

John drew it from his pocket. 'Everyone knows that a Dutchman is so addicted to eating butter, drinking fat drink, and sliding, that all the world knows him for a slippery fellow.'

Wyndham said, 'It seems to describe General Ahlfeldt – although that gentleman is a Dane.' They fell into over-loud laughter, and began to feel bolder.

'Come, let us warm ourselves with some of their schnapps,' suggested John, guiding Wyndham below. ''Twill chase away the glooms.'

Sitting on John's trunk, they drank from his pewter mug, but the strong spirit failed to lighten Wyndham's mood. Above, they could hear the soldiers drilling, and the sailors practising running out the guns.

41

'I still sense that I shall not return from these damned fjords alive.'

John looked at his friend with concern. He too had had a grim sense of foreboding. They sat in silence, then John blurted out, 'Do you think there is a state after death?'

'Yes, I have heard of those who communicate with the dead.'

'Pshaw! Do you dabble in witchcraft?'

'No, it can be quite orthodox. Have you not heard of the doctrine of the Communication of Saints?'

'Oh, that phrase from the Creed. I never understood it,' scoffed John as he took another mouthful of the fiery schnapps.

''Twas in that book of Glanvill's,' Wyndham continued doggedly. 'The one you lent me.'

'Indeed?'

'Yes, when he mentions those meetings held at the house of Lady Conway in Warwickshire.'

John smiled scornfully. 'A credulous old woman, and a pack of fat chaplains trying to curry favour with their patron! I don't believe it.'

'But you say Glanvill speaks the truth as far as it can be ascertained,' persisted Wyndham, 'derived from your personal knowledge of the case affecting Mr Cary.'

'Ah yes, my mother's neighbour,' John smiled. 'A most mysterious business.' He decided to indulge Wyndham over Lady Conway. 'Let us look at the book again.'

Standing up, they lifted the lid and rummaged around in the trunk, at last finding the volume. John read the relevant passage through. He looked up, smiling mischievously.

'Let us put this theory to the test. If the dead can appear to the living, let us make a pact that if either of us is killed, the spirit of the dead party will appear to the survivor.'

'Agreed,' said Wyndham, taking John's hand.

'Should we not make a formal vow to each other, such as is done in Scotland, in hand-fasting?'

'Aye,' agreed Wyndham. 'Let us swear – but by what?'

'Upon our honour as men – for in this matter we can swear by nought else, our belief in all other matters being subject to question.' John smiled, but the brilliant eyes were serious. 'I will start. I, John Wilmot, Earl of Rochester, do swear upon my word as a man of honour that should I die in tomorrow's action, whatever of me is immortal shall appear to my friend John Wyndham, to give him notice of a future state, should such state exist.'

'I, John Wyndham, do likewise swear that if I should die in tomorrow's action my spirit is to appear to my friend John Wilmot, Earl of Rochester, to give him notice of a future state, should such exist.'

Wyndham was just finishing as Montagu burst into the cabin. He looked at them in amusement. 'What happens here now, gentlemen? You look mighty serious.'

'We are charging our immortal souls to appear to the survivor, should one of us die in action tomorrow.'

Montagu was shocked. He looked at John sternly.

'Death and religion, my Lord, are no fit subjects for a jape."

''Tis not thought of as a jape,' retorted John indignantly, 'but as a serious experiment. If one of us dies, and does not appear to the other, we shall know that a future state does not exist, and that stories about Heaven and Hell are but tales put out by churchmen to fright us, as nurses do children.'

Montagu replied reprovingly. 'How will that be proof? You do not know that you will have the power to appear to your friend. Why should the veil of mystery which surrounds death be torn aside to satisfy your curiosity?'

'Why should it not? I am told that all that is required is the will. The will to appear to one's friend, and his readiness to apprehend one's presence. We have just willed ourselves to it.'

Montagu shuddered. 'Your lack of humility appals me. What is your will against the will of God?'

John shrugged. 'The will of God? What is that? Why should it be against the will of God that I should appear to my friend to convince him of the existence of a future state? Surely it would do religion a service, and convince doubters and unbelievers of the error of their ways.' He added decisively. 'If I do not appear to my friend it will be because a future state does not exist.'

'And I,' added Wyndham, 'believe the same. Will you not

join our pact? You too have had an intimation of death. Surely you would wish your fellows to know if this knowledge was rooted in the soul?'

Montagu drew back and crossed himself. The others exchanging looks, remembered that his brother was a noted papist. 'Is nothing sacred to you? Neither death, nor religion, nor love?'

John laughed, the tension breaking. 'Certainly love – but the other two? They need dispassionate investigation.'

Montagu sighed. 'To hear the way you talk of women, I would maintain that you were dispassionate about love too.'

'Never!' grinned John. 'Love needs the most passionate investigation possible.'

Montagu was not amused. 'Not reverence?' he said.

The two young men exploded with laughter. 'Obviously an admirer of old poet Randolph,' said John, and quoted:

> *I touch her like my beads with devout care,*
> *And come unto my Courtship as my prayer.*

'Does that sum up your philosophy for you, Ned?' gasped Wyndham.

'No,' frowned Montagu 'but neither do you. I believe that women are human beings needing our care and protection, not vessels for our use, and no more.'

'You maintain then that women have characters?' said Wyndham.

'Yes,' interjected John, 'some of them have characters, but those that do are usually disagreeable.'

Montagu was growing tired of the bright young men's exchanges and needed his bed. 'I trust, gentlemen, that you will survive tomorrow's action, and live to be disabused of your low opinion of women and of love. I had far rather you learnt that, than the secrets of life after death.'

He bowed. 'And now, my Lord, I am tired. I bid you good night.'

John grinned. 'I see, Wyndham, we are to be put to bed.'

He returned Montagu's bow. 'Sir, I leave you to dream of your goddess – of one who shall be nameless,' he added, rolling

44

his eyes. However, Montagu was busy with his hammock and was not to be drawn. John and Wyndham exchanged glances, then the young earl left to prepare for the night. As he settled into his own hammock he thought of Montagu's strange attachment. His devotion to Charles's unattractive Queen was certainly amusing. In matters of love, Montagu was all honour, devotion and the hero of ancient romance, Amadis de Gaul ... He must tell Harry Sidney of Montagu's sad tale. Sidney was showing far too much interest in the Duchess of York – he seemed to think her some sort of divine figure, poor fool! Still – at least she was handsome, which is more than could be said for Catherine! Sidney had good taste in women, though he was hopelessly romantic in his attitude towards them ... At this thought the memory of a pair of mocking brown eyes entered John's mind. He quickly pushed the memory aside. Yes, if women had character they were nearly always cold-hearted or disagreeable ... except for Sarah. He smiled. Yes, except for Sarah. She was deliciously alive, yet warm and affectionate too... He must see her again, if he got through tomorrow alive! But he knew now that he would. Sarah was something to look forward to.

* * *

During the night *Revenge* sailed for Bergen, but the roadstead was narrow and the water so shallow that by the time dawn had broken, very little progress had been made. When John and Wyndham came up on deck they found that the yard-arms of the ships were sticking in the very rocks, and that two or three hawsers had to be used for every ship, to be taken on her swing and so guided through the channel.

As *Revenge* cleared the gorge a pale, watery sun made a brief appearance in the sky. The crew were much cheered and by midday the fleet had reached deeper and broader water. However, as they reached Kaap Nordnes, the sky clouded again and the vessel ran aground. Teddiman had to wait for the tide to rise before his flagship could be brought off. The delay was tedious.

45

'Captain Langhorne should have his leadsman well flogged!' declared Stewart.

'But not until after the battle,' put in Harbord. 'We have need of every able-bodied man in the fleet.'

By six in the evening *Revenge* sighted Bergen, but the frigate *Foresight* came in so near to the flagship that the riggings of the two vessels became entangled, and great disorder ensued. Once free, the crew of *Revenge* were surprised to hear a shot whistle over their heads. It came from the castle at Bergen. The shot killed a man in the rigging of *Foresight*, and the crews of both ships sent up great shouts of anger.

'Let us give them a broadside,' shouted Clifford, 'while the seamen's blood is up!'

Teddiman was about to agree, but looking in the direction of the castle he saw a small skiff setting out.

'They are sending us a messenger. We must wait to hear what he has to say.'

He signalled to the fleet, and they lined up in half-moon formation, blocking the exit from the harbour. A sharp gale was blowing as the English squadron came to anchor within sight of the Dutch fleet, and the seamen gave a great shout of challenge to the Hollanders, who were lying one against another in the tiny harbour, incapable of firing a shot.

The Danish messenger came aboard. Harbord recognised him as Jens Toller, the official who had translated his letters of yesterday. Considerable indignation was felt that the Governor of the castle had despatched so lowly a messenger.

'Why did you fire upon us?' Harbord demanded angrily in French. Toller, recognising him, bowed, saying that Colonel Cicignon was outraged that the English fleet had omitted to salute the castle by striking topsails and flags.

'Good God, could he not see the trouble we were in, with *Foresight*!' demanded Stewart, shaking his fist in Toller's face.

'Gentlemen, gentlemen,' interrupted Clifford, making his way between them. 'We must treat Colonel Cicignon's envoy with courtesy. We were in the wrong in omitting to salute.' He took Toller over to Teddiman, and it was elicited that Colonel Cicignon wished to remind the English that according to the treaty the King of England had with his master, no more than five men-of-war could be allowed to enter the harbour at one time.

Clifford beckoned Montagu, and it was agreed that he should accompany Toller, see General Ahlfeldt, and explain the matter of the Secret Agreement. Montagu was also to point out that it was now evening, and far too late for the English to venture into the fjord unpiloted, even had they been willing to do so.

John and Wyndham watched Montagu depart in Toller's skiff. It was a cold depressing evening. Montagu wrapped his cloak closely about him to keep out the drizzling rain.

'This delay is proving invaluable to the enemy,' observed Wyndham, watching the Dutch move four of their ships athwart the harbour. 'They are now well placed to cover any attack upon the remainder of their fleet.'

'Yes,' added John, 'but they are still only four to our twenty-two fighting ships. The rest are but armed merchantmen, lying so close as to be incapable of defence.'

'Not if they combine with the Dane,' cut in Wyndham quickly. 'Look at that!' A party of Dutch seamen was dragging cannon from some of the larger ships which lay near the town, yoking them to drays, and taking them up to the fort.

'We should have attacked straight away!' cried John. They watched the preparation for battle until it began to get dark. Montagu returned to *Revenge* just before eight o'clock that evening.

'Ahlfeldt agrees that the whole fleet might anchor here until morning, and that six ships may be left to blockade the Dutch, but he denies all knowledge of the Secret Treaty, and will not allow us to make an attack upon them.'

'You received a rude reception?' enquired Clifford.

'Oh no,' Montagu was smiling with pleasure, 'Governor Ahlfeldt and Colonel Cicignon accorded me all the ceremonies due to an envoy of the King of England. They both came down to meet me with trumpeters and a guard of honour, and when I departed I was accompanied by a host of manservants carrying burning torches...'

'In the meantime, I have received a message from Colonel Cicignon,' interrupted Teddiman, 'telling me that if I do not retire within the hour he will have to deal with me "otherwise than he would desire". What does that mean?'

Montagu, a little deflated, explained. 'Colonel Cicignon is not our friend. He and Ahlfeldt seem to have had some disagreement over our reception. Ahlfeldt is full of compliment, and wishes to be accommodating, provided his "honour" can be protected. He was embarrassingly complaisant about the shot fired at our fleet. He said it was fired by an inexperienced Militia man, without orders to shoot into the vessel, and that if we wished the man hanged it should be done. I said that we had no wish to exact revenge for a mistake, but that as we were hoping for some assistance in effecting the capture of the Dutch, we should regard hindrance as an unfriendly act.'

'What did Cicignon say to that?'

'He spoke to Ahlfeldt in their damned outlandish tongue, then huffed out of the room.'

'And Ahlfeldt?'

'He said if we could reach some profitable agreement about the apportionment of prizes, he would undertake not to oppose our attack upon the Dutch, and that Cicignon would have to obey his orders.'

'What are the "profitable terms" he envisages?' asked Clifford.

'An equal division of the prizes between the King of England and the King of Denmark, and the exchange of hostages to ensure that this division is faithfully carried out.'

'Indeed? And what of his being a man of honour, as at his first conference?'

'He reverts to that argument now and anon, but says he wishes the English no discourtesy.'

Clifford and Teddiman considered that Ahlfeldt, with his half-hearted overtures, was just playing for time. While Clifford drafted terms for a possible agreement, Teddiman sought to improve the position of his fleet. It was now quite dark.

Montagu returned to Ahlfeldt with Clifford's proposals, but could not reach agreement with him about the division of prizes. He returned to *Revenge* several times during the night with counter-proposals. Ahlfeldt at one time expressed himself so delighted with Mr Montagu's company that he would be willing to accept him as a hostage, and would demand no other.

Towards dawn agreement had almost been reached, but Ahlfeldt would not accede to Clifford's demand that an ultimatum be sent to the Dutch by seven in the morning, with their reply required by nine. He felt that such a request, to a nation with which his country was not yet at war, would be discourteous, to say the least.

'He is unminded to cut their throats until they have breakfasted?' queried John sardonically, when Montagu visited their cabin just before four.

Montagu ignored John's irony and said he thought Ahlfeldt wished Teddiman to defer the attack for four days, until he had had time to send to Copenhagen for instructions and receive a reply.

'I am now returning to Ahlfeldt with Clifford's reply. De Ruyter is expected in the North Sea at any time and the business will brook no delay.'

Montagu, having failed to obtain Ahlfeldt's agreement to an early ultimatum, returned to *Revenge* just as dawn was breaking. Teddiman gave orders to begin the attack.

From his position at the forward rail of the poop, John watched the seamen making the yards gay with bunting. Great scarlet waist cloths were hung round the ships's bulwarks 'as well for the countenance and grace of the ship as to cover the men from being seen'. Just after five in the morning Teddiman let fly his fighting colours and poured a broadside into the enemy ships.

John was standing next to Montagu, a musket in his hand. He glanced at Montagu's strained face.

As soon as a break in the gunfire allowed, John enquired, 'Do you feel tired – lacking sleep?'

'No,' replied Montagu, 'exhilarated!' His eyes were bright, his manner strangely elated. 'Ahlfeldt is a damned rogue, but a pleasant one. I enjoyed my conversations with him.'

'Did he, in honesty, wish to come to some agreement with us?'

49

'Yes, he told me he thought it a great pity the King of England should break friendship for a few rascally prizes, and I told him that the remark was equally applicable the other way about.' Montagu smiled complacently. 'It was quite like the old days when I was often entrusted with his Majesty's business abroad.'

'Look!' yelled Harbord. 'Those plaguey Dutch are running to man the guns on the ramparts. They will fire on us, and Sir Thomas has expressly forbidden us to fire on the forts.'

The Dutch ships athwart the harbour were now beginning to reply to Teddiman's attack, and chain shot came tearing through the rigging of *Revenge*. Masts and sail crashed down, and a cable which had broken in two cut Sir Thomas Clifford in the face.

About a quarter of an hour later the Castle opened fire upon the English fleet. Soon all the Bergen forts were beginning to fire as well. Three hundred guns were trained on Teddiman's ships, obliging them to counter this as well as fire from the Dutch ships. The wind was with the enemy and it blew strongly out of the harbour, blinding the English with smoke.

John, his face blackened, and choking with the acrid smell of gunpowder, kept to his allotted station on the poop. So much was happening, and he felt useless as a mere observer.

Teddiman, unable to bear down upon the Dutch ships, at last gave orders to fire upon the forts.

'Mr Wyndham,' he called, 'pick those devils off the ramparts!' Wyndham was standing on the port side near the small fort called Nordnes. It had recently opened fire, and an additional party was running along to man another gun. Wyndham shot two of them with his musket, and had the satisfaction of seeing the rest of the team melt away.

'My Lord, I require your assistance on the starboard side,' called Teddiman. John looked round. A damaged English vessel was being blown towards *Revenge*. 'Help the men hold fire-booms, to keep them off!'

Eventually the ship was extricated from Teddiman's line of fire, and he was able to resume his attack upon the Dutch. For three hours the English fought, but they were exposed to an attack twice as fierce as they had expected. Towards eight Teddiman gave the order to retire.

Captain Langhorne, the commander of *Revenge*, moved towards the man in charge of the whipstaff, giving orders for the ship to be turned. As he did so, a cannonball tore across the deck, killing him. His blood and brains splattered Wyndham, who was standing near. Up till then Wyndham had been busily taking shots at Nordnes, but seeing the captain transformed within seconds to a mangled heap of blood and rags, he was seized with an overwhelming desire to be sick. He staggered towards the bulwark and hung on trembling, trying to overcome the feeling that his legs had turned to jelly.

Montagu, seeing Wyndham's fixed stare and grey green face, ran over to support him. 'Have you heard,' he quipped desperately, 'that the Dutchmen are running short of heavy shot, and will shortly be firing their round red cheeses?'

Wyndham gave a hysterical laugh as a second cannon ball tore through the bulwark, flinging both of them across the breadth of *Revenge*. Wyndham fell dead at John's feet, and Montagu, his belly swept away by the cannonball, staggered a few steps screaming. He fell to the deck and thrashed about as his guts flowed out of him.

John stood speechless, frozen to the spot. I am alive, he thought, and cannot move. Montagu should be dead, yet has the energy of twenty men. It is unbelievable that a man should suffer such agony. He started at the touch of a hand upon his arm.

'Lend me your musket, Sir,' said the boatswain.

Unthinking and unquestioning, John handed over his weapon and saw the boatswain turn it and strike Montagu a heavy blow to the back of his neck. ''Tis all as can be done for him, Sir. In an hour he will be dead.'

And it was as the boatswain said.

4

After Bergen

John spent the next few days in a state of dreamlike unreality. He was aware of all about him; he was, in fact, a docile and efficient automaton, but shock had removed the normal condition of unreflecting participation in the life around him. He watched himself performing, like a marionette.

The English fleet had limped from Bergen harbour, making their way up the narrow fjord as best they could. Had the Dutch taken it into their heads to pursue them, it would have gone ill with the whole fleet. Six ships were very defective in masts and hull and could hardly sail. Dead and wounded lay about the decks. John's back and arms ached with the fetching and carrying, and with the effort of pulling on ropes and oars. Every man's help had been needed to get the defective ships out of the line of fire.

'How we got out of that harbour, I shall never know,' declared Harbord, appearing from below with a fistful of cheese and ship's biscuit. 'I'm as ravenous as a dog – Here, want some?' he asked, offering John a morsel.

John shuddered and turned away. He had been watching a party of seamen carry a covered stretcher below. What was left of Montagu had been removed from the deck. It was now midday and they were anchored in Gjelte fjord, about five leagues from Bergen.

'The Dutch have not the courage to fight out of range of their friend's guns,' sneered Clifford, whose face was heavily bandaged. He peered fiercely up the fjord with his one good eye. He and Teddiman had taken stock of their position. The ships had been brought off safely, but with no profit. Provisions were getting low, so it was decided that as soon as the fleet was seaworthy they would sail for Bridlington, despatching a pinnace to take the unhappy news to Lord Sandwich. During the rest of the day the seamen were fitting new masts and repairing sails. Work continued until the light failed, then after a hasty meal the carpenters worked well into the small hours. The lonely fjord rang with the sound of their hammers, their torches of burning pitch clustering like fireflies about the broad hulls of the ships.

Dawn, when it came, was dull and mizzly but it was heartening to see the good repair which had been made to the fleet. The Dutch and Danes had left them alone to lick their wounds, and good use had been made of the time. Teddiman had posted guards all round the anchorage, but no movement had been reported. The seamen were bitterly resentful of the Danes' double dealing, and commanders were having difficulty in preventing men from making marauding expeditions upon the land around.

'Looting will be severely punished,' threatened the new captain, but the order was received with resentment below decks.

'Are we to have no profit, to compensate for the loss of our men?' muttered the bosun. 'The sneaking rogues deserve a drubbing.'

''Tis no fault of these ignorant fishermen, and stupid country hinds that their Governor is a rogue,' John argued. ''Twould be unfair to rob them, and we no better than pirates if we did so.'

The bosun looked at John contemptuously. A whey-faced lad, daintily telling a man twice his age his business? These namby-pamby gentlemen were more nuisance than they were worth!

Clifford came over to the Volunteers. 'My Lord, I wish you and Mr Stewart to transfer to *Breda* for a few hours. Twenty-nine of her men have been slain, including her captain, and fifty-five have been wounded. You must make yourself useful to the new captain in any way he thinks fit.'

Just as they were going, Clifford handed John a paper. 'Here is a list of precautions to be taken against the breeding of vermin. Give it to the captain, and tell him they are to be strictly carried out. When you return, bring me a detailed list of the wounded and what is required for their recovery. I am told there is a grave shortage of clothing and bandages, and that many of the men will need to be transferred to larger ships, better fitted with cradles and surgeons.'

Upon reaching *Breda* they found conditions appalling. The crew, mostly paupers pressed into service, had only filthy rags for covering. The few experienced seamen had nothing but contempt for them and treated them like slaves. The young lieutenant, recently promoted captain, was determined that discipline and efficiency should be instilled into his crew. He watched impassively as a poor shivering wretch was beaten towards the foremast and told to climb and disentangle a cut cable from the rigging. The unhappy wight, torn between his obvious fear of climbing, and his wish to avoid blows, was screaming and grovelling at the bosun's feet. John could stand it no longer.

'I will climb and do it.'

The bosun looked at him in amazement. 'Such tasks are not for one of your Lordship's quality.'

'But I wish to know how it is done.'

The man shrugged: such were the whims of young lords. He demonstrated the best way to climb, saying, 'Keep your eyes above you, or just in front of you – and don't look down.'

John leapt onto the ropes, climbing quickly, but slowing down as the ratlines grew narrower. Seeing that *Revenge*, across the fjord, was running up a new signal, he looked down to see if the captain had observed it. He was quickly reminded of the bosun's advice by the sudden sickening feeling in his stomach and the trembling of his hands on the ropes. He took a deep breath and turned his eyes upwards to the tangle of ropes above him. Luckily the cable could be released with one hand. Would he have had the courage to rely only upon the balance of his feet, had the use of both hands been necessary? He preferred not to think about it. Already his hands were wet and sticky.

Releasing the cable, and shakily descending to the deck, he returned with a greater respect for the abilities of ordinary seamen.

'You demean yourself in the eyes of these cattle, performing such tasks,' muttered Stewart, unimpressed.

John replied aggressively. 'Nonsense, had I failed, perhaps so, but I doubt if you could have done as well.'

'Touché,' Stewart sneered. 'The next time a sail needs changing, we must ask a peer of your Lordship's mettle to do it.'

'Seamen's work would be beyond my abilities, but I have an increased appreciation of their skills. You should try it yourself.'

'I have no ambition to acquire their mechanic arts,' sniffed Stewart. He turned away contemptuously.

'You starched poltroon!' threw out John angrily. 'You fear to try your courage in any way but that of a fine gentleman.'

Stewart spun round, his hand on his sword. 'No man calls my courage into question.'

'I do, you bloody prig.' Within seconds their swords were out, and they were fighting along the deck. The captain saw the fracas and fired his pistol into the air, ordering them to stop. 'Have we not trouble enough? The Dutch may soon be upon us!'

John, a little ashamed at having provided more trouble for the overworked captain, glanced at Stewart, who was glaring at him fiercely. He thought angrily that the ways of fate were puzzling. Why had this fool been spared, when Wyndham, curious, vital Wyndham had been killed?

The captain intervened. 'Come gentlemen, desist. The Commander needs our services.'

John put up his sword, and bowed to Stewart. 'I recant "poltroon" – in his Majesty's service.'

Stewart replied a little stiffly. 'You apologise then?'

'Yes, I apologise,' said John, thinking the matter ended. But Stewart's dignity had been mortally offended.

'Should your Lordship insult me again, in any manner whatsoever, I shall demand satisfaction, as soon as this campaign is over.'

'Hoity-toity!' mocked John. 'I shall be delighted to meet you ashore, but let us fight about something more serious than name-calling. Shall I leave you to think up a suitable quarrel?' He grinned. 'Come, Stewart, there is work to do here. Let us be friends.' He extended his hand.

Stewart took it coldly. 'Your Lordship is at times a little too free with his tongue.'

'Is not freedom the essence of friendship?'

'Licence is not.'

The captain, anticipating a renewal of the debate, decided to part the two young cockerels before further trouble ensued.

'My Lord, I believe you are to prepare a list for Sir Thomas Clifford. My lieutenant here will show you to the surgeon's quarters. Mr Stewart, take a party ashore, and endeavour to obtain fresh meat from the local people.'

During the next two hours John was busily employed noting the surgeon's requirements. The sights below decks appalled him. He passed between closely-packed rows of suffering men. The surgeon said that many would die, although he never ceased to marvel at man's powers of recuperation. The most dreadful flesh wounds, providing they did not turn gangrenous, would eventually heal, showing how little dangerous, after all, was the cutting of muscle in strong and healthy men. John thought the man's tone a little complacent, but upon reflection realised that the lack of emotion was purposefully cultivated. They stopped in front of a man who could not stop gasping and coughing. The surgeon looked serious, and shook his head. 'He will die,' he said. 'A mere puncture in the lungs or abdomen proves fatal.'

* * *

When John returned to *Revenge*, Sir Thomas Teddiman was receiving a deputation from the local inhabitants. They complained that a party of seamen had broken open their church doors and had stolen the vestments and chalice. Sir Thomas expressed regret, and ordered a diligent search to be made through the whole fleet. He promised that if found, the men involved would be hung.

John had a shrewd idea that Stewart's foraging party had

been responsible, but decided to keep his mouth shut. The captain of *Buda* had trouble enough, and he had no wish to provoke another quarrel.

He found Clifford was preparing a report for Lord Sandwich and another for Arlington, the Secretary of State. He presented him with the list of requirements for *Buda*. Clifford raised his eyes wearily, but smiled when he saw it was John.

'My Lord, a ketch is leaving with despatches for the admiral within one hour. If you wish to write to your kinsfolk, you must do it now. You may not have another opportunity for some weeks.'

John remembered a long-forgotten promise to his mother, so he retired to his cabin and took up a pen.

> *From the coast of Norway*
> *among the rocks.*
> *Aboard Revenge.*
> The third of August, 1666

Madam, I hope it will not be hard for your Ladyship to believe that it has been want of opportunity and not neglect, that has prevented me from writing to your Ladyship all this while.... He paused, wondering how he should continue. A letter full of compliment? Expressing his filial duty? No, after the experiences of the past few days a letter of convention seemed worthless. He would relate all that he could remember of the action but omit the horrifying details. He wrote steadily, unaware of the passage of time. *We shot at all and in a short time routed a number of men from one of their forts whence they had showered small shot upon us; but the castles were not to be fought down ... within three hours we lost 200 men and six Captains, our cables were cut, and we were driven out by the wind ... Mr Montagu and Tom Wyndham's brother were both killed with one shot just by me, but God Almighty was pleased to preserve me from any kind of hurt. Madam, I fear I have become tedious and beg your Ladyship's pardon, I remain your most obedient son, Rochester.*

Having sealed the letter, John went to find Sir Thomas

Clifford. Just as he reached the stateroom a sound of trumpets cleft the night air. John ran over to the window and saw a magnificent barge pulling in towards *Revenge*. It was resplendent with cloths of crimson and was filled with liveried servants bearing flaming torches. Clifford told him to make his way to the entry port and find out the identity of the visitor. He was told that it was General Ahlfeldt's clerk, Jens Toller, who had come aboard.

'We expected Ahlfeldt himself,' Clifford said later, 'considering the excess of state. However, 'twas but a message saying the general regretted using us "rudely".'

'Was that all?' queried John incredulously.

'No, I suspect that he has received instructions from Copenhagen, for he has requested that a suitable envoy be sent to discuss matters whereby "all mistakes and misunderstandings" would be resolved. Teddiman says I am to go myself with one attendant.'

John begged to be allowed to be that attendant, so early the next morning they set off for Langmandez Gaard, the governor's country residence, disguised as common sailors seeking to purchase bread and fresh meat. General Ahlfeldt had indicated in his message that he did not wish Cicignon to know of the negotiations.

Upon their arrival at his home, the general expressed regret at the 'glorious death of so brave a gentleman as his friend Montagu'. What was glorious about it? thought John bitterly. General Ahlfeldt much deplored the unfortunate necessity he had found to deal with the English 'so much otherwise than he had desired', but could still not be persuaded to afford any active assistance in an attack upon the Dutch. However, to ensure his future neutrality, he insisted upon the prizes being divided equally between the two kings.

While the governor served them wine, Clifford whispered to John, 'In truth, this connivance he offers is no more than a cock match, and he the umpire between us!'

Ahlfeldt resumed his excuses: his personal honour was at stake; he had given a promise to the Dutch that they could rest with safety in his harbour.

'How much,' said Clifford, 'do you think the Dutch East

India Fleet worth?'

On the governor's own estimation it was considered that the Dutch ships could not be worth less than six million pounds sterling.

'Surely,' Clifford continued, 'half such a prize would be worth a little effort on our behalf?'

Ahlfeldt, in reply, embarked upon a voluminous account of his family history and illustrious connections, and said he could not perform any act that would sully their memory. In execrable French he sketched out the difficulties he would have in dealing with Colonel Cicignon, and considered that if the Danish forts were silent during the proposed second attack upon the Dutch, he had provided all the assistance he could in honour allow. To ensure the agreed apportionment of prizes, he insisted upon the exchange of high-ranking officers, but hearing of John's nearness in the King's affections, he indicated his willingness to take the Earl of Rochester as hostage.

Clifford said he would have to consult with Teddiman before agreeing to the arrangement, and they parted with much compliment on both sides. On the way back to *Revenge*, John wondered what had been achieved by Montagu's death. They were no further forward than they had been three days ago, and many lives had been lost.

When Clifford recounted his interview to Teddiman, the admiral considered making a further attack, but the thought of having to divide the prizes with the Danes, without their giving any assistance in the fighting, decided him to sail for home instead. A powerful Dutch fleet might arrive at any moment.

The ship's company ate a sparse dinner that day. Very little fresh meat had been found available, and the seamen were already on half rations for beer. A quantity of fresh fish had been caught but would not last them long.

'It angers me more than I can say,' growled Clifford, 'that all our brave ships should slink home like whipped curs, because of the stupidity and avarice of the Danish governor. Here was at stake the whole wealth of the United Provinces, fifty-seven great ships all richly laden, ten of them East Indiamen, the rest from the Straits, Cadiz, the West Indies and Guinea.'

'I hear the Danish king is much in debt to the Hollanders,' said John.

'Aye, it is unbelievable that having now a treasure within his grasp, more by much than all his crown is worth, that he should not take his opportunity to break with them. He would have got into his hands the greatest treasure that ever was together in the world.'

The weather was rough that night and when John returned to his cabin he was unable to sleep. His thoughts kept returning to Wyndham and Montagu. The tiny cabin he had shared with them now seemed vast. Only their trunks bore witness to his friends' one-time existence. For what had they died? A squalid encounter involving high-level piracy? Nothing had been achieved, neither riches, nor glory, nor honour. What did they think now – if capable of recollection in the spirit state?

Suddenly he remembered the pact he had made the night before Wyndham's death. Would his friend appear to him? How? And if so, what would be the judgement of John's sophisticated friends at court? That he was a gullible fool? Before any credibility could be allotted to the experiment, Wyndham's ghost must appear to him before witnesses. He pushed away the remembrance of Wyndham's death. It had been swift, his friend had not suffered the agonies that Montagu had suffered, but the task of gathering what remained of his body had been just as grotesque. He deliberately turned his mind to other scenes.

He remembered discussing Italy with his friend. How fair life had been there ... Wyndham had enjoyed Italy too ... Just as he was sinking into sleep, John remembered his friend telling him of the Duke of Buckingham's interest in prophecies. Buckingham's father had been given ghostly warning of his own assassination at Portsmouth, but was said to have laughed it to scorn. All this had happened long ago in the late king's reign, but his son was said to be intrigued with the story. It was reported that Buckingham had in his employ a personal astrologer well informed in all occult practices ... The fellow might be able to assist with John's predicament. He resolved to question the Duke upon his return to court.

* * *

John and Clifford left *Revenge* with despatches and their pinnace reached *The Prince* next day, Lord Sandwich read the reports and discussed them with Clifford. He heard Clifford's complaints about the lack of medical supplies, and asked John questions about the state and number of the wounded.

Sandwich sighed when he heard of the shortages. 'His Majesty's servants ashore mind not his business, but only the profit their places afford. Much of the money assigned for the Navy, and actually reaching us in the form of provisions, is abysmally low.'

'But that is wrong,' put in John heatedly. 'If his Majesty's servants are dishonest, they should lose their positions.'

Lord Sandwich smiled wearily. The young Lord was both honest and able, but he had much to learn of the ways of the world. He decided to venture a gentle rebuke, saying smoothly, 'Even if they are related to my Lady Castlemaine?'

'Good God, most particularly if they are related to my cousin Barbara!' exclaimed John as he turned away fuming. Sandwich and Clifford exchanged knowing smiles.

It was arranged that Clifford should be despatched to Hull, to give the Duke of York a detailed account of the expedition. Before departing on *Drake*, Clifford recommended John's work to Sandwich, and suggested he be given the task of acting as his deputy for the sick seamen. Lord Sandwich agreed, and the fleet made for Southwold Bay, to put the sick ashore and obtain fresh men and provisions.

A glaring discrepancy had been found between the victuallers' statement of the drink said to have been provided for the last voyage, and that actually put on board. When Lord Sandwich had read John's report, he put his hand upon the young man's shoulder. 'You are right to put this in writing, my Lord, and I will draw attention to the discrepancy in my next letter to his Highness, but I doubt if much will be achieved by it, until the Duke returns to London.'

John sensed that he would have to content himself with Lord

Sandwich's promise: retribution for the King's unregenerate servants would have to wait its turn.

After many urgent messages were sent ashore, supplies began to arrive, and on the twenty-fourth of the month Mr Knight, a Court Surgeon, came aboard with a private letter for the admiral, from the King. Mr Knight was a great talker and brought the ship's company the news that nearly four thousand persons had recently died of the plague in London. John was relieved to hear that his mother was away from the town.

'The court is unlikely to return while the plague is rife,' said Mr Knight. 'His Majesty is at present at Salisbury, and the Duke of York is upon a Northern tour, and holds his court at Hull.' John heard that his mother was in attendance upon the Duchess and that she had one of his small nieces with her. The Duchess was said to be delighted with little Mistress Lee. Mr Knight, flattered by the young Lord's interest, continued to gossip. The Duke had been lavishly entertained by Sir George Savile at Rufford, and the Duchess had looked with favour upon Sir George's young kinsman, Mr Henry Sidney. He was now her Master of Horse.

John, glad to hear of his friend's promotion, asked if there was any news of Sir George's brother, Henry. 'Aye,' said Mr Knight, 'Mr Savile is now Groom of the Bedchamber to the Duke and will attend upon him when he returns south. Parliament is to be called to Oxford in October, and the whole court goes there then.'

For the next two days the repairing and provisioning of the fleet hurriedly continued. Then, on the twenty-seventh of August Sandwich heard that de Ruyter's battleships had reached Bergen. 'The Dutch convoy must sail for home before the winter storms,' said Sandwich, 'so we have hopes of catching them yet.'

The next day, in fearful weather, they weighed anchor and sailed for the Dogger Bank. At a council of war it was agreed that the large battleships should hold themselves in readiness to fight in line against de Ruyter's men-of-war, and that the frigates should attack the merchantmen, and take the prizes.

Sandwich asked John if he would care to join one of the frigates. 'Prize money,' he smiled, 'being a great inducement to young men of valour, but no fortune.' John agreed enthusiastically and it was arranged that he should transfer to *Lion*, under the command of Sir Edward Spragge.

'Ah, my Lord, I am glad to see that the Danish guns failed to strip you of your red coat,' said Spragge jocularly. 'We may have need of it yet.'

John, remembering his discomfiture at the Admiral's dinner some weeks ago, coloured slightly, but managed to reply smoothly that his life, nay his very clothing, was at his Majesty's disposal, should the exigencies of the service require it. Spragge turned his sharp blue eyes upon the young Volunteer, and seeing the ghost of a smile twitching about the corners of John's mouth, laughed aloud, saying that he could see his Lordship was a subtle rogue who knew how to take a little raillery in good part.

'I sense we may have good sport once we know each other,' said Spragge, as he took John below and brought out some Irish whiskey. 'A good brew, from the land of my birth,' he pronounced, pouring out two good measures. 'To our better acquaintance,' he toasted. By the end of the evening they thought each other capital fellows.

Sir Edward Spragge was courtly, well-dressed and eloquent, with only a hint of brogue betraying his Irish origins. He was a notable contrast to the 'tarpaulin' captains of Teddiman's type. Teddiman was a valiant fighter and a good seaman, but he was rough and inarticulate in his speech, and could scarce put pen to paper. Spragge was ambitious, with relations at Court to help him, and he intended to make his way in the world. Sea service was to be but the first step in his career. John had heard from others of his skill and bravery. He was now to hear of it from the man himself. Sir Edward was charming and able, but modesty was not one of his virtues.

Spragge had been knighted for his service at the Battle of Lowestoft, where his actions had been favourably observed by the Duke and Prince Rupert. He now intended to acquire money to support that favourable position, either by the capture of a Dutch prize, or by marriage with a rich widow. 'But my dear Jack,' he said, 'I had far rather it were the Dutch prize. Marriage is not to my taste; I like variety. A choice of pretty pullets abroad, rather than one hen at home!'

'My sentiments entirely, my dear Sir Edward,' said John, laughingly at his ease as Spragge refilled his glass. He was flattered by the confidences of this accomplished and authoritative man some years his senior, and was glad he had made the move to *Lion*. Lord Sandwich and the officers aboard *The Prince* were a professional and formal body of men. General conversation was inclined to be dull. Spragge was a jolly fellow, and had a good voice. He and John sang a few catches together when the Lieutenant and two other Volunteers came to join them at the evening meal.

As the night wore on, the gale strengthened, and Spragge was informed that *Lion* had sprung a leak. He took John below with him. The men were hard at work with the pumps, while the carpenters sought to repair the damage. But water had entered the gunpowder hold: it was essential that the barrels should be removed. John saw his pleasant drinking companion transformed immediately into a professional commander. Spragge gave orders for the safe stowage of the gunpowder, transferred several members of the crew to assist with the pumping operations, directed sail-makers, cooks and cabin boys to assist by putting the whole force of their weight against the planks while the carpenters did their work, and did not scorn to put his own back against the wood. He inspired his ship's company with such a wholeness of will, that it was marvellous to watch him. John recalled the unhappy atmosphere aboard *Breda*, and pondered upon the difference in commanders. Spragge was no harsh disciplinarian, but he had energy, interest and ability, and the men responded to his call.

At last the leak was stopped, and most of the ship's company staggered to their hammocks to get some rest. The weather was foul and the ship rocked and shuddered so much that John got very little sleep that night, and was badly sick. The next morning he refused food, but attempted to stagger about the ship, remaining upright by an effort of will.

'The Dutch must be in league with Lapland witches,' said Sir Edward. 'Never in my life have I known such a gale.' De Ruyter was eluding them, but although the storm was preventing them from finding him, it was at the same time frustrating the Dutchman's efforts to keep his convoy together. One after another the Hollanders were dispersing in the storm, and all de Ruyter's attempts to reassemble them were proving vain.

On the third of September visibility improved, and seven or eight of the stragglers were seen as they made their way towards Texel. It was reported that the great East Indiamen, foul after their long journey and difficult to manoeuvre, were rolling about helplessly in the North Sea. Sandwich gave orders for *Hector* to attack *Phoenix*, an East Indiaman estimated to be worth more than two million pounds. One of de Ruyter's frigates was in attendance and trained numerous broadsides upon *Hector*. The Dutch guns tore immense holes in her superstructure, she gave a great list and sank and the main part of her crew were drowned.

'Poor wretches,' shouted Spragge. 'I'll be revenged for them!' He bore down upon the Dutchman. John, deafened by the gunfire, wondered if he would come through this second experience of battle alive. His orders were to observe the activity on the upper gun deck, but to hold himself in readiness with his sword, should there be an opportunity of boarding the Dutchman.

The disciplined efficiency of the gun team inspired his admiration. The sweat was rolling from the men's bodies, in spite of the cold wind and showers of spray. Their gunfire reduced the Dutch frigate to helplessness. Spragge manoeuvred close enough to board her, and his men invaded her with barbarian cries. Swords, pistols, cutlasses, meat-axes, marling spikes and clubs were the weapons they carried. They murdered impartially and systematically. If you failed to kill the Dutchman in front of you, he would kill you. John attacked a Dutch officer with his sword. His opponent riposted skillfully and John would have been a dead man had it not been for his steel breastplate. As the Dutchman withdrew from his lunge, John penetrated his guard and ran him through the body. It all happened so quickly he could scarcely believe he had killed his first man. He had little time to reflect upon it because another Dutchman was upon him with a club. John quickly dodged away, then brought his sword down upon the man's arm. His opponent would not wield his club again.

Looking around he found Spragge at his side, smiling triumphantly. 'The frigate is ours – now for the prize!' Leaving a party on board to secure the prisoners, John and Spragge returned to *Lion*, and together with *Adventure* they pursued the rich Dutch merchantman, *Phoenix*. Her commander, having watched the unhappy fate of the frigate, decided to surrender. They took a Dutch vice-Admiral prisoner, together with several hundred men. As soon as the prizes were secured the whole English fleet tacked westward, to avoid the dangers of a lee shore.

When an account was given to Sandwich, they learned that *Plymouth* and *Milford* had taken another rich prize, *Slothony*, together with its Dutch rear-admiral, and fourteen hundred men. Of the smaller vessels taken one was a merchantman from the Straits, and the other a Malaga man. The only English loss was *Hector*.

For another week they weathered the storm on Dogger Bank. The atmosphere remained thick and mizzly. Break of day on the ninth brought fifteen more Hollanders into view, accompanied by some of de Ruyter's frigates. There was a sharp encounter, and it was heard that *Revenge* had lost her captain, but by nine in the morning the English fleet had taken four men-of-war, one merchantman and nearly a thousand prisoners.

The Admiral, directing operations from *The Prince*, was informed that thirty more Hollanders were passing on the horizon. The battleship gave chase, but the wind rose to a gale, and sight of the Dutch was soon lost in the spray. It was decided to give up pursuit and take home the prizes already secured.

John, staggering across the foredeck of *Lion*, and hanging on to a bulwark to avoid being swept away by the wind, had never before seen such a great sea. An enormous wave came crashing over the ship, but miraculously the vessel came through. John, wet from head to foot, was glad to get below. The wind dropped a little overnight, and the following morning a messenger came from Lord Sandwich requesting the Earl of Rochester to return to *The Prince*. John was glad to see the messenger was Harbord, and they exchanged news of all that had happened to them since they had last seen each other.

Soon after John reached *The Prince*, another gale blew up and the vessel's foresail and topsail were carried away. John was glad to have a cabin to himself again. He realised with surprise that the company of Harbord and Stewart was proving less amusing than in the past, and that he no longer cared whether or not their opinions of him were favourable. He and Stewart had patched up their relationship, but they both discovered they had little in common. The company of Clifford and Edward Spragge had accustomed John to the conversation of men of authority and judgement, and Stewart and Harbord, although sobered by their fighting experiences, seemed like boys in comparison. John was glad of the work he had to do in connection with the sick and wounded; time wasting debate with young companions was no longer an agreeable pastime.

About five in the evening all on board were heartily relieved to see Yarmouth steeple on the horizon, and some hours later the whole fleet of about eighty sail anchored in Southwold Bay. Sandwich called John to his day cabin.

'My Lord, I intend to despatch you tomorrow with a letter for his Majesty. Can you complete your report on the sick and wounded by tonight?'

'Yes, but I shall have to visit those ships which have just come in,' John replied. He noticed that one of them was *Success*, in which he had embarked from Yarmouth a bare two months ago.

Captain Grove welcomed him aboard, well pleased with the expedition. 'We have taken some fine prizes, my Lord.'

John grunted. 'Aye, but not as fine as those we could have taken at Bergen.'

Grove, surprised at the impatience of his tone, looked at him closely. 'Ah, I heard you were at Bergen. A sorry business, I fear.'

'Yes,' said John shortly. 'I lost two of my friends. Have you many casualties on board?'

'Six dead, and fifty wounded. I will take you below.'

They climbed down an ill-lit companionway to the orlop deck, where the wounded were accommodated below the waterline. As they reached the bottom, a scream burst through the fetid air. The surgeons were about their work, and the floor was littered with baskets containing the severed limbs of their patients. The bulkheads, painted dull red to disguise the presence of blood, added to the pervading sense of gloom and pain. John recognised an old sailor moving amongst the wounded, water jug in hand. 'How are you, Frank, I am glad to see the Dutch did not fell you.'

The seaman peered at John, and set down the jug. 'Ah, 'tis you, my young Lord! Faith, but y'are older already. Was it but eight weeks ago ye boarded *Success*?' Frank knelt down and gave a drink to a patient. The man's leg had been amputated a week ago, and the stench from the wound was appalling. 'This young fellow be like to die, Sir. He has the fever.'

John looked at the inflamed face, and the wild staring eyes of the man beneath him. The patient had caught hold of Frank's arm and would not let go. 'Yes, yes, lad, I promise,' said the old man trying to quiet him. 'You must rest now, rest.'

He got stiffly to his feet, muttering to John, 'He will not last the night.' John tried to recall where he had seen the patient before. Suddenly he remembered the worried lad he had seen on the quay – how many lifetimes ago?

'He be fearsome troubled, about a lass heavy with child,' whispered Frank. 'Was pressed the day afore their marriage, and now fears she will fall upon the parish when her time be come.' He clicked his lips impatiently. 'Foolish young creatures! But I promised to see that she gets his pay – I had to do him that last service.'

John nodded, wondering how many more tragedies the war would cause. He turned aside; there would be countless numbers, no doubt, but none of his concern. He found himself a clear corner and busied himself with his work. Just as he was leaving, the young man died. Making a final adjustment to the numbers of the dead, John completed his report and bade Frank Jones farewell.

* * *

Wine and fresh meat were provided at the Admiral's table that night and John enjoyed the best meal he had had for weeks. Lord Sandwich was in a jovial mood; toasts were numerous, and the Commander thanked his Flag Officers and Volunteers for their services. He congratulated them upon the capture of so many valuable Dutchmen.

Sir Roger Cuttance ventured a question. 'When can we take our prizes, my Lord?'

'When the Commissioners have made a computation of their value.'

'Faith,' growled Teddiman, 'and when is that to be?'

'When all the court rascals have had their pickings!' shouted Sir Thomas Allen, a rough 'tarpaulin' officer. The bottle had circulated several times and was loosening the gentlemen's tongues. 'Why should so many damned land-lubbers have first choice when those who won them have to wait their turn?'

Sir Thomas, his face red as a turkey-cock's, brought his fist down on the board. 'I, for my part, would take my prizes now, whilst they are at port, under my hand!' Sandwich was by now pleasantly fuddled and sought to pour oil upon troubled waters. 'Lord Rochester is to ride to the King tomorrow. I will mention the prizes in my letter. When the King considers the unexpected good fortune of our expedition, he may be inclined to grant us privilege.' A growl of agreement went up round the table. 'We may receive a reply by the time we reach Buoy of the Nore.'

Sir Edward Spragge cheered. 'To my Lord Rochester, may he bring us good news!'

John acknowledged the toast and proposed the health of all those at table. Pledge followed pledge, and Sir Edward entertained the company with a song. John followed it with an amusing imitation of General Ahlfeldt listing his illustrious ancestors. Harbord danced a hornpipe whilst the company whistled a tune. Bawdy tales were told; the party grew uproarious and did not disperse until the early hours of the morning.

5

St Giles and Oxford

September 1665

When John arrived at Salisbury, he was told that the King was staying at St Giles, Lord Ashley's house in Dorset. He started on the road again and passed under Ashley's handsome gate-house at five in the afternoon. The King and his host were still out hunting, so he was shown into Lady Ashley's oak-panelled parlour.

'I hear you bring good news from the fleet, my Lord. How prospers my Lord Sandwich?'

John bowed over Lady Ashley's hand. 'In good health. We have taken many fine prizes.'

Lady Ashley beamed with pleasure. 'You bring welcome news. How long have you been upon the road?'

'Four days. I left Oxford at first light this morning.'

'Have you dined?' John shook his head.

'Then you must be famished!' Lady Ashley turned and called a young girl who was sitting in the window sewing.

'Jane, go to the kitchen, and tell them to send up the cold leg of mutton, with fresh bread and cheese, and some ale.'

The maid rose, and John saw that she was but a child, although tall for her age. A cap covered her hair, and the modest collar which lightened her plain brown dress, gave her the look of a nun. Grey eyes regarded him seriously as he took off his cloak.

'Heyday, but you'll stare me out of countenance!' said John

gaily. Jane blushed, and dropped her eyes. Long black lashes veiled their grave regard. Curtseying, she ran upon her way.

'An obliging, modest maid,' said Lady Ashley. 'She is the child of our local curate, who died of the smallpox this summer. As she has no kin of her own, I took her in to be my waiting-maid, and I have not been sorry.'

John bowed politely. 'Assuredly a pretty child – and industrious too?'

'Aye, most clever with her needle,' continued Lady Ashley. 'She makes all her own clothes, and embroiders mine to perfection.'

John noticed Lady Ashley's fine gown. The costly yellow silk was lavishly embroidered with tiny sprigs of multi-coloured flowers. 'Did she work upon your yellow gown?'

'Yes, is it not fine? The child is a very paragon, and has so many useful accomplishments.'

Lady Ashley prattled on. John contrived an interest in all that was said, and was in consequence considered a very well-bred, civil young man.

Jane returned and set food upon the table. Lady Ashley bade him sit down, and then turned to Jane.

'Bring your guitar, and sing to us while my Lord eats,' said Lady Ashley. 'He tells me he loves music, and wishes to hear what is new-written at court.'

'I know only the old songs,' came the grave reply.

'Tush, child. Sir Charles Sedley has been teaching you one of his new compositions.'

'Yes, but I have it not to rights yet.'

John smiled indulgently. 'Is it very hard?'

'No, but Sir Charles says it should be sung with vivacity, and says it is a quality I lack.'

John, looking at the sober little figure, could not in honesty bring himself to disclaim the remark. 'Have you something more suitable in mind?'

'I know several of Shakespeare's songs. My father loved them greatly.'

'He is a favourite of mine too. Pray sing one of those.'

Jane's solemn eyes took in the young Lord's appearance.

71

How handsome he was, his dark hair shining against the rich red of his coat. Such a magnificent young man, and brave too ... he had been in battle, he had looked upon death. The thought brought her pain, she must not think of her father. She must sing. She picked up her instrument and struck a few chords.

> *Come away, come away, death,*
> *And in sad cypress let me be laid:*
> *Fly away, fly away, breath:*
> *For I am slain by a fair cruel maid.*

Her voice was good, and she sang with feeling. Too much, thought John ruefully, as the song brought to mind the mocking eyes of his own cruel enchantress. Would she have cared if he had been killed at sea?

> *Not a flower, not a flower sweet*
> *On my black coffin let there be strown:*
> *Not a friend, not a friend greet*
> *My poor corpse, where my bones shall be thrown.*

Jane's voice, trembling upon the edge of too much emotion, finally broke, dissolving into sobs. Lady Ashley hurried over to her.

'Child, child, you must not take on so! You spoil the pleasure of our guest.'

John, his mouth full of food, looked at them with some concern but wished that he could have eaten alone.

Jane looked up. 'Oh, my Lady, please forgive me ... and you too, my Lord.'

'Why of course, my child. Go to your chamber and rest. You must sing to my Lord on another occasion.'

Bobbing a curtsey to them both, Jane fled from the room.

'I hope you will excuse her, my Lord. She is still much distressed for the death of her father, and I fear the unhappy choice of song brought it back to her mind.'

'Mistress Jane's daughterly affection does her much credit.' Just then the sound of a hunting horn and the barking of dogs broke the rural silence of St Giles.

Lady Ashley went over to the window and saw a party of horsemen clatter into the yard. ''Tis his Majesty returned. I will let his Majesty know that my Lord is here.'

John took a hasty gulp of ale as Lady Ashley left the room. Opening his doublet he took out the packet from Lord Sandwich. There was not much time to eat further, for he heard a deep laugh and the sound of swift movement on the stairs.

'Johnny, Johnny, I hear you bring good news.'

John dropped to one knee as his Majesty entered the room. Charles, his humorous face alight with pleasure, went over and raised him quickly. 'Nay, lad, I do not wish to spoil your meal, but give me your letters quickly. When I have read them you must give me a first-hand account of the engagement. I am glad to see you well. Brown, is he not, Sedley?'

He turned to Sir Charles who stood just behind.

'Weather-beaten, Sire, rather than sunburned.'

'Aye' said John, 'we had foul weather in the North Sea.'

'You must tell me about it when you have eaten,' said the King. 'Attend upon us in an hour.'

The King went and John was left to finish his meal in peace.

About ten minutes later there was a shy knock upon the door, and Jane re-entered the room.

'My Lady says evensong is about to be read in the chapel and has sent me to show you the way there.' John had not bargained to make his devotions so soon, and said that he must hold himself in readiness to attend upon the King.

'Oh, but Sir Charles Sedley says he will summon you from the chapel should you be required before the service is over.'

John looked a little nonplussed.

Jane added, with a ghost of a smile, 'Sir Charles also said I was to tell you "the hour of deliverance is at hand."'

John murmured, 'My thanks to Sir Charles.' He looked at Jane and saw that she was carrying a prayer book. 'Who gave you this, your father?'

'No, my Lady Ashley. She is excessively kind to me, and it is one of my most treasured possessions.' She handed him the book, bound in fine calf, with golden lettering on the spine.

'It is indeed a very fine book.' John handed it back to her. 'Do you use it regularly?'

'Ah yes, twice a day for service, as well as for private study.'

'And you derive great benefit from these exercises?'

'Of course,' said Jane gravely. 'How can we live virtuously without the spirit of Grace to guide us?'

John smiled. What a funny little piece of solemnity! 'But you read other books, I hope?'

'Only the Bible, and some few books of devotion – and Shakespeare.'

'Thank heaven for Shakespeare!'

Jane looked up and saw that he was smiling. In a spirit of confidence she volunteered, 'I sometimes steal into my Lord's library, when he is not there, and look at the books about foreign lands.'

'Those interest you?'

Jane nodded as John continued, 'I have recently returned from abroad.'

'Did you see many strange sights?'

John smiled mischievously. 'Yes, in Bessarabia there are men with tails two yards long.'

Jane opened her grey eyes wide.

John went on, 'Which they carry elegantly over their arm as they walk along.'

Jane, unwilling at first to believe that he was lying, had at last to smile. 'I don't believe you.'

'My dear young lady, how can you imagine that I should wish to deceive you?'

'Perhaps you would not deceive, but I think you rally me a little, do you not?'

'A little,' admitted John, as they both laughed. 'But the pity of it,' he sighed 'that our fops here lack tails upon which they could tie a ribbon or two – or wear a very fine ring.'

Jane was convulsed with laughter. 'Fops like Sir George Hewitt?'

'Yes,' grinned John. 'Does that prancing clothes horse visit here?'

'Occasionally. He is a kinsman of my Lord Ashley.'

74

They had reached the chapel door. Jane raised a finger to her lips, and adopted a suitably grave expression. 'We must be quiet,' she whispered.

'I shall have to continue my tales of foreign travel upon another occasion?'

'Yes, funny false ones.' Her grey eyes were sparkling. John was beginning to think Sir Charles wrong: the child was not entirely without vivacity.

* * *

> *And after singing Psalm the Twelfth*
> *He laid his book upon the Shelf,*
> *And looked much simply like himself.*
> *With eyes turned up, as white as ghost,*
> *He cried, 'Ah, Lord of Hosts*
> *I am a rascal, that thou knowst.'*

The lines from *Hudibras* danced through John's mind as he watched Lord Ashley read the lesson. This artful man was acting a favourite part – the benevolent patriarch seeking the spiritual welfare of his dependants. The St Giles household had gathered in respectful silence to hear their Lord Temporal expound the instructions of the Deity. The proceedings seemed endless, but at last the chaplain read the benediction and the company made solemn procession towards the door. John was glad to see Sir Charles Sedley waiting there. He told him the King was ready to receive him.

'What's this I hear about little Mistress Jane being reduced to tears in your company?' bantered Sir Charles.

John shrugged. 'The child wept for the death of her father.'

Lord Ashley overheard their conversation. 'The Roberts child is most affectionate, and devout too...'

'I have already received a detailed account of her virtues from my Lady, your wife,' put in John quickly.

Lord Ashley understood and smiled. He said drily, 'There is not much to talk of in the peace of St Giles. London and the great world are far away.' He paused. 'His Majesty tells me Lord

Sandwich has written upon the matter of prizes. As you know I am one of the Commissioners. You may tell Lord Sandwich that no doubt he and I will be able to come to some amicable arrangement for the furtherance of his Majesty's business.'

John gave a sardonic smile; in furtherance of your own, he was thinking.

Sedley changed the subject. 'I hear the fair heiress pines for you at Oxford,' he whispered as they climbed the stairs.

'You are misinformed,' said John. 'She makes mock of me, and refuses to reply to the many letters I have sent her.'

'Nevertheless, she pines,' Sir Charles insisted. 'She had only that dull rogue Hinchingbrooke for company.'

'Lord Sandwich's son?' enquired John, surprised. 'I did not know he was my rival.'

'He had to stand down when Lady Castlemaine spoke to the King on your behalf, but of course, after your escapade in May, he is now free to make his addresses.'

'But Bess could never stomach that silent awkward coxcomb,' said John indignantly.

'I agree,' shrugged Sir Charles, 'but he now has the King's permission to address her.'

John considered this information. Was that why Lord Sandwich had been so reserved? To be sure he was not forthcoming with any man, but the remark about the preference shown to my Lady Castlemaine's relations now made additional sense. Could a man be fair to his son's rival?

'Ah, Johnny, there you are,' said the King. 'I have been reading good things of you. "Brave, industrious, and of parts fit to be very useful" in my service. I must make use of this industry Sandwich speaks of.'

'Assuredly,' put in Lord Ashley. ''tis a quality rare at your Majesty's court.'

Charles smiled benignly, turning to John. 'I hear you were of some assistance to Sir Thomas Clifford, who tells me there was a great shortage of medical supplies.'

'Yes, but that was not all,' John added indignantly. 'On our arrival at Southwold, we found that we had been debited with twice the amount of equipment supplied.'

Lord Ashley watched John with some amusement. 'My Lord fears his Majesty is ill served,' he sneered.

Charles, catching the glint in Ashley's eye, declared, 'I know that I am, but every rogue I employ thinks he must have his pickings.'

'But that is wrong!' fumed John, his eyes alight. 'Those who cheat your Majesty are traitors and felons and deserve to be hung.'

'Dampen your ire a little, Johnny. If I hung every dishonest servant, I should have very few left.'

'A household takes its tone from its master,' purred Lord Ashley. 'And those who attack his servants, attack the King.'

'Better to have few servants, and loyal,' said John hotly, 'Than an army of grasping hangers-on!'

Charles smiled coolly. 'Ah, but if I dismissed all those hangers-on, they would form a faction against me. Better to be served lukewarmly than opposed strenuously.'

'Your Majesty is more lenient than I would be,' said John haughtily.

'Aye, Johnny, but I can give you some years, and I learned leniency in a hard school.' He looked at John's stern face. 'One should not be too unconscionably moral, but know one's servants thoroughly, their virtues and their weaknesses – and use both.'

John seemed unconvinced. Charles viewed the young man's set jaw. Where is the son of my merry companion? he thought. Those plaguey St Johns and their damnable morality! His stiff mother and her friend Clarendon had exerted a suffocating influence in the boy's early years. An idea occurred to the King. 'My Lord Clarendon is moral, industrious and honest is he not?'

John nodded.

'But many of my subjects find him haughty, censorious and impatient?'

John looked at Charles, and saw that he was smiling. He replied with a smile, 'I fear so.'

Charles put an arm around his shoulder. 'In my young days I benefited from my old friend's good qualities; now I suffer his bad. It is a matter of picking the right servant for the right task.

I cannot be everywhere at once, and a little inefficiency must be taken in our stride. There are many to be satisfied – yourself included!'

John, sensing it was time to lighten the conversation, held out his hand. 'What about my prize money?' he said saucily.

Charles grinned. 'I was coming to that. I have a task for you. Tomorrow you must take a message to Lord Sandwich. I wish all the flag-men to have some token of my gratitude. Tell Lord Sandwich I shall support him in any decision he sees fit to make in the apportionment of prizes. The fleet is to be laid up for the winter, and I shall look forward to having your company at Oxford, whither I go a week today.'

Charles then dismissed the young man with a wave, and John understood that the interview was at an end.

'That boy has many good qualities,' said the King thoughtfully, as the door closed. 'I hope to make good use of him one day.'

Lord Ashley's thin lips uncoiled into a smile. 'But not, I should imagine, in a diplomatic capacity?'

'Why not?' said the King.

'His moral sense is too highly developed,' purred Ashley.

'How very unfortunate!' laughed Charles, as they made their way to dinner.

* * *

December 1665

'Have you heard the news from the Duke's court?' Frances Stewart asked Elizabeth, as they sat at a window in Merton College.

'About the handsome Sidney making eyes at the Duchess?'

'Oh, that's old news,' said Frances. 'My Lord Rochester has returned to court, and is now reading his verses to Anne Temple.'

Elizabeth felt a stab of pain; had his 'hopeless despair' at the loss of her been so soon overcome? She tossed the long ringlets of her rich brown hair.

'The lying cheat. I was right not to trust him.'

'Yes, and that is not all,' added Frances. 'Goditha Price tells me he is pursuing one of the Duchess's serving maids too.'

'Marry come up! He is busily employed.'

Frances studied her friend, noticing the downward curve of the mouth, and the hands tightly clenched as they lay in her lap. She continued, 'I pity Temple really. Goditha tells me the attention he pays her is only a cover to allow his friend Sidney some intimate little conferences with the Duchess.'

'Whilst the Maid is engaged, the Mistress converses unobserved.'

Frances gave a tinkling laugh. 'Yes – they say the glances between the Duchess and her Master of Horse are becoming a blatant scandal.'

'Does the Duke know?'

'Good Heavens, no! He is busily engaged elsewhere, trying to seduce the new Maid of Honour, Frances Jennings.'

'I hear she laughs in his face.'

'Yes, and scatters his little notes all over the floor,' added Frances. 'I admire her spirit.'

'So do I,' said Elizabeth. 'I hate the Duke – such a solemn lecher.'

'Aye,' Frances agreed. 'A womaniser should be gay, or the whole business becomes too unseemly for words.'

Elizabeth, lost in thought, agreed dreamily. 'Gay and charming...' She noticed that Frances was laughing at her and immediately riposted, 'like the King?'

Frances fell quiet. Elizabeth knew she trod upon difficult ground, but wishing to help, pressed the question. 'Do you love the King?'

Frances was silent as she looked out over Christchurch meadow, the winter sun gleaming on her soft bright hair. She began slowly. 'Of necessity, my relationship with his Majesty is something of a puzzle, but I know I can rely on your discretion.' She spoke with some difficulty. 'If he were in a position to marry me ... I would do so ... and would love him well – for who would not choose to be Queen?' She drew a deep breath, 'But I will not be his whore!'

Elizabeth laughed gently. 'Many would say you were foolish. He treats his women generously enough, and you have no money of your own.'

''Tis not lack of money that disturbs me, but the lack of a good marriage. I am a conventional person and need a respected place in society. When I first came to court, it was with the idea of making a suitable marriage. I did not bargain for the King's interest in me.'

'They say the King loves you greatly, and that, should you choose, you could wield even greater power than Castlemaine.'

'The King loves me because power does not interest me. It is as simple as that. Castlemaine has influence, money, jewels, practically anything she wants; but I would not be spoken of as she is by the men at court – and by his Majesty himself, when in a cynical mood.'

'Men are two-faced wretches!' said Elizabeth emphatically.

'Oh Bess,' Frances sighed, 'I am reduced to that extremity that I would take a personable man of but £1500 a year, if he would have me in honour.'

Elizabeth laughed. 'Reduced to extremity indeed! But such a man would incur the King's enmity if he married you.'

'If he married me in spite of the King's displeasure, I should know he really loved me. Most of my so-called adorers' declarations amount to nothing.' She laughed, drawing a note from her pocket. 'Listen to this, from Buckingham: "You are in everything a goddess, except that you are unmoved by prayers"!'

Pealing with laughter, Elizabeth reached out and snatched the note. 'But it is very clever,' she said, as she read it through.

'Aye, I have no doubt he was thinking that as he wrote it,' Frances replied.

'Most of the men at court are in love with their wit, more than with the supposed object of their admiration.'

'Assuredly, they are naught but a vain crowd of barn-yard cocks!'

'Flapping their wings and crowing "she dies for me"!' added Elizabeth, indignation gathering in her voice, 'when you do but give them an ear for your diversion.'

Frances, noticing the vehemence of her tone, smiled teasingly. 'But Hinchingbrooke is modest enough, is he not?'

'Aye – but deadly dull,' Elizabeth sighed. 'I have a good mind to ask if he would run off with me, just to observe his reaction.'

Frances giggled. She was about to question further when a knock on the door announced the arrival of a maid, with a mercer's woman. They hurried to view her wares, and were soon lost in the insoluble problem of deciding the respective merits of embroidered satin and turquoise tabby silk...

* * *

The winter sun set in a red glow behind the roofs and turrets of Oxford as a merry party of riders turned in at Christchurch Gate. John and Killigrew were entertaining the Maids of Honour with fantastic impromptu stories. Frances Jennings, witty and resourceful, had contributed to the entertainment, but red-haired Anne Temple was listening open-mouthed and speechless.

'And so,' drawled John, 'the Princess Aleophangina, having seen her doughty knight wounded in the huckle-bone, wept copiously...'

'Where is the huckle-bone?' demanded Anne Temple, finding her voice at last.

'My dear young lady, I could not possibly tell you, but perhaps you will one day permit me to show you...'

'Get on with the story,' cut in Frances.

'Mistress Jennings may command me anything,' murmured John smoothly. 'Having, as I said, seen her doughty knight wounded, the Princess knew him no longer capable of serving his Mistress as a good knight should...'

'Where the devil have you been?' interrupted a troubled voice. A stocky young man had appeared out of the dusk of the courtyard. 'You are damnably late.'

'What's that to you, Savile?' sneered Killigrew. 'Worried about the Duchess? Concern wasted I should say.'

'Yes,' added Frances, laughing. 'She was so well attended by

81

her Master of Horse, that they spurred ahead, and we should have had much ado to keep up with them.'

'A pity you did not,' hissed Savile. 'There's been a devil of a pother here, I can tell you!'

'Why, what has happened?' enquired John hurriedly as the party dismounted.

'The Duchess is in tears, and the Duke is like a bear with a sore head.'

'Good Heavens,' said Frances Jennings. 'Where is Mr Sidney?'

'Banished the court,' Henry Savile replied. His brown eyes, usually merry, were now filled with concern.

'Banished the court?' they repeated incredulously. 'He was with us but half an hour ago.'

'I know,' said Henry. 'Whatever happened occurred swiftly. The Duke, damned tetchy all day, in spite of good hunting, took it into his head to return early, going straight to his wife's apartments. I was left to wait outside the door, then out dashes Sidney, his face the colour of flame, saying he has to leave court immediately!'

Savile's audience stood in Christchurch Quadrangle, mouth agape.

'Next thing I know is the Duke storms out, says I am to see that all Mr Sidney's effects are cleared from court, and that he has been dismissed for presumptuous and imprudent behaviour. Well, I was dumbfounded, I can tell you, stood there like a stuck pig until the Duke glared at me saying, "Neither qualities, I must impress upon you, being desirable in gentlemen who seek to serve Princes!" We hopped off pretty swiftly, I can tell you.'

'What did Sidney say?' asked John.

'I could get nothing from him, except that he did not wish to appear an even greater fool than I knew him to be already. He sets off for Penshurst now, but he won't get far before dark.'

'Well that finishes his career at court,' said Killigrew with satisfaction.

'Yes,' agreed Savile sorrowfully, 'but at least he doesn't rely upon his court appointment for a livelihood.'

Killigrew's eyes narrowed. 'Hmm ... I heard that his mother

had made him her heir, and that he has fair estates in Kent.' He turned to the girls and started tattling. 'It put his elder brothers' noses out of joint, I can tell you. Lady Leicester left them but £500 apiece and all the rest, unentailed, to Henry...'

'You Maids had better hurry,' interrupted Savile. 'My Lady Rochester is in one of her haughty moods, and wants to know why the Duchess was left so ill-attended.'

He turned to John, and catching the troubled look in his eye, whispered, 'I daresay you know more of this affair than it would be wise to say. Keep your mouth shut and stay out of the Duke's way.'

* * *

Who ever loves, if he do not propose
The right true end of love, he's one that goes
To sea for nothing but to make him sick

'Insolent! You are not to quote your lewd verses to me,' exploded Lady Rochester.

John's eyes widened in mock innocence. 'I do but quote from the writings of the revered Dr Donne.'

'Dr Donne, in later life, expressed regret for the looser writings of his youth.'

'Ah, in later life – the essential phrase.'

John rose from his seat and wandered restlessly about the room. He wondered if the interview was at an end. Summoned by a peremptory note to attend at her lodgings, his mother had reproved him at length upon his attentions to Anne Temple. The girl had no fortune, and did not possess qualities Lady Rochester thought desirable in a daughter-in-law. From there the rebuke had veered towards the 'wild and immoderate behaviour of Mr Sidney towards the Duchess' and how he was lucky to have escaped with his life. John, his face a smooth mask of concern, had listened solemnly as his mother told him, 'It would have gone ill with the Duchess had I not been present in the next room, heard all, and been able to vouch for her modesty of conduct.'

83

'It was indeed fortunate that you were present.' John had been silent for some minutes, thinking of Sidney's infatuation and of the Duchess's undoubted "prudence". He burst out hotly, 'Sidney loved her to distraction, and she encouraged him to think that she had some kindness for him.'

'Certainly some kindness – but no more than that! Had he rested satisfied in his knowledge of the Duchess's esteem, this unfortunate occurrence need not have happened.'

John smiled ironically. His mother's cosily enwrapped self-satisfaction had irritated him, tempting him to quote Donne.

He looked out into the courtyard where the links burned fitfully in the chill December night. The short day had gone. His mother's love for his father must have been like winter sun, he thought: soon down, and scarce warm at its highest. He turned, adopted a sphinx-like expression, and waited for a further storm to break.

'Young men,' continued his mother with asperity, 'must I suppose, seduce a maidservant or two to prove their manhood. But, my son, for your own safety and for the well-being of your family, remember that the wives of Princes are inviolate.'

John looked at his mother with surprise. 'I can assure you, Madam, I have no improper thoughts concerning the Queen or the Duchess of York. They are a little too plump for my taste.'

His mother was not amused. 'And Sarah Cooke is not?'

John started. So that was the way the wind was blowing. How did his mother know of his friendship with Sarah? 'You are well informed of my activities, Madam.'

'I make it my business to know of all that concerns your welfare.'

John sighed.

'You must stop turning little Sarah's head. I am but urging you to follow your better nature. You know you cannot support a woman, either in or out of wedlock, and it is an unkindness to the girl to continue paying her attention. I should think very ill of you, should you abandon a young maid to shame and ruin.'

'You run ahead of me, Madam. Sarah Cooke is not my mistress.'

84

John's mother looked at him in surprise. 'Then break off the association at once, before it goes further, and you both come to harm.'

'Madam, you must by now allow me to know what is harm and what is not. You reared me with firm moral precepts. Pray allow them to work for themselves; they no longer need your urging.'

Lady Rochester nearly choked with indignation. John knew that he had overstepped the mark of her tolerance. Ready to do all in her power to make members of her family happy, secure, and successful, provided they were content to be her indulged and ordered puppets, they would nevertheless feel the blast of her displeasure should they show signs of independence. They would suffer the cutting courtesy of her formal answers to their questions, the chilly silences which sentenced sociability to death.

For a few moments the silence was oppressive, then Lady Rochester announced in her iciest tones, 'I will desist from my urgings – and with the payment of your allowance.'

'The payments from Adderbury – from my father's estate?'

'From my estate – I renewed the lease with my own money. Your father died greatly in debt.'

'Have I no money of my own then?'

'None at all, other than by my favour.'

'Then I will earn my bread, Madam, and relieve you of a troublesome burden!' He bowed curtly, and flung out of the door.

* * *

Seething with rage, John stalked out into St Aldates and bumped into Harry Killigrew.

Harry laughed. 'How now Jack, whither in such a hurry?'

He matched his pace to John's. ''Tis a fine pother about Sidney, is it not? He was about to do the Duchess's business, and the Duke did as much for him!' Killigrew staggered into the wall, hugging his little joke.

John looked at him with distaste. Since his return from sea

he had found Killigrew's scoffing manner increasingly jarring. 'I would have thought Sidney's misfortune a matter of concern for his friends, not merriment.'

'Faith, Jack, don't look at me so haughtily. Y'are the image of y'r Lady mother. Has she read you a lecture lately?'

John, sore from his interview, and appreciative of an ally, relented in his attitude. 'I have just come from one now.'

Killigrew whistled. 'I thought it would not be long. Goditha Price informed her of your friendship with little Sarah, y'know. Said it was for the girl's own good, not wishing her to come to ruin, and suchlike stuff.'

John stood dumb for some few seconds, then gave vent to a powerful expletive, greatly impressing Killigrew with his virulence. 'May ten thousand devils run off with these damned interfering hags! How many more young maids are there to be protected from my "evil advances"? What have I done to wrong them?'

''Tis their own lack of opportunity they resent,' sniggered Killigrew. 'You know Price is hopelessly angling for Chesterfield, and pines at his lack of interest.'

'So that's the reason...,' John smiled slowly. 'I'll make her smart.'

Killigrew's interest sharpened. 'How?'

'Why, by making her intrigue public – as she has made mine! What a revenge! Poor stubby Mistress Price, and her hopeless passion for the haughty Chesterfield – what a fine subject for a lampoon!'

6

London and Putney

February 1666

My Lord,
These are the gloves that I did mention
Last night, and 'twas my intention
That you should give me thanks and wear them...

'Have you seen this supposed letter from Goditha Price to Lord Chesterfield?' asked Hinchingbrooke of Elizabeth. 'They say it is one of my Lord Rochester's lampoons and that the whole town is laughing over it, but damn me if I can see anything funny in it.'

Elizabeth read it through. 'It is mildly funny,' she said, 'and is not as unkind as some other court satires, but my Lord Rochester's unkindness lies in the way he has made Mistress Price's name public, and in pointing out that Chesterfield does not care for her at all.'

'I think Rochester a malicious knave.'

'He can be, if he thinks himself wronged. But he does not always seek to harm. He has a great fund of good nature for his friends.'

'I can see that you still regard him with some favour.'

Elizabeth shrugged. 'He can be very amusing, and he writes clever verse. He used to write to me in complimentary terms, but that has fallen off of late.'

'Why so?'

'I refused to answer his letters.'

Hinchingbrooke saw his opening and tried to be gallant. 'For my sake, I hope.'

Elizabeth smiled non-comittedly, and smothered a yawn. Why had she come to visit Lady Sandwich? She had no wish to encourage Hinchingbrooke, but her step-father had said she must at least cultivate his acquaintance, so that should she refuse him her decision would be based upon sound knowledge, and not upon petulance and pride. She knew Hinchingbrooke well enough now. He was a conventional unimaginative prig. How much longer would the ridiculous farce have to continue?

Lady Sandwich hurried over to her. 'My dear, my husband tells me young Lord Rochester has called to see him. If he brings him to the parlour, to meet the family, would this discommode you?'

Elizabeth, surprised to hear of the visit, thanked Lady Sandwich for her consideration, and said that since Lord Rochester had written letters of apology to her grandfather and to her parents, her family bore him no ill-will. She turned and walked over to the window in some agitation. Perhaps if she hid in the embrasure, he would not see her. Why did she want so much, and yet at the same time, not want to meet him?

Her feelings were still greatly disturbed when Lord Sandwich brought her ex-suitor into the room. He cast no glance in her direction but went straight over to Charles Harbord, Lord Sandwich's young kinsman. The two young men engaged in what seemed to be an endless conversation. Elizabeth turned, and found to her annoyance that Hinchingbrooke was still at her elbow. When someone does not appeal to one, devotion, even the flattery of admiration, is unbearable. Hinchingbrooke, with his heavy insensitive earnestness, with his minute observation of the proprieties, was an appalling bore.

She said to him cruelly, 'I wish to hear what my Lord Rochester has to say. Do you wish to accompany me?'

She bore down upon the young Earl, a well turned-out frigate on manoeuvre, with a reluctant tender in its wake. 'I hear, my Lord, that you are now in love with Anne Temple. No doubt you address to her those poems you once addressed to me.'

John, unaware of Elizabeth's presence in the room until this

88

moment, was overcome with surprise and bewilderment. He stared at the challenging goddess before him, unable to remember what she had said to him, so great was his surprise to see her in that company.

'Well, my Lord, have you lost your tongue? I believe you are now in love with Mistress Temple.'

John gathered his wits about him. 'I fear you are misinformed. Mistress Temple and I have a merely platonic relationship.' He smiled seraphically. 'She is kind enough to listen to my verses.'

Elizabeth snorted. 'The ones you wrote to me, I suppose.'

John looked at her in surprise. 'No, of course not. I have no need to repeat myself. I have written an ode celebrating her beauty.'

'Then you are in love with her.'

'If heaven had made me susceptible to impressions of beauty I should never escape her chains.' He smiled impishly. 'But I am not, thank God, affected by anything but intelligence, and I can enjoy the most agreeable conversation with her without running any risk.' He bowed to Elizabeth saying softly, 'The slave of your wit still carries his chains.'

Elizabeth, aware that their interchange was of interest to the whole room, felt foolish and exposed. 'Your double tongue still hides your double heart,' she spat out indignantly.

John raised a brow in surprise. 'I fail to understand why my verses should interest you. Hinchingbrooke, I hear, fills my place as suitor.'

Elizabeth nearly choked with indignation. 'As suitor, yes, but I have not yet chosen.'

'A goddess fair but cruel! Why keep your unhappy slaves in suspense?'

This sally raised a laugh from Harbord, and from Hinchingbrooke too. Elizabeth could have cried with vexation. 'I shall no longer tarry to bring you sport,' she declared, sweeping out of the room, with Hinchingbrooke somewhat reluctantly following.

'What did I say to displease her?' asked John. 'I spoke most truly when I said I was still her slave.'

'She thinks you make sport of her,' laughed Harbord. 'In a court addicted to malicious wit, your Lordship's variety of self-mocking humour can be misunderstood. I think the lady loves you, and you would do well to renew your suit.'

John looked at Harbord closely. He suspected him of insincerity but could detect no sign of it upon his face. 'She has, in the past, made sport of me. I am trying to forget her. In any event his Majesty has forbidden me to approach her whilst Hinchingbrooke is making his addresses – and I would not wish to disoblige my Lord Sandwich in his time of trouble.'

'You mean the scandal about the prizes?'

'Aye, I believe my Lord's appointment as Ambassador to Spain is but being "kicked upstairs".'

John was disturbed at Elizabeth's unexpected appearance and verbal attack, and thought it best to hide his concern by speaking rapidly of other matters. He remembered his return to Buoy of the Nore last September. Following the message he had brought from the King there was great spoil of the East India ships. The rapacity of the flag-men was quite breathtaking. 'I hear Lord Sandwich took goods to the value of five thousand pounds, which was no more than he would have received as his justifiable perquisite at the hands of the Commissioners. I managed to get a few bales of silk for my shirts and three bags of gold, but the greed of some of the commanders was quite appalling.'

'I hear there was great ignorance of the value of much of the spoil.'

'Yes, in one ship pepper lay scattered in every chink of the planking, and in one hold I walked in cloves and nutmegs up to my knees.'

'Is it true that the common seamen sold a bag of rubies for thirty-five shillings?'

'I cannot vouch for that, but seeing their betters grabbing riches with avidity, the seamen thought themselves entitled to do the same. I was told that at Gravesend it was possible to buy cloves at a ridiculous price.'

'And now Lord Sandwich suffers for it!'

'Aye, it is said to be a bad precedent to allow a General to take what prizes he pleases. My Lord's defence, that much more was taken away then he intended, is not believed.'

'Hmm. It is not believed because others desire him out of the way. Albemarle and Prince Rupert both have a wish to command the fleet.'

John laughed. 'Yes, those who wax most moral about the prizes, have a mind to the commander's place. His Majesty has advised Lord Sandwich to accept the appointment as Ambassador to the Spanish Court, and to be out of the country until the furore dies down.'

'Such is the way business is conducted at court. Will you go to sea in the spring?'

'Most probably,' gloomed John. 'I am still damned short of money, now that my mother has disowned me. His Majesty has promised me the next place to fall vacant in the Bedchamber, but Heaven knows when that will be available. The King has awarded me a pension of £500 a year in consideration of my father's service, and he looks for me in his entourage, but my pension will not support me in a place about the Court. I suppose I must sponge upon my uncle at Battersea for the next couple of months, before I go to sea.'

'I know Sir Edward Spragge will be glad to have you aboard his ship. I was dining last month at Sir William Penn's and Spragge spoke highly of you.'

John beamed with pleasure. 'I am glad, for I greatly admire him.' He looked at Harbord's honest, jovial face. The fellow was a wag in company, but he had a good heart, which was more than could be said for many at court. Also, he had shared with him scenes of great hardship and danger, and links fostered in such circumstances were not easily broken. 'I shall welcome seeing you, if our paths cross again. My regards to Sir Edward. I must leave now to visit my uncle Apsley who lives across the Square. He has a fine hawk for me to take to Sir Walter at Battersea.'

* * *

May, 1666

Sarah, bored and languid, looked about the tiny garden of a

cottage in Putney and scuffed the gravel path with her foot. The river gleamed in the distance and hot spring sunshine warmed the backs of Mrs Cooke and her sister Mrs Joyner as they sat upon a wooden bench outside the kitchen door.

'Well, sister, 'tis a pretty box, in a fine situation, and well kept. But how long will it last? How can you put your trust in that mad young Lord?'

'My Lord Rochester? If it had not been for him we would have starved. Living on green cheese and ox-cheek we were, in nasty lodgings, until he sought us out. If he had more we should not want it. But it often goes hard with him.'

'Huh, the sweet bits you swallowed have made young Sarah's belly swell. Well, Sarah, after all your junketings there will be a bone for you to pick. They say he is a wit, and wits are nothing but deceivers of women, and spenders of other people's money.'

Sarah looked at her aunt with distaste. 'He has spent plenty on me. Did he not give me my embroidered shawl, and my first silk gown? Has he not taught me to dress, talk and move well?'

'He has taught you to talk indeed.'

'Nay, you are too tart with her, sister' interrupted Mrs Cooke.

'Tart, indeed. I warned you what would happen, months ago, when I saw them coming out of the Mulberry Garden, hand in hand together.'

Sarah ignored the interruptions. 'My Lord is teaching me to act. He says he will put me on the stage when the playhouses open again. He says I am like Mistress Nell Gwynne, and that I have her gamine charm.'

'Gameen? What's that I pray?'

'A fine French word, like a lot of others he uses. It means "saucy",' said Sarah proudly. 'My Lord knows a lot of fine words.'

'Aye, and a lot of fine tricks 'tis not good for a young maid to know, I'll warrant!' added Aunt Joyner.

'Why should I not go on the stage and have as good luck as the others?' threw out Sarah. 'And as good clothes, plate and jewels, even if it does turn the neighbours sick with envy?'

'Ha! You wont get that by Rochester's assistance. I hear the wretch goes on tick for the very paper he writes those lampoons on. If you had to turn whore, why for mercy's sake didn't you pick a man with money?'

Sarah's eyes, up till now defiant and contemptuous, filled with tears. 'It wasn't like that at all. I love my Lord, and he loves me. I didn't sell myself to him.'

'Hoity-toity, more's the pity. What's to happen to you when his fine "love" has worn itself out?'

'When love fades, friendship will still be there. He says he will always be my friend and look after my interests.'

'Fine words butter no parsnips. How long is the rent paid here?'

'My Lord has taken the lease for a year. He says when the child is born we will put it out to nurse, and I shall go on the stage.'

'Huh – 'twas a pity you lost your good place at court. Did the Duchess know you were with child?'

Mrs Cooke, annoyed with her sister's badgering, elbowed her way into the conversation. 'No, the trouble was over that scene between Mistress Hobart and Mistress Temple.' Mrs Cooke sighed. 'Sarah was held to blame, although the poor child had done nothing except tell my Lord of the dreadful calumnies Hobart was spreading about him. She told Temple those lampoons written on Goditha Price had been written about her, and that she must speak to him no longer. Naturally my Lord planned revenge. Sarah had the bad luck to be taking a sly bath in the Duchess's closet, when Temple and Hobart came in, not knowing she was behind the curtains. Hobart attempted to embrace Temple, who pushed her away and had a fit of hysterics.'

'Yes,' giggled Sarah, her tears forgotten. 'It was uncommonly funny. You see Temple and Hobart had arranged to walk in the Mall, masked, in each other's clothes. I told my Lord of their plans, and he and Mr Killigrew pretended to be taken in by the masquerade. Mr Killigrew took Temple aside and implied a number of incredible things, such as that Hobart was a man in woman's clothes, who got maids with child, and all that kind of thing, and of course, the fool believed him. That evening I was taking my unlucky bath, when Temple ran back to the Palace, to the bath, and couldn't change out of Hobart's clothes quick enough. When Hobart followed her in and tried to find out the trouble, Temple had her screaming fit. It disturbed all the other Maids of Honour, who came crowding in, and found me behind the curtains in the bath. They said I had no business to be there, and they would report me to the Duchess. The next day Aunt and I had to go along and tell the Duchess what all the trouble was about.'

'Unfortunately,' said Mrs Cooke, 'the Duchess would hear no ill of Hobart, preferring to disbelieve us. She said that Temple was a silly girl, and that my Sarah was a malicious trouble-maker. Of course, I couldn't stand for that, and I said that Sarah had found Mistress Hobart a very odd person herself ... but the Duchess would hear nothing of it, and so we were dismissed the court.'

'A fine kettle of fish! That's what comes of tattling of the Quality's business.'

Sarah's eyes flashed. 'Why should I not tattle of theirs? They tattled of mine!'

'Tattled of yours? Who would concern themselves with a serving maid, pray?'

'My Lord tells me Goditha Price was the one who informed his mother he was helping us. Lady Rochester told him he was not to see me any more, and cut off his allowance when he refused. My Lord says it was then that he realised he loved me, and that he would always be my friend.'

'And where is your fine friend now?'

'Gone to sea. His Majesty told him that every available gentleman was needed to fight the Dutch.'

'Well, I hope you see him back. Still, at least the rent is paid for a year.' Mrs Joyner gathered herself up. 'Let me know when the child is born. You will need help then.'

7

At The Gunfleet

The twenty-second of July 1666

'I hope,' said George Digby, a younger son of the Earl of Bristol, 'that we shall not see a tarpaulin in charge of a ship within these next two months. Thanks to the influence of Prince Rupert, the sons of gentlemen are now volunteering for service at sea.'

John looked scornfully at the speaker: the wine was going to the insolent cur's head. Digby had been put in command of a ship, with scarcely one year's experience at sea. He was expatiating upon the necessity of having his Majesty's fleet commanded by gentlemen.

Gathered around the table of Sir Jeremiah Smith, Admiral of the Blue, were his Vice-Admiral Sir Edward Spragge, his Rear-Admiral Keynsthorne, the captains of his frigates, and several gentlemen Volunteers. The conversation had turned upon the mismanagement of the Battle of the Downs, fought against the Dutch scarcely more than a month ago.

'Of course, we were put at a great disadvantage because of the need to divide the Fleet,' offered Spragge. 'The French had just made their Treaty with the Dutch, and had declared they would attack us in the Channel.'

'Yes, and two days were wasted, looking for the cursed mounseers!' swore Sir Jeremiah Smith.

'But the Duke of Albemarle himself,' put in Digby, 'maintains that not above twenty of his captains fought as they should have done.'

Privately, the more experienced officers considered the lack of success was due to poor seamanship on the part of the joint commanders, Prince Rupert and the Duke of Albemarle. Albemarle had attributed it to cowardice on the part of the captains.

Everyone was tired of Digby's voice. John was surprised that none of the older men had put the young braggart in his place. Silence fell as Digby paused for breath. John ventured a reply.

'Better some rough tarpaulins who know how to handle a ship in all weathers than gentlemen with the talents of our French friend Du Tell.'

Digby turned haughtily. 'And what do you know to the discredit of Monsieur Du Tell? In spite of his nationality, he is a gentleman commissioned by his Royal Highness, the Duke of York?'

'I know this,' said John, 'that he was ignorant of which tack lost the wind and which kept it, and that he fired more shot into Albemarle's ship than into that of the enemy. The Duke cried out that there was a little Dutchman to the right of his ship, that did plague him more than any other, and when he looked – it was Du Tell!'

There was a growl of agreement round the table. 'But for the interest it was known he had at Court,' contributed Sir Edward Spragge, 'Albemarle would have had him hanged at the yard-arm, without staying for a court-martial.'

'I believe 'twas a fine gentleman responsible for the order which ran *The Prince* upon the Galloper Shoal,' said Sir Jeremiah Smith with some heat. 'How my spirits sink when I think of the loss of that fine vessel.'

Digby looked at his commander with scarcely veiled contempt. Smith had risen from the decks in Oliver's day, and was certainly no gentleman.

''Tis pity,' ventured Digby, 'to see his Majesty's fleet entrusted to the command of soldiers, merchant seamen, and miserable snivelling anabaptists,' his eye flicked over Smith's person, 'who can scarcely be said to dress like gentlemen.'

The company, acutely embarrassed by the insult offered to their commander, regarded Digby with silent contempt. Smith was an odd fellow, but he kept his religious persuasions to himself. John yearned for the cold, yet civilised authority of Lord Sandwich. His previous commander had been displaced by Albemarle and Rupert, and had been sent Ambassador to Spain. The smooth and ready tongue of Sir Roger Cuttance would also have been appreciated, but the Admiral of the White had already sailed to meet the Dutch.

John tried to turn the conversation to other channels, ignoring Digby's rudeness by refusing to acknowledge what had been said. 'The Duke of Albemarle is under the impression that he is still ashore, with a troop of cavalry at his command. "Right wheel", he roars from the poop, and the poor tars at the whipstaff have to puzzle out his meaning.'

Digby looked challengingly at John. 'The Duke of Albemarle is an able and valiant commander.'

'No-one doubts his courage,' murmured John, 'or his ability to command troops. But it could be wished that he would dampen the fire in his belly when at sea, before the sea does that service for him.'

'How so?'

'On the first of June there was a heavy swell, and many questions of wind and weather should have been taken into consideration before making the attack. The wind being high, and we to windward, we were unable to use our lower tier of guns against the Dutch.'

'You are quick to air your seafaring knowledge,' sneered Digby, 'but none too anxious to maintain your assertions in a fight.'

'Very few causes are worth a fight.'

'There speaks a worthy son of Sir Allen Apsley.'

John, puzzled at first, caught the look in Digby's eyes, and knew he was seeking a challenge. Digby was a clever duellist and had often sought to harry the young Earl. John had extricated himself from trouble on previous occasions with the readiness of his verbal exchanges, but he knew he could not excuse the implied insult to his mother. Mentally, he gritted his teeth, but replied calmly, 'You are mistaken, Sir. Sir Allen Apsley is my mother's cousin, not my father.'

Digby raised his brow. 'You surprise me,' he sneered. 'You have his own over-tender spirit, and his dislike of cold steel.'

John recognised the threat, and awaited the next sally in silence.

'Besides, 'tis well known he whored Lord Wilmot's wife.'

John rose, flung back his chair and struck Digby full in the face. 'My father knocked that lie back into your father's throat – some eighteen years ago! Why do I have to do the same for you?'

Digby was furious. He attempted to staunch the blood which was pouring from his nose. 'You will give me satisfaction for this, my Lord.'

'I think not. The blow was my satisfaction for your insult to my mother.'

'You refuse a challenge, my Lord?'

'Certainly, I have no intention of allowing you to murder me with ceremony.'

'Coward.'

'This quarrel has gone far enough,' interrupted Sir Jeremiah. 'Leave the cabin, Mr Digby. You have allowed yourself far too many freedoms at my table.'

Digby stared insolently at Sir Jeremiah for some minutes, but seeing the inflexible expression on his commander's face, he bowed carelessly and left the cabin.

The rest of the company heaved a sigh of relief.

'That ruffling bully deserves a lesson,' declared Spragge emphatically. 'We shall be all of us obliged when you send him your challenge, my Lord. I shall be happy to act as your second.'

John, a little surprised, shrugged his shoulders. 'The fire-eater has been put down well enough for tonight.'

'But the fellow called you a coward!' reiterated Spragge indignantly. 'You cannot lie down under that.'

'Who cares for the opinion of Digby? I have friends enough to support me in the eyes of the world, without accepting a challenge from every hot-mettled ruffler who considers himself entitled to kill me.'

The company looked at him in astonishment.

'You must fight him' said Spragge. 'Your position as a

gentleman requires it.'

John looked round the company. Few of them had had the stomach to challenge Digby themselves, thought John. He had no relish to be led like a lamb to the slaughter. However, having been assigned to Sir Edward's ship *Victory*, he was anxious to retain the good opinion of his commander. He attempted to lighten the situation.

'I am a gentleman only when it pleases me. Most of the time I prefer to be a man – and a live one!'

Spragge was plainly shocked. 'Then Digby will have no alternative but to proclaim you a coward through the fleet.'

'Falstaff has always appealed to me more than Hotspur.'

The flippant remark failed to lighten the solemn faces around the Admiral's table: many of the seamen captains were totally unacquainted with the plays of Shakespeare.

Sir Jeremiah asserted his authority. 'My Lord Rochester would be ill-advised to send a challenge. His Majesty has expressly forbidden duels amongst the officers of his fleet. No doubt my Lord will give us full proof of his valour when we meet the Dutch. Ninety of their fleet have been sighted off Orfordness. We must address ourselves to the business in hand. I will give you my fighting instructions for tomorrow.'

John was no longer the cynosure of all eyes, but he remained uneasy, sensing Spragge's disapproval. The man was his commander and they had agreed famously last year, but the fellow had a fighting man's punctilio about honour and pursuing a feud. John shrugged. He supposed it was Spragge's Irish blood; the Irish loved a fight, he had heard, and revenge was sweet in their mouths.

* * *

Later that evening Henry Savile came aboard *Victory*. He had a message for Sir Edward from Prince Rupert. Accompanying Savile was Sir Robert Leach, a foppish middle-aged bachelor who had volunteered for service. He was shown below and was directed to share John's cabin. John was unenthusiastic about the arrangement, but he welcomed the new man politely before hurrying away to catch a word with Harry before he departed. They greeted each other warmly.

'Dear Jack, how good to see you. I have a hundred good tales to tell you, but time presses. I must be back with the Red Squadron before midnight. We sail at four in the morning.'

John smiled. 'I wanted to ask you about Sir Robert Leach. He seems a strange fellow.'

'Yes, almost as queer as your Rear-Admiral, Sir Jeremiah. Everyone was surprised when Smith was given command of *Loyal London*, our magnificent new ship. But concerning Sir Robert, he is a good subject for baiting: he sees visions.'

'No!' grinned John. 'Tell me more.'

'You will find out for yourself,' laughed Harry. 'I wish I could see your face when you encounter him, but I fear you will find him a tedious cabin companion. I had a much better partner on Albemarle's flagship – Lord Mulgrave, do you know him?'

John shook his head.

'He writes poetry and plays, and discusses the value of words, endlessly, just as you do. I anticipate you would have much to say to each other should you meet.'

'I shall look forward to making his acquaintance – if we survive tomorrow's action.'

'Yes, indeed. I hear your commander is more careful of men's lives than is ours. On the third day of the Downs battle Albemarle threatened to fire the magazine of our vessel rather than surrender. He would have denied us the chance of saving our lives by jumping into the sea. Buckingham and I, in a laughing way, most mutinously resolved to throw him overboard if we should ever find him going down to the powder room!'

'You had no mind that Albemarle should be your executioner?'

'The Dutch, yes, but Albemarle? I should resent it extremely. I must depart, the ketch is here. Give my regards to young Mr Middleton who has just come aboard. He is only sixteen, and very enthusiastic. Of your charity, Jack, look to his welfare.'

'Do you make me his bear-leader?'

'Aye, train him well!'

John turned to Middleton and said he would take him to Sir Edward Spragge. The young man came from Cheshire and had already had experience of sailing his brother's yacht in the Mersey and the Irish Sea. He was excited at the prospect of serving on a ship of the line and said he looked forward to learning about the management of large vessels.

'Have you seen the Rear Admiral's flagship *Loyal London*, provided at the cost of the City?' asked John.

'No, but I hear she is a most excellent vessel, making extraordinary speed with her new type of rigging, and that she is built to a model more exact than any formerly.'

'Aye, her guns are more than five feet from the water in the lower tier – which will obviate the difficulty found at the Downs when we were unable to direct the full force of our broadsides against the Dutch.'

'I hear that because the Duke was to windward, he was unable to use his lower tier against them. I should imagine that with the continual squalls and choppy sea 'twas impossible to fire with any accuracy?'

John nodded, impressed with the young man's grasp of the situation. 'Have you any experience of fire-power at sea?'

'Yes, two years ago my brother organised an expedition of local merchants to clear the seaways of Irish pirates. My brother obtained six pieces of ordnance for our vessel: we had four sakers and two falconets and did the villains much damage.'

'Do you intend to make a career in his Majesty's service?'

'Aye, there is little scope for a younger son at home. My brother cannot afford to give me any part of the family estates. He has a family of his own to provide for.'

John was impressed by the boy's confidence and knowledge. He guessed that before many years had passed he would be in charge of a ship of his own.

Spragge, when they found him, was much distracted by work. He greeted the young Volunteer and explained that he was extremely short of accommodation. He addressed John and said that he would be obliged if he and Sir Robert Leach would make room for Mr Middleton. John could not refuse, especially as Savile had told him that on *Royal Charles* gentlemen were sleeping four to a cabin.

When John and his charge reached their quarters they found Leach on his knees in an attitude of prayer. They exchanged grimaces but sat down quietly on their trunks. They watched as Leach opened his eyes, breathed deeply, and then made a deep obeisance towards the floor. 'This is holy ground,' he declared.

'You mean holy deck,' said John. 'All our surroundings are made of wood, and we are floating on water.'

'I have just had a vision in which I was told that I shall kill de Ruyter with my musket.'

'Indeed,' mused John. 'What form did your vision take?'

'Seven aerial men appeared before me.'

'Seven?' repeated John incredulously. 'It must have been uncommonly crowded in here. The three of us can scarcely pass each other.'

'Such men are not limited by earthly space.'

John decided that Sir Robert was quite mad and would need to be humoured. 'In what mode were they dressed?'

'In the English mode, with crimson velvet cloaks and purple stockings.'

John shuddered. 'What vile taste they have in the ethereal regions!' Young Middleton looked at John and smothered a laugh.

Sir Robert Leach, armed with a childlike faith, and a complete lack of awareness of the amusement he was causing continued to enlarge upon his heavenly visitors.

'I first saw them in the company of Dr John Heydon, the noted alchemist and astrologer.'

'Tell me more of Heydon,' said John. 'Does he often see these beings?'

'Aye, they are aerial men of the Fourth Sphere, who are born and die as we, but live much longer. The lowest sort amongst them are genii to the best amongst us, such as the basest men here are the trainers up of the best sort of dogs.'

'A happy simile,' murmured John softly. 'And do the bodies of these aerial men appear real? Can you feel and touch them?'

'No, one can see them only. The tenuity of their bodies is

such that they can do no hurt, saving by inspiring terror in a guilty conscience, or joy in those who love and practise virtue.'

'Do you see them often?' John was intrigued, in spite of himself.

'No, they visit but rarely, and impart only matters of vital importance.'

Suddenly John was put in mind of the oath he and Wyndham had taken at Bergen the previous year. 'Do these aerial persons regard vows taken by mortals as binding, even after death?'

'Only if the vows are given in accordance with the requirements of true religion.'

'And what religion do they consider best amongst us?'

'The Protestant,' answered Sir Robert stolidly, 'and they consider Episcopacy the best form of church government.'

'They speak exactly like my Lord Clarendon.' John was unable to hide his mirth longer. 'You must tell me more when we are at greater leisure. I suggest we sleep now. We must be up betimes.'

That night a great wind sprang up and none of the gentlemen could get much sleep. The wind ceased just before dawn and by morning the sky was clear and visibility good.

8

The St James's Day Battle

The twenty-fifth of July, 1666

The battle was hot,
And bloudily fought,
The fire was like rain
And like hail was the shot.

Old Naval Ballad

At six o'clock in the morning the Dutch were sighted well to the south, making for the mouth of the Thames. The British fleet had the windward position and Rupert and Albemarle gave the order to bear down upon the Dutch in line abreast. The fleet was in good heart, having been re-manned and victualled in record time after the harrowing and profitless four days' fight with the Dutch, scarcely more than six weeks ago. Today ninety ships of the line, sails filled and pennants flying, seemed to fly across a fair smooth sea.

Standing upon the deck of *Victory* in the company of his commander, Sir Edward Spragge, several officers and other Volunteers, John felt carefree, almost elated. The muddles, delays and quarrels of the past few weeks were forgotten, or perhaps could be atoned for by this day's action. Momentarily, the thought that he might not see the end of it drove a sliver of ice through his stomach, but for the main part the idea of death left him feeling strangely detached.

He was young, he had much to hope for from life, despite its recent disappointments. The realisation that he would never possess the only young woman whose personality interested him, his alienation from his family, and a gathering boredom with his life with Sarah, left him listless and cold. As for ambition, what was that? To be thought well of by fools if one was a successful knave? To be hated by knaves if one was an honest man? Surely the fate of Lord Sandwich was proof that honesty and ability went unregarded when the envious and powerful had a mind to your place?

If he died today, he told himself, it would be in a worthy cause. The Dutch must not be allowed to lord it in the Channel and the North Sea. If he died perhaps Sarah would grieve, for a while... At least she need not worry about the child. His mother would see to that. She would not let a grandchild starve. Of course, his mother would be furious when she read his letter, but then it would be easier to pardon the indiscretions of the 'glorious dead' than the peccadillos of an impecunious son... If he survived this day's action, he would have to make his own arrangements for the support of his love-child... What problems one's pleasures brought in their wake! All life was a cheat really. At the bottom of his heart he knew that his swift response to the King's request for Volunteers had been prompted by a desire to escape London and its complications. Sarah was pretty and gay, but she had no real interest in the actor's craft, except that she thought it would bring her money and fame. And her appreciation of words – their quality, their power – was non-existent.

The sudden sound of gunfire brought him out of his reflections. The company on the poop could see that Sir Thomas Allen, leading the Van and having the full advantage of the north-east wind, had already reached the Dutch.

'Gentlemen, it is now ten of the clock,' declared Sir Edward. If the wind does not increase, we of the Rear cannot hope to reach the Dutch before twelve. A precipitate attack by the Van, before the whole of the fleet is enabled to get in line, would seem to me to be unwise.'

'The Dutch line is worse formed, Sir,' called Middleton, handing back the glass to his Commander. 'More of a crescent than a line I should say... Albemarle and Rupert will be able to get up with de Ruyter before he is in a position to assist his Van.'

'De Ruyter – I dreamt of him last night,' declared Sir Robert Leach, in his squeaky voice. The rest of the company burst into laughter. He was still convinced that he was to kill de Ruyter with his musket.

Increased roars of gunfire told Sir Edward that more of the Dutch were engaged with Sir Thomas Allen, Commander of the White Squadron.

'The Red will soon be upon them,' he said, training his glass upon the Dutch Fleet. 'It would appear, from the standards flying, that we of the Blue are to meet Van Tromp.' He fell silent. 'I must warn you, gentlemen, that Van Tromp is the most tenacious of the Dutch commanders. We must expect a bloody fray.'

'Such a pity that Digby will not be here to enjoy it,' murmured John. 'With luck a Dutch cannonball would have rid us of that troublesome hornet forever.'

'Is your Lordship not to do that for us?' queried Spragge, his brow raised.

'Not if I can keep out of his way!' laughed John.

Spragge shook his head. 'Digby will pursue you. He took your remarks, about his enforced stay in Harwich, very ill.'

John smiled mischievously. Two nights ago, while anchored in the Gunfleet, they had experienced a most violent storm. Thunder and lightening had disabled Digby's ship. Her masts had suffered from a thunderbolt and *Jersey* had had to repair to Harwich for a refit.

'Providence does not intend that you should die in battle, Digby,' John had jeered. 'Presumably you are preserved to be hanged.'

Digby, his face white with hate, had reached for his sword, but had been prevented from drawing by others of the company. Sir Jeremiah had ordered Digby to his ship, and the young captain had turned abruptly on his heel, saying nothing.

'He was furious to think you considered him anxious to miss the battle,' continued Spragge. 'I hear he went over Smith's head, to Prince Rupert, to ask if he could transfer to a ship under his command. Rupert refused, of course. He told Digby he should comply with the orders of Sir Jeremiah, and stay in port. Enough trouble has been caused already by the insubordination of captains. However, you know how Rupert favours these hotheads; he smiled on Digby and told him that his zeal for service would be remembered.'

Spragge raised his glass and looked along the line. 'Speaking of hotheads, I see Rupert has appointed his old friend Sir Robert Holmes to be Rear-Admiral of the Red. He is flying his standard in *Henry*.'

'Holmes must be happy to find himself, once again, at Rupert's right hand.'

Spragge smiled ruefully. 'I thought his Highness was going to appoint me to his Squadron, but on the appearance of our hero of Guinea, he assigned me to the Blue.'

John had heard of the rivalry between Holmes and Spragge for Rupert's favour, and tried to think of an accommodating reply.

'Unless Holmes is adequately rewarded for his efforts he will no doubt tear up his commission and fling it at the feet of his commander, as he did to the Duke of York last year. I have not met the man, although he started his career in my grandfather's service in Ireland. I hear he has very little control of his temper.'

'True,' frowned Spragge, 'but I will say the man has courage, and his Highness draws out his better qualities. They are besides, old comrades in arms, having fought together in the Civil Wars, and then later with Prince Maurice in the West Indies, in Oliver's time. He will have to be remarkably indiscreet to lose the Prince's favour.'

'I hear,' ventured John 'that Sir Jeremiah is a great favourite with Albemarle.'

'Aye, the jump from mere captain to Admiral of the Blue, in little more than a year, is a remarkable achievement. When he saved the Duke of York's life at Lowestoft, it brought him to the notice of the mighty.'

They turned their gaze towards *Loyal London*, which was bearing down on Van Tromp.

'The command of the King's newest battleship has been given to a mere seaman,' pontificated Sir Robert Leach. 'The fellow smells of pitch and tar...'

'And was no doubt swaddled in sailcloth!' added John with an ironical smile. 'Does that make him any less effective as a seaman and a fighter? Albemarle himself reeks of beer and tobacco.'

Just then a burst of gunfire put a stop to further conversation. Rupert and Albemarle were now engaged with de Ruyter. The commander of *Victory* knew he would soon be in action – and a hush fell on the company. Spragge, through his glass, could see that Keynsthorne in *Defiance* was well ahead of Sir Jeremiah, and was bearing down upon Van Tromp's Rear-Admiral. A slight increase of wind had developed, and the space between the English and Dutch rear was narrowing rapidly.

Keynsthorne was directing his fireship to bear down upon the Dutch. John knew that fireships, converted merchantmen soaked with oil and tar, and sailed by a skeleton crew, could only be used from a windward position. At the critical juncture, the captain would bind his rudder, set fire to the fuses, and jump into his waiting longboat, whilst the burning vessel crashed alongside the enemy. However, Keynsthorne's man was unlucky. The Dutch saw his approach and opened fire before he was ready; the hold of the fireship being full of combustibles, went up in a sheet of flame. Those of the crew who could save themselves jumped into the sea. The rudder of the burning vessel had not been tied on course towards the Dutch before the unlucky hit. The fireship became a hazard to Keynsthorne himself, and he had to tack about. This exposed *Resolution*, the next in line, to the full force of the Dutch guns.

The fireship, severely shattered and out of control, drifted across the English line of sail. Sir Jeremiah closed his wind to avoid her, thus missing his chance to fire upon Van Tromp. The Dutchman, finding no obstacle in his way, despatched a fireship of his own towards *Resolution*. The rest of the Rear watched helplessly as the Dutch threw their grappling hooks upon her, lit their fuses, and escaped in their longboat unharmed. *Resolution's* rigging went up in flames.

'Unless Sir Jeremiah re-tacks he will be unable to help *Resolution*,' stammered John.

'I imagine he intends to leave her to her fate,' said Spragge. 'See, her men are jumping into the sea.'

'The small ketches are picking up as many as they can reach, but hundreds will drown!' cried young Middleton.

Spragge turned his attention to the narrowing distance between himself and the Dutch. *Loyal London* had tacked about and was again bearing down upon Van Tromp. *Victory* had by now reached the rear of the Dutch vessel.

'Fire!' ordered Spragge. The guns went off in perfect unison. The sound was deafening; a few seconds later John could hear the echo of the crash as the shot entered the enemy's hull. A gentle wind swept smoke along *Victory's* bulwarks, clouds of it billowing in dark waves amongst the company on the poop. The din was continuous now; guns fired, carriage trucks rumbled, and gun-captains bellowed orders. John was well-nigh dazed and stupid with the noise.

A red glare, an ear-splitting bang, took possession of his consciousness. He could see Spragge fumble with his speaking trumpet. The crews were working admirably, the guns going off singly as the sergeants made sure of their targets. The flash of a gun illuminated a vessel close on the port side. It was a Dutch ship with a dangerous list to her side. She could do them no harm, her sails miserably shattered and her men jumping into the water. Nonetheless, it was puzzling to know how she had gained the weather of them.

By now it was impossible to see what was happening because of the smoke, but the look-out man called to Sir Edward that another Dutch ship was bearing down upon them.

Soon nothing existed but the roaring thundering monster that discharged huge missiles into and upon *Victory*. However, the Dutch firing was lamentably inaccurate and was failing to hole the vessel. The Dutch commander transferred his attention to the rigging of the English ship and peppered it with chain shot. Dust, debris, splinters, torn yards and rigging came flying through the smoke which had replaced the breathable air. A rain of metal fragments, cloth, and even pieces of human body began to fall from aloft. John, his eyes wide open, yet convinced that he was dreaming, seemed bolted to the deck when scarcely a few yards away young Middleton's arm was torn from its socket. Blood, thought John. Blood everywhere. He watched in horror as the red river gushed from Middleton's shoulder. 'That is his life's blood!' He jerked himself from his daze. Remembering what he had learned in the aftermath of Bergen, he snatched up a piece of cord, tore at the rags of clothing, and exerted pressure on Middleton's shoulder. The boy was screaming with pain. 'Lie still!' John snapped, shutting out emotion as he went about his desperate work. The surgeons at Bergen had been strangely abrupt and unsympathetic but self-possession was their armour; some of their patients had survived.

The pressure John exerted on Middleton's shoulder was beginning to staunch the flow of blood. He was about to call for help to remove his charge below when a grinding and rending of wood sent a quiver through the ship. A Dutch man-of-war was alongside and beginning to grapple with *Victory*. Soon her crew were springing over the bulwarks and pouring onto the deck. The soldiers, who up till now had borne no part in the fight, fell upon them with spirit, but the Dutchmen's weight of numbers bore them back.

Three of the enemy came running onto the poop. One was an officer brandishing a sword and the other two had cutlasses. John released his hold on Middleton to draw his pistol. The blood once more began to pour upon the deck. Spragge fought the officer and ran him through with his sword. John shot one of the Dutchmen through the head. Sir Robert Leach despatched the other with his musket.

By now, the sailors had snatched up their boarding pikes and axes. Step by step the Dutchmen were driven back to their own ship. Spragge's lieutenant made to follow them, but the Dutch cut the ropes of their grapnels and the ships drifted apart. Some of their last men were forced to jump into the sea.

Sir Robert Leach looked up into the Dutchman's rigging, spied the look-out man, and shot him. The man screamed and fell with a sickening thud onto the bulwark. His brains spattered over the sides of both ships. Leach, strangely untouched by the horror around him, laughed delightedly and congratulated himself upon the accuracy of his firing. He is like a child, thought John: he is utterly absorbed in what he is doing, and delighted to find he is doing it well. The horror of the action does not trouble him.

John turned to Middleton, left unattended during the Dutch boarding. He lay in a pool of blood, his face stark white, and his breath weak. He motioned John to raise him. 'If I lie flat ... I shall choke,' he gasped. John held him in his arms, as he called for a surgeon. By the time a stretcher party arrived the boy was sinking into unconsciousness. 'Will I die?' he croaked. 'No, of course not' said John. He called impatiently for men to clear the way. Middleton murmured something weakly. John bent to hear. 'Beowulf ... death ... is the hazard of the warrior.' They were his last words. By the time they got him below he was dead.

John returned to the poop with a heavy heart. During his absence the cannonade had been renewed. Smoke enveloped *Victory* and covered the sea for several hundreds of yards. It was difficult to see where the main line of the fleet now lay.

Spragge, although elated with the retreat of the Dutchman, was now burdened with the problem of communicating with his Admiral.

Albemarle had issued Sailing and Fighting Orders before the commencement of the year's campaign, and had impressed upon captains the necessity of regaining their stations once they had repulsed their immediate adversaries. The instructions laid down various evolutions and signals for their execution. The problem of manoeuvring a large fleet was much facilitated by the Order of Battle, which specified each ship's station in the line, with distinguishing signals for each individual ship. With the great increase in the number of signals, it was realised that smaller vessels would be required to repeat the Admiral's signals all along the line. One such vessel was allotted to each flag officer.

Several of *Victory's* masts were severely shattered and had lost their distinguishing flags. Spragge flew a signal from his foretopmast directing his signalling ketch to approach. He was hailing its lieutenant through his trumpet when a Dutch ship appeared out of the murk. She carried no guns and was silent. Sir Edward stiffened with fear; undoubtedly she was a fireship and would burst into flames as soon as she collided with them. Only the signalling ketch lay between him and the certain disaster of *Victory* catching fire. He ordered the ketch commander to put his ship by: the Dutch would not ignite their fireship to burn such a minor prize.

Spragge was correct. When the ketch turned towards the Dutch fleet, the fireship turned aside. No sooner was it done, however, than a great Dutch battleship appeared to windward and opened fire on the ketch. Raked fore and aft by the Dutchman's guns, the frail craft sank before their eyes.

'All hands to the guns!' Sir Edward roared. He realised from the standard flown by the Dutchman that he was about to engage Van Tromp himself. 'What has happened to *Loyal London*?' he asked himself. 'I must inform Smith of our position. With my signalling ketch gone, and Van Tromp bearing down upon us, I have no time to hail another vessel.'

He turned and addressed all those standing on the poop. 'Who will go in the ship's longboat and deliver a message to Sir Jeremiah Smith? He must be informed that we are unable to return to our station, and that we are heavily engaged with Van Tromp.'

No one hastened with offers of help. Van Tromp was making speed towards them and would soon be within firing distance. John was surprised to hear himself say, 'I will go.'

Spragge, his face drawn, nodded briefly. 'A longboat on the port side for my Lord!' he called. He turned to John.

'*Victory* will shield you for the first few hundred yards, but you will soon be in open sea, in full view of the Dutch line. With luck, you may be able to get out of range before they sight you.' He smiled, pressing John's arms hard with his two hands. 'May good fortune and the holy Saints protect you, my Lord.' He turned away quickly. Van Tromp's great battleship had opened fire.

'Make haste, my Lord. If Sir Jeremiah cannot assist us, we

shall be dead men.'

John hurried down to the waist of the ship, and was greeted by a sergeant with four seamen. 'I can spare you few men, Sir. It takes a minimum of four to row the longboat.'

'Is it necessary to use it? If you provide me with a row-boat, I can go by myself.'

The sergeant stared at him in surprise. 'But my Lord, it would not be in accordance with your rank.'

John shrugged with impatience. 'My dignity can spare the risk of four men's lives in the circumstances in which we find ourselves. If the longboat is sunk, five men's lives will be lost. If I go alone, and am lost, another can be sent in my place. A row-boat, if you please.'

He was taken to the entry port and let down with ropes. His rowing practice on the Thames now proved useful. Using long powerful strokes of the oar, he was soon clear of *Victory*. With luck, amongst all the confusion, a small rowing boat might pass unnoticed. The sea was calm, and dimly he could see the English line. If he could reach one of the ships before being observed by the Dutch, he would soon be within reach of Sir Jeremiah. He rowed steadily for five to eight minutes and was congratulating himself upon his progress, when a cannonball screamed over his head. A few seconds later a spout of water announced the arrival of another. Had he been sighted by the Dutch? 'I must be a difficult target at this distance,' he thought. 'They cannot keep it up for long.'

He passed a small ship belonging to the Blue squadron heavily engaged with a Dutch frigate, and the air became thick with flying shot. John kept his head down and continued to row steadily. The heat of the day was oppressive, and although his helmet and breastplate shielded him from flying pieces of metal, the weight of his armour was rapidly becoming unbearable. It seemed to him that he was rowing through boiling sea and red-hot rain. His only thought was to keep going. He must reach the English line and deliver his message before death claimed him. Nothing else mattered.

At last he reached an English ketch from Sir Jeremiah's own squadron. The captain came to his aid and John was soon upon

113

the deck of *Loyal London* giving an account of the sorry condition of his own vessel. *London* had also suffered badly. The decks were alive with activity, and every available hand was employed in remedying the damage she had suffered. Many of the crew were occupied in cutting away the wreckage of the mizzen mast, and trying to clear the stern from sail and ropes. Carpenters were lowered over the side and were nailing pieces of wood over the shot holes near the waterline. Men swarmed aloft knotting and splicing ropes and fishing in the water for damaged spars.

'Van Tromp gave us a stiff battle for well above an hour,' said Sir Jeremiah, 'when suddenly he tacked about and made towards his rear. We saw very confused fighting in your direction, and presumed that his Rear Admiral had signalled for his assistance.' The air was clearer at this end of the line, and John noticed with some surprise that it was a beautiful day. How incongruous it was to remember the bright sparkling sea of the morning. In the distance, John could see a small fleet hove to, flying the standard of the Red squadron.

'Those of the Red are taking their ease,' said John, nodding in their direction.

Sir Jeremiah smiled. 'So it would appear. But to be fair to Sir Robert Holmes, he was involved in a close tussle with *Zeven Provinien* and completely dismasted de Ruyter's flagship before being forced to come out of the line to refit.'

'Sir,' said John urgently, '*Victory* is in sore condition. Can you make all haste to assist her?'

Sir Jeremiah looked at him, as though for the first time. The lad was exhausted and as taut as a drumskin. The commander fumbled awkwardly at his belt and brought out a bottle of water. 'Here lad, drink this. Y'are uncommonly pale.'

John drank the water greedily. Although of a brownish colour, and warm, it tasted like nectar. Sir Jeremiah turned and paced the deck. John watched him and considered that he scarcely looked an Admiral: his dress was slovenly and his gait shambling. 'He is really a rather comic fellow,' thought John, 'but good-natured. It was good of him to think of the water.'

Sir Jeremiah returned. 'Holmes has brought his ships about.

We thought he was coming to assist us, but presumably the manoeuvre was in accordance with an order he had received from the generals, further along the line. He has not moved towards us, and now we must bear away to assist Sir Edward.'

He looked at John. 'Are ye better, boy?'

John nodded.

'We are much obliged t'ye. 'Twas a brave act to bring a message through such heavy fire. My ketch is at your disposal. Tell Sir Edward to keep Van Tromp engaged for as long as possible. As soon as I can put on enough sail *Loyal London* will make all speed to assist you.'

By the time John returned to *Victory* she had lost more than a third of her men. Dead and dying lay strewn about the decks, and ruined masts and rigging impeded passage along them. Her guns were still firing at Van Tromp, but both vessels presented a pitiable appearance. The hulls, but two hours ago so trim and smooth, were splintered and jagged. Portholes were knocked into one, bulwarks had been carried away. Van Tromp's stern gallery was gone, his sails riddled with shotholes, though strangely enough his masts remained intact.

'Van Tromp is still manoeuvrable,' gasped Sir Edward, when he saw John. 'But with our masts gone we are like sitting ducks before his guns. What of Sir Jeremiah?'

As John delivered his message the new English battleship appeared off their port bow. She was making good speed, although unable to carry all her sail, as the repair work had had to be curtailed. As she drew near the wind freshed and turned towards the south-east. Van Tromp drew off to meet his old adversary again. He now had the advantage of the windward position.

Van Tromp seemed tireless and bore down upon *Loyal London* firing his guns furiously. Spragge ordered the captains of two of his frigates to tow *Victory* from the line of battle. He was well behind the Dutch line, unable to move and completely at the mercy of any unengaged Dutchman who might appear. The vessel was in tow when de Haan, Van Tromp's Vice Admiral, appeared with a fireship and set it on a course for *Loyal London*.

Sir Jeremiah was making a valiant stand against Van Tromp, but the fireship was too great a hazard to be ignored. He tacked and pulled away from the Dutch line, but not before the fire ship laid its grappling hooks upon him. His men slashed at the ropes and eventually freed *London* from the fireship's greedy embrace. Pushing her off with fire-booms they succeeded in turning her bow, only to have her stern brush dangerously near their stern gallery, setting the Master's cabin alight.

Spragge, watching the fire spreading and powerless to assist until essential repairs had been completed, sent two of his frigates between Sir Jeremiah and Van Tromp. He asked his look-out to see if there were any English ships within signalling distance. He was in dire need of help, but the main body of the fleet was in full pursuit of de Ruyter.

'What is the small fleet, to the north-east?' he enquired. John told him it was the Rear-Admiral of the Red. 'He will be unable to help,' said John, 'his flagship *Henry* is dismasted.'

'He could send his frigates to assist us,' groaned Spragge. 'Has not the man eyes? What is he doing over there?'

They looked towards *Loyal London* and saw that Sir Jeremiah was rapidly pulling away from the Dutch line. The fire was gradually being brought under control, but it was a hard struggle. Van Tromp was preparing to give chase when, mercifully, the wind dropped. Not a breath of air would fill his sails.

It was now about six o'clock. The opposing fleets spent the last hours of light desperately effecting repairs, and desultorily firing at any enemy vessel that drifted within their range. As the smoke cleared, they saw the main body of the English fleet disappear over the horizon. By nightfall only Holmes's small fleet remained in view.

During the night a little wind had sprung up from the north-east, giving the English the windward and offensive position. Considerable repairs had been carried out, but the Blue Squadron was far from ready to re-engage. Should the wind change and Van Tromp attack them, they wished to be in as strong a defensive position as possible, with sails and rigging in place.

116

John ate a hasty breakfast, not realising how hungry he was until the food appeared. He had not eaten since the same time the previous day. The help of every able-bodied person had been needed in the night. He himself had been busily employed taking the wounded below. The remembrance of some of the scenes he had witnessed in the orlop last night suddenly quelled his appetite for ham and ship's biscuit. Surely, he thought, death would be better than enduring some of the wounds he had seen?

He was aroused from his thoughts by a great shout going up all around the ship. 'The Dutch are fleeing!' He clattered up on deck and saw that Van Tromp was signalling his fleet to withdraw. Relief suddenly possessed the crew of *Victory*. The sailors laughed and hugged each other, dancing impromptu jigs on the spot.

'God knows why the Dutch are fleeing, gentlemen,' said Sir Edward. 'At the first turn of the wind they could have had us at their mercy.'

'We have been protected by holy forces,' declared Sir Robert Leach. 'I have seen three aerial men hovering over our vessel.'

'They were certainly in control of your musket yesterday,' said John with a smile. 'You wreaked havoc amongst the Dutchmen – although de Ruyter has so far escaped the attention of your friends.'

'The Spirits will chastise him in the ripeness of time.'

Spragge exchanged looks with John. 'Ripeness is all,' he laughed.

Leach knelt on the deck to pray but his devotions were interrupted by a call from the look-out. Sir Jeremiah was signalling all captains and commanders to come aboard his ship. Sir Edward Spragge directed John and Sir Robert Leach to accompany him, and for the next hour they were occupied attending a Council of War aboard *Loyal London*.

* * *

'The wind is very light, gentlemen, and the Dutch are making slow progress with their withdrawal. My masts are now complete, and preparations can be made to pursue the Dutch into their waters. I should be glad to hear of the progress being made in the rest of the Squadron. Sir Edward, is *Victory* yet manoeuvrable?' Smith himself was confident of recovery.

Sir Edward was about to give his account when the whole company was astonished to hear an explosion. The ship quivered, as they heard a sound of rending wood. They rushed onto the poop deck, expecting to see a Dutchman upon them, but the enemy was well away upon their lee. To the windward was an English frigate, flying the standard of the Red. She fired three more shots across their bows before clapping on all sail to rejoin her commander.

'What in Hell's name is happening?' roared Smith as the frigate drew near *Henry*. When Holmes saw his frigate approach, he clapped on more sail and both vessels were soon off in pursuit of the Dutch.

'What does that purblind bilge maggot think he is up to?' swore Sir Jeremiah. 'I'll have an explanation from that damned madman, if it is the last thing I do!'

'Does he wish to indicate that he is to join with us in pursuit of the Dutch?' puzzled Keynsthorne.

'He could have chosen a more courteous way of letting us know,' murmured Spragge.

The company returned to Sir Jeremiah's burnt-out state-room. It was decided that *Loyal London* should take the main body of the Blue in pursuit of the Dutch, whilst Sir Edward remained behind to protect those vessels still effecting repairs.

'I should be glad if you would spare your young Volunteer for my service,' said Sir Jeremiah to Spragge. 'I have need of a courageous young messenger.'

It was arranged that John should transfer to *London*, and upon his return to *Victory* his trunk was brought up and he said his farewells.

On the new vessel he was assigned a cabin of his own, for which he was greatly thankful. He was blackened with smoke and his shirt, jacket, and body armour were spattered with dried blood.

He realised with a start that the blood was Middleton's

Suddenly yesterday's tragic death came back to him with great immediacy. He fought against the feelings of loss, but they were overwhelming. He wept bitterly, glad that during those few minutes he was blessedly alone. He struggled to regain his self-possession, then washed his face, changed his shirt and cleaned his armour. When he presented himself for duty Sir Jeremiah said his services would not be required until they contacted the Red Squadron. He would then be needed to take a message to its Rear Admiral.

* * *

The entry port of *Henry* loomed above the longboat and, ignoring the sickening feeling in his stomach, John steeled himself to climb the wooden rungs. Above him two villainous-looking seamen had thrown down a rope, but even with their assistance it would be difficult to make a dignified arrival. He had been sent with a trumpeter in attendance, to deliver a message to the formidable Sir Robert Holmes.

'Ye'll find Sir Robert a deal haughty,' Sir Jeremiah had said, 'so wear your court finery, well be-sprinkled with baubles, and perhaps he will deign to speak wi' ye!'

John laughed. 'I will endeavour to do *London* no shame.' With his scarlet coat well brushed, breastplate and head-piece newly burnished, his tall figure presented a well enough sight. Sir Jeremiah considered it would impress even the most querulous of commanders.

'Take no nonsense from the braggart,' he growled, and sniff out his plans if ye can. 'Tis a fine riddle to know whether his ruling passion is misliking me or hating the Dutch.'

John, remembering the tales he had heard of the fiery Sir Robert, anticipated the meeting with mingled feelings of curiosity and trepidation. His reception, once aboard *Henry*, was not encouraging.

'Sir Robert be on poop.' One of the villains jerked his head to the right, implying that John was to follow him in that direction. Every rogue they passed bristled with weapons. Noticing the assortment of daggers thrust into his guide's belt, John felt

119

that the fellow would plunge one into his person at the blink of an eye. He considered he was amongst pirates, rather than King's men.

John was led before a figure resplendent in gold-laced coat and feathered hat. Sir Robert was a tall man, whose heavy features could once have laid claim to good looks. His piercing black eyes raked John from top to toe.

'And what has the Admiral of the Blue to communicate to me?'

'Sir Jeremiah Smith requests you presence aboard *Loyal London*, Sir. He feels you have much to discuss.'

Sir Robert laughed harshly. 'Oh ho, my young coxcomb so I am to dance attendance upon Sir Snivelling Smith, am I?'

'I would hesitate to phrase such a message,' said John coldly. 'The Admiral of the Blue has courteously requested the conversation of the Rear-Admiral of the Red.'

Sir Robert looked closely at John's impassive face. Smith's messenger was no damned half-pay lieutenant, one could tell that. But he was young – and green.

'Tell him I am unable to come. I received a hurt in yesterday's fight.'

'So we were informed.' John continued ironically, 'But Sir Jeremiah gathered from your four-gun salute of this morning that you were anxious to confer with him.'

'Anxious to confer with him?' roared Sir Robert. 'No, my young jackanapes, I have no wish to confer with him, but you can take him a piece of advice if you like.'

He looked at John fiercely, trying to shake his calm.

'What is that?'

Sir Robert grabbed John's arm, and thrust his face close. 'That he would do well to get his flags together,' he said fiercely, 'and fall upon the body of the enemy!'

John stiffened. 'It is our intention to do so, but our Vice-Admiral is disabled.'

'Ye can leave him behind.'

'We shall be less in number than yesterday, and the enemy is a considerable squadron.'

'So...'

John freed his arm and stared at Sir Robert haughtily. 'If it is your intention to join with us, Sir, the numbers would be equal, and we would support you.'

'Support me, indeed! As you supported *Resolution* yesterday, I presume?' Sir Robert sneered.

'I know nothing of the reasons for abandoning *Resolution*, but I do know that the enemy has a number of fireships still in his squadron, and that they will form a considerable hazard should the wind change.'

Sir Robert's face expressed interest; his professional curiosity was aroused. Smith's lieutenant was a gentleman and certainly no empty-headed court popinjay. He knew something of tactics. 'Tell Sir Jeremiah he should intercept them with his frigates and force them to leeward.'

'We should need a stronger wind than we have at present. Fireships must be dealt with quickly.'

Sir Robert grinned wolfishly – the lad had spirit.

John continued. 'There is not sufficient wind to overtake and destroy them before the main body of Van Tromp would be upon us.'

Sir Robert's heavy brows came together. 'So, you would argue strategy and seamanship with me, would you, my fine fellow? I was sailing frigates before you were out of pissing clouts.'

'That I can well believe,' said John, 'for were you not my grandfather's footboy?'

Sir Robert, taken aback, quickly resumed his bantering tone. 'And who was your grandfather, my young cockerel?'

'Wilmot of Athlone.'

'Aha – blood tells!' Sir Robert seemed unaware of the sneer implied in John's remark. 'Your grandsire was a great fighter, and resourceful – and a good friend in a tight corner.'

John, momentarily embarrassed by the generous response to his equivocal remark, felt that the conversation was getting off the point.

'I had far rather you argued strategy with Sir Jeremiah than with me, Sir. It is his intention to follow the Dutch, just out of range, and then surprise them with fireships during the night, should the wind allow it.'

'And should it not do so?'

'We will bear down upon them at dawn, with our guns.'

Holmes rubbed his chin, seemingly lost in thought. 'Tell your master I will be more kind to him, than he was to *Resolution*,' he said grudgingly, 'and that I will stick by him whatever he does.'

John, surprised, questioned further. 'You will join with us when we bear down upon the Dutch?'

'Aye, I shall await your signal. Farewell.'

* * *

The Blue harried the Dutch during the rest of the hours of daylight, keeping company with Sir Robert's squadron, but the wind, blowing from the quarter was not strong enough to allow them to overtake the enemy. Many of the Blue, having lost much of their sail in yesterday's fight, lacked the manoeuvrability necessary for offensive action. By nightfall, they were dangerously close to the Dutch shore.

Sir Jeremiah's pilot was well acquainted with the area; he warned that they were getting into very shallow water, and at any time might run ashore upon one of the Dutch shoals. Smith signalled to his Squadron that they were to drop anchor for the night, and continue pursuit at first light. But when morning dawned the Dutch were gone, and Sir Robert's squadron too was out of sight.

Sir Jeremiah decided to sail towards Flushing, hoping with a good wind to pick up the enemy, but nothing was sighted until, by mid-day, the main body of the English fleet came into view. They drew near the generals' flagship, and the Blue Squadron was signalled to anchor. The commanders were called to a Council of War aboard *Royal Charles*.

John accompanied his commander to the flagship, thankful for a change of scene. Smith, although an admirable enough person, was very odd. The urbane and worldly Spragge was much more to John's taste. The previous night, at Sir Jeremiah's sparse table, the conversation had limped along. Everyone was disappointed at missing the Dutch, and they wondered how fortune had dealt with the rest of the fleet. Smith, noting that John was drinking rather freely, broke the silence by saying that at one time he too had been a notable drinker, but now touched nothing but water.

He warmed to his theme. 'When I was aboard *Mary*,' he reminisced, 'there was a young Quaker who refused to eat or drink anything for five days, because he had been pressed and would not take the King's victuals – which would have committed him to service. I had to discharge him in the end. He had a strange power about him...'

'Aye, I know these Quakers,' broke in *London's* captain, 'there's no breaking them – and they have an unsettling effect upon the men. Y'have to get rid of them. They're like one bad apple in a barrelful – they turn the rest rotten. Prison's the only place for them.'

Sir Jeremiah seemed unaware of the interruption. 'I had a colic upon me, and before he was sent ashore he said, "Friend, drink nothing but water, and the Lord will favour thee. Drink spirituous liquors and thou wilt be dead within the year." Well, I was in such pain that I followed his advice for a few days, and then felt so much better that I have touched nary a drop of liquor since.'

John, meditatively sipped his watered wine, and no longer wondered why such vile stuff was served at his commander's table. The fellow had no palate himself, and was unaware of the outrage he inflicted upon his guests' stomachs.

'And you, my young Lord...' John suddenly realised that Sir Jeremiah's eyes were upon him 'would do well to restrict your drink to water and small beer. Ye will live longer and happier for it.'

John looked up. 'But much duller, I fear.'

Sir Jeremiah shook his head. 'Ye know nothing of the compensations a healthy body and quiet mind can bring to those who have looked into the pit of Hell. 'Tis a state of mind I hope your Lordship will never suffer.'

John shifted uncomfortably in his chair. The conversation was getting damned heavy. It was obvious the man had a touch of religious mania. He laughed lightly and attempted to change the subject. 'I am obliged to you for your concern, but contemplate Hell no more than I do Heaven. I am content with earthly delights.'

'Ye will find them nought but dust and ashes in the mouth. Hell comes with that realisation.'

John, noticing that Sir Jeremiah's quiet grey eyes betrayed real concern, felt touched and embarrassed. What a puzzling fellow he was! Religious bigots usually regarded one as a mere sounding board for their own opinions. One could deal with them upon their own terms. But sincere madmen? They were the very devil!

Luckily someone turned the conversation to the general shortage of beer on board. The captain wished to divert the conversation from the poverty of the victuals. He commented that it was getting late, so the company broke up and retired to their hammocks.

By the afternoon of the next day, when the longboat reached *Royal Charles*, John was more than ready for a change. Sir Jeremiah led the ascent to the entry port. John noticed his commander's darned stockings. His eyes travelled over the rest of his apparel, and came to rest upon his chief's ancient headgear. The hat band was stained; it was adorned with a battered and tarnished silver buckle. Smith was such an odd rag-bag of courage and diffidence, of authority and ungainliness, that John's respect was mingled with exasperation, his admiration tinged with pity.

Upon the deck they were joined by Sir Edward Spragge, who had also been summoned. The generals' flagship had suffered much damage and it could be seen that she was in no condition for another engagement. It was now nearly four o'clock. The commanders had been assembling since two. As they entered the stateroom John was surprised to see Sir Jeremiah jostled by a tall fellow with one arm.

'Holles, ye stand in our way,' said Sir Jeremiah evenly. 'Pray be good enough to move.'

'Pray,' sneered Holles, as his eye ran over Sir Jeremiah and his companions, 'aye, one can expect no more from whining anabaptists – and sneaking papists! 'Tis all ye are good for. A

124

man of spirit ignores such advice.'

'Sir Frescheville, are ye drunk? Stand aside, we are here upon the generals' business,' maintained Sir Jeremiah authoritatively.

'What is the trouble at the door, gentlemen?' called Prince Rupert. 'Ah – Smith ... and Spragge.' He glanced at them coldly. An unnatural hush fell upon the room. 'We should be glad of an account of the action of the Blue.'

John, looking at the faces assembled around the commanders' table, wondered why the atmosphere was so tense. Rupert and a few others were seated, but Albemarle remained standing. John remembered Albemarle had received a bullet wound in the buttocks at the Downs battle in June, and had since found sitting painful. Whether it was due to his wound or to the matter in hand, Albemarle certainly looked extremely uncomfortable.

He cleared his throat. 'We had hopes, Sir Jeremiah, that you would have been with us before now, chasing Van Tromp into our arms. Unfortunately he has slipped into Flushing between us.'

'Aye, under our very noses!' fumed Sir Robert Holmes. 'And who was to blame for that? The coward – Sir Jeremiah Smith!' With an abrupt movement he flung round from the table and struck Smith across the face. His victim staggered clutching at a chair for support.

There was a shocked silence before Albemarle cut in. 'I will have no brawling here, Sir Robert. You will apologise to the Admiral of the Blue.'

'I will not,' said Holmes. 'I insist upon my charges being brought before a court-martial.'

'Court-martial?' repeated Sir Edward Spragge, unable to believe his ears. He turned to Prince Rupert. 'Your Highness, what wild talk is this?'

Rupert looked acutely embarrassed. 'Sir Robert Holmes has a number of criticisms of Sir Jeremiah Smith's conduct in yesterday's battle, and insists that he be brought before a court-martial. His Grace of Albemarle does not agree. As for myself, I am reluctant to believe Sir Jeremiah a coward, and would be glad to hear his account of the events of the past two days. I hope we will be able to reach a just decision in the matter.'

Smith looked stunned, and declared that he would be glad to give an account of the action of the Blue.

'A chair for the Admiral,' called out Albemarle.

The assembled commanders listened to Sir Jeremiah's account of the battle. As he concluded, Holmes turned upon his heel and left the room.

'Gentlemen,' announced Prince Rupert, 'I think we can acquit Sir Jeremiah of cowardice in this action. A more experienced commander would perhaps have questioned the advisability of chasing the Dutch into their waters, but recriminations will not help us now. I must report the whole of this matter to His Majesty and will await his decision upon the necessity of calling a court-martial. In the meantime Sir Jeremiah Smith is still Admiral of the Blue, and will be accorded all the respect due to his rank and person.'

Albemarle growled his agreement. 'I will myself write upon this matter – to the Duke of York. He knows the value of my old friend, and will give no credit to the slanders of a loud-mouthed jackanapes. Never fear, Smith.'

The Council of Commanders then turned its attention to the future prosecution of the war against the Dutch. An expedition was to be prepared for a raid upon the island of Terschelling, where the Dutch kept vast warehouses for their Indies trade. It was decided that the severely damaged English ships were to return to the coast for repairs, and to land the wounded men.

John, feeling a hand upon his arm, looked round and recognised Sir Thomas Clifford. 'My dear young Lord,' said Clifford, 'how good it is to see you again.'

John smiled. He had not seen Clifford since Bergen. 'The last time I saw you, Sir Thomas, was in a raging storm, just before you were sent to Hull with despatches.'

'Your Lordship has an excellent memory. I am to be despatched tonight upon a similar task. Do I understand that you were with the Blue during the last engagement?'

'Yes, we fought like furies. Holmes must be mad.'

'Indeed? I should be glad of an account.' Sir Thomas listened with close attention as John gave an emphatic denial of Sir Robert's charges, and a detailed résumé of the crowded events he had witnessed during the past two days.

Clifford, silent for the main part of the narrative, interjected a few pertinent questions when some points needed amplification. 'Thank you, my Lord. I am to give the King an account from as many eye-witnesses as possible. He will be interested to hear of the experiences of one as brave, and as high in his favour as yourself.'

They parted with many promises of further acquaintance, and John returned to *Loyal London* with Sir Jeremiah Smith.

The next morning they anchored in Southwold Bay, and landed their great numbers of wounded. In Albemarle's despatches they would be described as "gallant men" and "valiant wounded", but John considered "animals in pain" a better description. Five hundred valiant wounded meant five hundred separate tragedies. Their deaths and sufferings, cast in heroic terms, mocked the bitter truth as he had witnessed it. Accurate descriptions, such as blown into bloody joints of meat by a cannonball, and burnt alive enveloped in burning rigging, might jolt the politicians and merchants at home into a greater realisation of the cost of their ambitions. John's face hardened as he remembered Lord Ashley's ingenious excuses for not paying the seamen their prize money last winter. Next winter, he thought, when these ships are laid up, will the seamen's fate be any better?

Bells were rung in Yarmouth and London to celebrate the victory of St James's Day. Rupert and Albemarle had succeeded in beating de Ruyter home to his ports. The English, for the month of August, ruled all in the North Sea. On the fourth, the Red Squadron, under the command of Sir Robert Holmes, attacked the island of Terschelling and set fire to two Dutch warships and one hundred and sixty-five merchantmen sheltering in the Vlie. It was a terrible blow to the Hollanders. Van Tromp was court-martialled, whilst de Ruyter poured all his energies into getting a sizeable fleet out to sea before the storms of autumn put an end to all combative activity for that year.

'Holmes's Bonfire' cheered the King and court, and when the

thanks of the London merchants had been conveyed to Sir Robert, his overweening arrogance knew no bounds. He was determined to pursue his vendetta against Smith, and by exerting influence through Prince Rupert and his friends at court, he had succeeded in moving the King to write to Albemarle. His Majesty considered that as the complaints against Sir Jeremiah Smith were so universal, he thought it necessary that he should brought before a court-martial. Albemarle replied lengthily, supporting his old friend, and by the end of August had obtained agreement that the hearing could be deferred. It would be held before the King himself, at Whitehall, when the present campaign was over. In the meantime Sir Jeremiah was to remain in charge of the Rear Squadron.

When repairs had been effected to *Loyal London*, Smith had taken his ship towards the Dutch coast and in a short engagement had sunk six of Evertsen's squadron, and had succeeded in removing seven brass guns from the wrecks as they lay in the shallows. Brass was in great demand at the Navy Office.

All through August the Admirals sent constant demands to the Navy Office for fresh provisions and new supplies of men. Money and manpower were short, and in desperation many of the press gangs were kidnapping the crews of the merchant supply ships. Many of the King's vessels still awaited provisioning and failed to receive it, because there were no men available to transport the supplies to them. However, by the twenty-ninth of the month some provisions were available at Solebay, and Rupert and Albemarle replenished their holds. They gave orders to sail at seven the next morning.

It was rumoured that de Ruyter had succeeded in getting the remnants of his fleet in fighting order and was planning to rendezvous with the French near Calais. The English fleet sailed for North Foreland without meeting him, and then proceeded into the English Channel. However, the weather proved so violent that both sides had to abandon their plans for warfare and seek shelter from the elements. De Ruyter decided to return homewards, but was delayed by adverse winds and had to anchor in Boulogne roads. The English, having heard that the French had retired to Brest, decided to shelter in the

Solent. They would be well placed to challenge either adversary, should they decide to combine their forces when the weather improved.

By mid-day on the second of September the Isle of Wight was sighted, and His Majesty's fleet came to anchor in St Helen's roads. John was once more aboard *Victory*. The vessel had been repaired and re-provisioned at Harwich, and was again an effective fighting unit in the Blue Squadron. Sir Edward Spragge had loyally supported his commander and it was the general opinion in the fleet that Sir Jeremiah had suffered an unjustified attack upon his reputation.

When the Fleet anchored in the Solent a General Council of War was held. Sir Thomas Allen was directed to take the White Squadron to sea, to watch any movement on the part of the Dutch or the French. Rupert and Albemarle went ashore, to call upon the Governor of Portsmouth, Sir Philip Honeywood, who had despatches for them from the King.

9

Portsmouth

It was on the fifth of September that the astounding news reached the fleet. There had been a great fire at London and the city had been burned to the ground. It was now little more than a smoking ruin. The King requested the Duke of Albemarle's return. He had need of his energy and organisational ability. Prince Rupert was to be left in overall command of the fleet.

The new arrangements were disastrous for the fortunes of Sir Jeremiah Smith. He was ignored at many of the Councils, and was subject to many insulting remarks by Holmes and his toadies. The wind continued high and it was impossible to put to sea. Prince Rupert accompanied Holmes to his stronghold on the Isle of Wight. Sir Robert was in such favour with his commander that had it not been for the loyalty of the officers of the Blue, it was probable that Smith would have been imprisoned at Portsmouth.

On the ninth of the month Prince Rupert returned to the mainland and dined with Sir Philip Honeywood, the Commanders of the Red Squadron, and many of the gentlemen Volunteers from *Royal Charles*. When Harry Savile visited John the next day, he gave him a detailed account of the proceedings.

'Holmes was lording it everywhere, with his crony Frescheville Holles in attendance,' said Savile. 'God, how I hate that pair of ruffling villains!'

'Why are they such boon companions?' asked John.

'Henry smiled. He said banteringly, 'I don't know how much

130

you are aware of sailor's habits, young fellow, but shall we say that they are brothers-in-arms of long standing, and great drinking companions.'

John wrinkled his brow.

Henry continued, 'When the *Henry* lost her topmasts on St James's day and became completely unmanoeuvrable, it was Holles who towed her out of the firing line. Had he not, Holmes could well have lost his ship.'

'So Holmes owes Holles a favour?'

Henry grinned again. 'Yes, amongst many others. Shall we leave it at that?'

John, a little puzzled at Henry's mysterious jocularity, shrugged, and said, 'I hear Holles made an amazing recovery after the Four Days' Battle, when he lost his left arm.'

'Aye,' agreed Henry, 'the man has guts and stamina – perhaps that is his attraction for Holmes. Sir Frescheville has few other qualities to recommend him.'

Sir Edward Spragge entered the room. 'Did I hear Holles mentioned? The man is a barbarian, and has the manners of a meat porter. He continually insults my religion, although I fear I am a scandalously negligent papist, and make no great clack of it abroad.'

'The man enjoys a fight,' said Savile. 'It is as if he cannot rest until he sees blood flow.'

'A fit companion for Digby,' laughed John.

'Aye,' added Spragge. 'They are well acquainted. I fear we shall have to meet them ere long. The Red are forming a faction against the Blue, and we shall have to guard our backs if we walk the lanes of Portsmouth after nightfall.'

'There is no likelihood of visiting Portsmouth at present,' said John. 'Sir Jeremiah tells me that we have to keep our station in St Helen's roads in case Sir Thomas Allen sends for our assistance.'

Five days later news was given of the approach of eight sail of French, and *Victory* was ordered to pursue them. The warship caught up with them off Dungeness. Spragge assisted in the capture of a French frigate, and took the commander prisoner. The Frenchman was considered a civilised member of his nation, and by the time *Victory* returned to Portsmouth, he had become a popular member of Sir Edward's stateroom. The company heard that Monsieur de la Roche had lost his trunk of clothes when his ship had been handed over to the local Commissioner for Prizes. Sir Edward sent a courteous message to Prince Rupert, asking him to use his influence to have it returned. Amazingly enough, this was done. It was thus agreed that Prince Rupert was no barbarian, although many of his adherents were unruly pirates.

The weather continued foul, and there seemed no better way of passing the time than staying under hatches, drinking and talking. John brought out his flageolet, which had lain buried in his trunk for the past two months. Monsieur de la Roche taught him some French songs. For the young earl it was a great pleasure to be able to practise some music.

On the twenty-first of the month Sir Jeremiah sent a message requesting his officers to attend a Council, and afterwards stay and eat dinner. His invitation was not received with any great enthusiasm: his abstemious habits had given him a reputation for meanness amongst the officers of the fleet.

On their arrival aboard *Loyal London* Sir Jeremiah told the officers that orders had been given for the fleet to sail for the Gunfleet in three days. It was considered that the French and Dutch would give no further action during the year, the weather proving so thick and foul. Officers and Volunteers alike were permitted to go ashore for two days, to replenish their stores and clothing. Volunteers who wished to return to their homes were free to do so, but Sir Jeremiah expressed a preference for them to remain on board should their commanders so wish. Sir Edward asked for John's company until *Victory* was de-commissioned at the Gunfleet, and John was happy to comply. He had no home to return to, whilst relations with his mother remained strained.

Sir Edward Spragge escorted his French prisoner to the Governor of Portsmouth. Sir Philip Honeywood now had the responsibility of guarding him. Sir Edward suggested that he and John should take rooms for two nights at 'The Man in the Moon', a noted Portsmouth hostelry. They could bathe there, eat and drink well, and be entertained by local musicians, with perhaps a wench or two to sing and provide comforts.

John agreed with enthusiasm. He was beginning to tire of the cramped accommodation aboard ship. He had lived in the same suit of clothes for the past month, and felt dirty and windswept. He had his trunk brought ashore and hired a woman to wash his shirts. He walked about the town and bought new shirts, wine, fruit and cheese. However, he was not impressed with the amenities of Portsmouth. He found the town dirty and provincial, and nothing but a long straggling High Street behind the dockyard. The road was full of pits and ruts, with dungheaps piled in front of every stable door. The most notable heap was that outside Sir Philip Honeywood's residence, he remarked.

He met the Mayor of the town when he and Spragge delivered Monsieur de la Roche to the Governor's residence. The man's name was Ben Jonson. When John asked him if he was related to the great poet, he looked puzzled, replying that 'such London rogues' were no kin of his.

Spragge went visiting his cousin George Legge, who was a Member of Parliament for the town. He would be returning to the inn for evening supper. Invitations were extended to Smith, de la Roche (who the Governor agreed could be let out of prison on parole), and several officers and Volunteers from the Blue. Sir Edward agreed to an invitation being extended to John's friend, Henry Savile, and left him to perfect the arrangements for the evening's entertainment.

John interviewed the proprietor of the inn, Master John Fitzpains, who was overjoyed at the sudden increase in his trade. He would be happy to arrange for musicians to call and entertain the gentlemen. However, he had one proviso: all festivities must cease before twelve on the Saturday evening, as fiddling and drinking were strictly forbidden on the Lord's day. When John protested, he agreed that the local justices were ridiculously puritanical, but maintained that he had to be careful because the local schoolmaster, who lived opposite, had given evidence against him a year ago, and he had had to pay a heavy fine. Fitzpains was, he said, extremely reluctant to curtail the gentlemen's pleasure, but could not afford another

133

amercement during the current year.

John, laughing, said he appreciated the innkeeper's predicament, and added that they would all need to be abed betimes. They had to return to the fleet by six on the Sunday morning.

As John went up to his room, he saw Robert Julian, Spragge's secretary, at the hall door. The man had a satiric wit and appreciated it in others. He and John had concocted an entertaining piece of doggerel on the subject of Sir Robert Holmes – on the model of Marvell's satire, *A Second Advice to a Painter to draw the Duke by* – which had set all Oxford laughing the previous winter.

'I can't get it printed, my Lord. The fellow tells me Holmes has too much power in the Portsmouth area, and it would go ill with him did it become known that he had produced it. If he took our money now, he would pay for it dearly after our departure.'

'A pity,' said John, 'but we can sing it tonight if the fiddlers know of a suitable tune.' Later, John and Robert Julian rehearsed the musicians, and their voices rang loudly as they sang their doggerel to a popular air.

'You find much sport in singing of my friend,' said a deep voice at the door.

John looked round and saw Frescheville Holles standing there. He was a giant of a man, well over six feet tall.

The young Earl bowed mockingly. 'We have to make our own pleasures in this flea-bitten town.'

'I have heard that you plan some junketings tonight. Take care lest they give offence to powerful men.'

'We are preparing a private party. I had not heard that you had been extended an invitation.' John resented the intensity of the man's gloating gaze.

Holles turned on his heel abruptly, and left without further comment. John shrugged and turned back to the musicians. 'We will repeat that phrase just once more.' The preparations for a pleasant evening were going very well.

The dinner proved greatly successful. Legge had sent half a buck to 'The Man in the Moon', with his compliments to Sir Edward, and the company had enjoyed fresh meat for the first time in months. Fitzpains' wine was good, and the company became boisterously merry. At length, Sir Jeremiah decided it was time for him to go. He thanked Sir Edward and the young Earl for their hospitality, and said he had to leave as he had much work to do aboard. He wished them a pleasant evening, consonant with the desires and interests of youth. Rochester and Spragge, viewing him with bonhomie engendered by wine, accompanied him to the inn door.

When they entered the courtyard they found the exit into the road blocked. Holles, Holmes, Digby and several of their bravoes were standing under the arch.

'Let us give this gawk a drubbing,' said Holles. He and Holmes drew their swords.

Smith, knowing there was no escaping them, drew his rapier and advanced upon Holmes. 'Out of my way, Sir Robert.'

'So you think to fight with gentlemen's weapons?' sneered Holmes. 'If this is to be a duel, who will be your seconds?'

'Our Admiral does not lack friends,' declared Spragge roundly. He turned to his servant. 'Get my sword from my room'

'And who will you fight?' grinned Holmes.

'Your friend Holles,' said Spragge stoutly. 'He and I have quarrel enough to justify a bout.'

'Aye,' agreed Digby, stepping forward, 'and I challenge my Lord Rochester to render satisfaction for his blow at the Gunfleet.'

John, having expected a pleasant evening, was taken unawares by this sudden turn of events. He looked around the group in the courtyard; menace was thick in the air. He knew that the quarrels of the past two months would have to be resolved in this hour, and in this place. There was no escape.

He sent for his sword and declared to Digby, 'I shall be happy to slit your throat.'

'You'll find the opportunity a rare thing,' retorted Digby, rejoicing to find John at his sword's end at last.

By this time most of the gentlemen gathered in the dining room had crowded into the yard. When it was heard that formal challenges had been extended between the quarrelling parties, the company formed a ring around the courtyard and declared they would ensure fair play.

Savile, on hearing what was afoot, advised Fitzpains to alert the Governor and the Justices, saying that the King had given strict instructions forbidding fighting amongst the officers of the fleet. The Governor had powers to have it stopped. Savile also sent for a surgeon.

Sir Jeremiah advanced towards Sir Robert and briefly saluted. They were soon heavily engaged. Spragge, although an experienced fighter, found it hard to maintain his guard against his one-armed opponent. Holles, with the advantage of his build, had a long reach, and although the wound he had sustained in June had weakened his ability for a long bout, he seemed tireless.

Digby lunged at John, but the young Earl had a quick eye and nimble feet, and parried the thrust. Digby lunged again, but failed to penetrate John's guard. John riposted, and had a great stroke of luck; Digby's foot slipped on the mud of the yard, and as he fell backwards John's sword grazed his chin and cheek. It was only a flesh wound, but Digby became rattled. He regained his feet and began to thrust wildly at his opponent. John was a defensive fighter, and skillfully kept up his guard, but after several minutes he was stretched to the limit. He wondered how much longer his luck would hold. He became dimly aware of a tramp of feet in the road outside.

A cry went up: 'The Governor's men are here!' A party of soldiers marched into the inn yard. 'Hold, in the King's name!' shouted the officer. 'You are all under arrest.'

Three soldiers approached each party of fighters. They flung up the swords with their halberds. John found his arms grasped from behind, and all the standing protagonists were frogmarched into the inn. Holmes had to be carried in, as just before the arrival of the Governor's men, Smith had wounded him in the shoulder. Sir Robert had suffered severe loss of blood and lay unconscious in the mud of the yard. He was moved inside, where, owing to Savile's foresight, a surgeon was waiting to attend him.

The young officer assembled the remaining combatants in

the dining room. All the gentlemen were breathless and in a state of shock. They were indignant at being manhandled by the soldiers; none had been restrained with such lack of ceremony since a boy at school.

Frescheville Holles was the first to break the silence, and demanded to be taken to his injured friend Holmes. On hearing the name of the injured man, the young lieutenant knew that he would have to act with circumspection. He learned, further, that three of the combatants were Admirals, and that the fourth was a Lord from London. He decided the matter too weighty for his handling, and confiscated the gentlemen's weapons, demanding that they should give an undertaking to depart peaceably to their lodgings. They were to give an oath that they would appear before Sir Philip Honeywood the next morning. As all were officers of the fleet, the matter would have to be reported to Prince Rupert.

None of the combatants was in a position to argue. Those who had been anxious for the fight were still staunching their wounds. The peaceable parties were glad that the action was over. Each of the gentleman gave the undertakings requested.

The surgeon appeared and told the lieutenant that Sir Robert Holmes had been run through the shoulder. The wound was deep, and the muscle cut and bruised, but luckily the weapon had not permanently damaged the artery. Provided the wound did not turn gangrenous, Sir Robert should be a fit man within six weeks. Having been assured that no fatality was likely to occur, the lieutenant was visibly relieved. Sir Jeremiah was allowed to return to his ship. Holmes and Holles were accommodated in the innkeeper's best room. Digby was having his flesh wound examined by the surgeon. He had two silk sutures placed in his cheek. Ashen-faced, he departed without speaking.

John and Spragge turned to each other, dazed with surprise and relief. They looked around the ruins of their dinner, and burst into uncontrollable laughter. They would be in grave trouble with the civil and naval authorities tomorrow, but at least they were alive. When they learned of Savile's role in the matter, they were grateful to have such a sensible friend. If it had not been for his good sense and prompt action, they realised, they might well now be dead men.

* * *

John retired early and fell into an exhausted sleep. He had no idea of the time when he was awakened by a soft but persistent knocking at the door. He drew on his breeches and caught up his sword, unsheathing it before opening the door. John Fitzpains was standing there with a candle, carefully shading the flame with his hand.

'My Lord,' he whispered, 'her Ladyship and her two nieces are below, refusing to go without attendance money. What am I to tell them?'

John frowned. What on earth was the man talking about so furtively – and in the middle of the night?

'What o'clock is it?'

'Near midnight, Sir. I have told them to go, but her Ladyship insists on seeing you.'

John, his brain fuddled with sleep, drink and exhaustion, tried to get his memory to function.

'You must be mistaken. I have no acquaintance in Portsmouth.'

Fitzpains persisted, in obvious embarrassment.

'Her Ladyship will not go without payment and I beg your Lordship will manage the matter with discretion. I have the reputation of my house to think of and I cannot risk another disturbance this night.'

Suddenly John realised the implication of the conversation. During the afternoon he had asked one of the musicians if they knew of two fresh young wenches who would sing and entertain the company in the latter part of the evening. With a laugh, the fellow said he would pass word on to the appropriate quarter.

Fitzpains continued in an urgent whisper, 'Sir Edward is below and requests your assistance.'

John was irritated and annoyed, He had planned an evening of merriment and song, not fighting and venery. What a damnable nuisance. He had scarcely gold enough to meet his reckoning in the morning, but obviously the whores would have to be paid off. He nodded to Fitzpains and said he would soon be below. He retrieved his purse from under his pillow, and met Spragge at the bottom of the stairs. He could see that his commander was torn between amusement and irritation.

'Good God, Jack, have we not been exercised enough this day, without requiring the services of two doxies? Do you want your girl, or shall we pay the harridan off with attendance money?'

'Pay them off, for God's sake. I requested singers, not whores. How much does she want?'

'A guinea apiece for the girls, and two for herself.'

John whistled. 'A bit high – for a couple of unsung ballads!'

Spragge laughed. 'It is obvious that her Ladyship thought weightier services would be required. She has been telling me how careful she is to ensure that her girls are clean and that both Sukey and Meg are virgins. You must know they cost more.'

'I know nothing of the sort!' snapped John. 'I have no need to buy women, and venery is the last thing on my mind. All I want is sleep.'

'I agree entirely,' said Spragge. 'Let us pay them off. Fitzpains is anxious to avoid a rumpus.'

John opened the door of the parlour and bowed to the bawd. 'I apologise for wasting your time, Madam. I understand a payment of four guineas will compensate you for the inconvenience?'

'Well, if you don't want my girls, I suppose it will have to do – but fine girls they are, if your Lordship will but look at them.'

'I have tonight fought a duel, Madam, and have not the inclination. I cast no aspersions upon the quality of your merchandise.' He placed the money in her hand.

One of the girls giggled and ogled him. 'What a fine gentleman. I would allow him some liberties free of charge!'

'Not in my employ, young Meg. Come along, Sukey, we waste our time here.' Her Ladyship pushed Meg through the door, and roughly grasped the arm of the younger girl. Sukey raised terrified eyes as she was hurried away. She burst into tears as the women crossed the hall. 'I would ha' done it,' they heard her say. Meg gave her a push and burst into roar of coarse laughter as they entered the inn yard. Fitzpains shut and locked the door behind them.

Spragge whistled. 'We are well rid of that baggage. I doubt if Meg was yet a virgin.'

John, disinclined for jollity, replied coldly, 'The younger girl was no more than a child.'

Spragge shrugged. 'She was perhaps fourteen. If she has no father or even a brother to protect her, she is bound to lose her maidenhead ere long.'

'But she looked terrified.'

'I expect she was told that she would be beaten if she did not please us.'

'But that is devilish.'

'I agree. I take no pleasure in reluctant maids, especially when the world is full of young women who are willing.'

'I hear you are courting a rich young widow.'

'Aye, one who I hope will confer the blessing ere long.'

'Then I bid you pleasant dreams, Sir. I must sleep. We must be up betimes.'

As John returned to bed he remembered Sukey's frightened eyes and wary silence. He would not have desired her in the best of circumstances, but her air of apprehension inspired his pity. It was appalling that the child should be enslaved to that harpy. It could not be right, however much one judged her ultimate destiny to be that of servant, drudge or whore.

* * *

The next morning John and Spragge attended at Sir Philip Honeywood's residence, and learned that Prince Rupert and the main fleet had sailed for the Straits of Dover during the night. Holles had made arrangements for Holmes to be carried to his ship, and had sent a message to the Governor saying that the necessities of war had demanded their departure.

Sir Philip Honeywood understood that Smith, Spragge and Rochester were the attacked parties, and that they too, should not be impeded in their departure. However, he warned them

140

that all participants in the previous evening's affray would be subject to arrest for breach of the peace, should they enter Portsmouth on any subsequent occasion. When they left Honeywood's presence, Smith and Spragge said they need not be concerned; the fracas would be all forgotten as soon as the fleet had sailed.

On the next tide, the Blue Squadron left St Helen's roads and they passed the Straits of Dover on the afternoon of the next day. Instructions were received from London that the whole fleet should proceed to Buoy of the Nore, to be laid up for winter, as de Ruyter had returned to his home ports.

When *Victory* reached the Gunfleet John heard that Sir Robert Holmes had prepared his articles against Smith, and had hurried up to London on the last day of September. Smith and his two Vice-Admirals, Spragge and Keynsthorne, prepared their defence and had no fear that they would be cleared of Holmes's charges by any independent panel of arbitrators. John was thankful that Smith's court-martial was to be heard before the King himself. At least his Majesty would be above the factions in the fleet.

On the third of October John said his farewells to Spragge and the many friends he had made on board *Victory*. If the war continued he would no doubt meet many of them again, though already there was news that the Dutch were asking the French to negotiate a peace. In London, his Majesty was declaring that he had no more money to prosecute the war, and the City was in no mood to finance it, following the disaster of the Great Fire. It was reported that not a building was left standing between the Tower and Temple Bar, and that some of the ruins were still smoking. The King's Treasury was empty and the seamen were being dismissed with tickets instead of money. This practice was causing dangerous discontent, as many of the men's families were desperate for money. The seamen were having to part with their tickets to speculators who were demanding a heavy discount for their services.

John himself was down to his last few guineas and as no prizes had been taken on this campaign, he would receive no recompense for his services unless the King made him a present. He thought of Sarah and wondered how his mother had taken the news contained in the letter he had sent her on the eve of St James's Day. Would she be glad – to see him back alive, or angry – that Sarah was to bear his child?

He decided that his best course of action would be to call upon his uncle Apsley in Lincoln's Inn Fields. He would be able to gather news there and reconnoitre about the court. He was confident that Apsley would give him a warm welcome. Sir Allen was his mother's cousin, and he had always had a strong affection for John. Sir Allen had helped him out of many a scrape when young. His aunt Frances kept a well-ordered house, and kept it cheerfully, so he would not encounter there the air of disapproval which marred his visits to the St Johns at Battersea.

He knew he would not be allowed to enter the Duke's court to see his mother. The Duchess had banished him last spring following the contretemps with Sarah and Anne Temple. How long ago it seemed now! He would have to visit Sarah as soon as he had gathered some money together. Money was the priority now – even if it meant appeasing his mother. He was hoping that Sir Allen would perhaps smooth the way.

10

An Audience and A Visit

The Apsleys had a townhouse in Lincoln's Inn Fields, a country house at Battersea, and the use of lodgings at Hampton Court. John decided to try the London House.

Apsley welcomed him with great affection. He was an honest, reliable, and tolerant man. Perhaps his only weaknesses were that he relished gossip and loved a good bottle of wine overly much, but in John's eyes these were not faults; he knew that his uncle would be the ideal person to put him in touch with affairs at Court.

'You are a secretive fellow, Jack, to steal away to sea, and tell no-one where you were going. We were worried about you when we heard you were forbid the Duke's court.'

'I did not think my company would be welcome. The Duke and Duchess were so incensed against me that I thought they would look acidly upon you had it become known that I had called here.'

'Dear Jack, you are a foolish and troublesome young jackanapes, but you did not commit treason. The Duchess would not carry her ire so far as to set it against me, her old friend and servant.'

'What is happening at St James's? I hear another of the York children is sickly.'

'Aye, and little hope of a new child. The Duke neglects his lady, and is wholly taken up with a new love, my Lady Denham.'

'Old Sir John's wife? The young and beautiful Margaret Brooke?'

'Aye, and she has spirit as well. Says she will not go up and down the privy stairs, as others have done, but will be owned publicly, and so she is. The Duke goes at noonday, with all his gentlemen with him, to visit her in her lodgings in Scotland Yard.'

'And how does old Sir John take this?'

'He is ill, and keeps to his bed.'

'He bides his time, for I hear he is a vengeful man.'

Apsley nodded. He was ready to enlarge upon the character of Denham, but John was anxious to change the subject. He wanted to know how the exploits of the Admirals had been judged at Court.

'What kind of reception did Prince Rupert receive from the Duke?'

'Cool. Albemarle and his friends have the ear of the Duke, following the very good service they rendered after the terrible fire last month. Albemarle is defending Smith against the charges of Holmes, who as you know is Rupert's crony.'

'Only too well. I can tell you much about that.'

'I was hoping you would do so. I look forward to hearing of your experiences after dinner... In the meantime, I think you ought to know that Albemarle and his adherents have produced a report in Cabinet saying that the fleet has returned in a very bad condition.'

'Hardly surprising, considering the weather and the fighting we endured.'

'Aye, I think all reasonable men would acknowledge that, and you have a good fighter in Rupert. He rose up and told the Cabinet that whatever was said he knew he had brought home his fleet in so good a condition that it could have stayed out longer, and fought the enemy, but that he was bedevilled by the weather and the contrary instructions received from the King's Council. Of course, the King smoothed matters over, but outside the room, Albemarle quarrelled with Rupert, and then the Duke of York quarrelled with Albemarle, so they are all at sixes and sevens.'

'How does the King view the matter?'

'He looked very bored at Council. The only time he bright-

144

ened was at the end, when he announced that he was about to set a new fashion in clothes – a plain black vest, with white facings.'

'It sounds very sombre – even puritanical.'

'Aye, but a good thing at this present time. Economy and humility are being called for on all sides.'

'Because of the great fire?'

'Yes, Tuesday is to be a day of fast and prayer. A collection is to be made for the victims of the fire.'

'Money is expected from us then? I have absolutely none.'

'I will lend you fifty pounds, until you can see the King. I expect he will make you a present for your service at sea.'

'I certainly hope so. Where does the King hold his levee this month?'

'At Whitehall, on the seventeenth. He is to wear his new costume, and all those attending are expected to dress in the same fashion.'

'Then I must visit my tailor, without delay.'

* * *

On the appointed day, John duly appeared at Whitehall, resplendent in black and white. Diamond buttons were sewn on the short black surcoat which fastened over a calf-length vest cut in the Persian mode.

Harry Killigrew greeted him enthusiastically. 'It's good to see you, Jack – and I see you are in the new style. God's blood, but we all resemble a group of magpies! I hope the mode will not last long.'

'I hear the King favours it.'

'Aye, but he will be laughed out of it ere long. We hope you will help there, Jack.'

'Not yet. I have just acquired this suit at considerable cost.'

'I can believe that,' said Harry, his small grey eyes fixing enviously upon the diamond buttons.

John did not tell him how he had cajoled his elderly relation Lady Manchester into lending them to him. She had worn them at the King's coronation five years ago. Now, although sick and probably on her death bed, she declared that she could refuse her winning young rogue nothing. He made her laugh so much with his scandalous tales.

'I visited little Sarah, at Putney,' continued Killigrew, 'and took her some oranges. She pines for you, y'know, and expects her time to be up next month.'

'I know,' said John, 'and I intend to visit her ere long. But I must establish my fortunes first. It will be of no purpose to visit Putney without money.'

'I think you wrong her,' said Killigrew quickly. 'She wants you before your purse.' He reflected with some bitterness that he wanted Sarah for himself, but he rarely had any success with women.

'I do not wish to imply that Sarah lacks a good heart. She is a fine girl, but her needs at this time will be many. There will be the child to think of soon.'

'Aye, her aunt chatters endlessly about the expected babe, and continually questions me about your return from sea.'

'I shall see her next week.'

Their conversation was arrested at this moment by the appearance of the King.

'Why Jack, how pleasant to see you. You look so well in our present mode of black that I am persuaded it should never be changed.'

'There are some here, your Majesty, laying wagers that your present mode will be changed before the year is out.'

'Do not put your money on it, boy. The fashion stays until my fortunes change for the better.'

'So I shall be forced to wear this suit until your Majesty finds me some lucrative employment. I have spent the last of my money upon it, so shall be an interested party in preserving it.'

The King laughed. 'It is good to have you back, dear rogue. I must have some private conversation with you.' He turned around. 'Sir Thomas Clifford here will let you know when to attend.' He waved Clifford over in John's direction, and nodded a dismissal.

'My dear young Lord, I rejoice to see you looking so well. I

146

hear you were involved in a skirmish with Digby. I feared at first that you might have suffered injury, but I hear it is quite to the contrary, and that it is our young cockerel who is nursing his wounds.'

John bowed. 'I understand that my assailant will suffer no permanent injury.'

'Except for a scar to his face.' Clifford made the remark with such satisfaction that John knew it implied approval.

'I am surprised to hear the town has heard of the fracas at Portsmouth – and of the results.'

'My Lord, the fleet is ringing with the details of your exploits. I heard of them last night, at the table of Sir Edward Spragge.'

'Sir Edward is a practised raconteur. He has no doubt exaggerated the tale.'

Clifford smiled. 'I imagined that was probably the case. I gave no credence to the tale of the two virgins which followed later.'

John, a little taken aback, murmured, 'I am amazed at the extent of Sir Edward's invention.'

Clifford laughed. 'Sir Edward was deep in drink at the time – but we waste our time with idle talk. His Majesty wishes to see you privately. I suggest you call at my lodgings tomorrow, after the play.'

'I have received no invitation to attend.'

'His Majesty expects you to be there. I look forward to receiving you.'

John bowed his thanks as Clifford rejoined the King's procession.

Killigrew jogged John's arm and laughed. 'God's wounds, Jack, have they many fine whores in Portsmouth? You lost no time taking your pleasure, I gather. I must tell the Ballers of your exploits.'

John, although a founder of the bawdy drinking club, was unenthusiastic in his reaction. 'I do not wish the tale to be spread abroad.'

'How so? Savile told me you asked for two girls to attend.'

John nodded. 'Savile was there, but he doesn't know the

147

whole of the story. It was something of a misunderstanding, and you have heard a garbled tale.'

'And I'll wager 'tis a good one, you lecher!' Killigrew sniggered. 'Two at once!' He elbowed John in the ribs, and hurried away to join Buckhurst and Arran.

John saw them grinning and glancing in his direction. He felt irritated and exasperated. The truth of what happened in Portsmouth would not be believed in a twelvemonth. He recalled the danger of that September evening. The terrible experiences of the summer and autumn seemed belittled and trivialised now by the circulation of a bawdy tale. He could see that Killigrew was providing him with a gaudy reputation as duellist and lecher. In truth his role had been neither that of hero nor villain. The irony of the situation was laughable; he shrugged off his irritation. There was naught so false as common fame.

The next afternoon John attended the performance of *Mustapha*, held in the Queen's apartments. The Queen was with the Duchess of York, and as they both smiled upon him when he paid his respects, he knew that the escapades of the previous spring had been forgiven. Lord Broghill's play gave a stirring account of the exploits of a Turkish warrior. John resolved to buy a copy of the play as soon as it was printed. There were some fine parts in it for women-players and he would rehearse Sarah in the part of Roxalana, as soon as her condition would allow.

When the play ended John found Sir Thomas Clifford at his side. Clifford motioned him to a side door, and guided him through many anterooms and corridors before arriving at his lodgings. The comfortable room was warm, with a brightly burning fire in the grate. The silver dishes and gleaming goblets on the polished oak table reflected light about the room. A discreet manservant lit extra candles before Clifford motioned him to withdraw.

Sir Thomas Clifford was proving a most useful servant to the King. His efficient administration, his energy and his quick intelligence encouraged Charles to employ him in many capacities besides those of Commissioner for Prizes and

148

Comptroller of the Household. Clifford was tactful and knew when to hold his tongue. He was courageous and would speak his mind honestly when called upon to do so. The King made use of him to approach men secretly. Clifford would arrange a number of important meetings under cover of a pleasant evening's entertainment.

There was a knock at the door and Clifford admitted the King. John knelt before Charles, who extended his hand. The King raised him immediately.

'No ceremony tonight, dear John, we must be at ease. I wish you to tell me of your life at sea.'

'Truthfully, or amusingly?' asked John.

'Truthfully and factually' said the King emphatically.

Charles was in a quandary. The charges brought by Holmes against Sir Jeremiah Smith were causing a strong element of partisanship throughout the court. The King was finding it hard to discover a man who would give him a dispassionate account of the actions which followed the battle of St James's Day.

Clifford had volunteered to arrange meetings where the King would be able to converse freely and where he would not be overheard by adherents of either Rupert or Albemarle. Albemarle had sworn he would not return to sea unless Sir Robert Holmes's commission was taken from him. He would support his old friend Smith throughout the whole proceedings.

Prince Rupert was growing increasingly irascible. In the aftermath of the Four Days' Battle in June, a block had fallen upon the front of Rupert's head. The wound had failed to heal and his physicians were becoming increasingly concerned about his state of health. Pain, and the shame of disfigurement, it was said, were turning the Prince's brain. The King was disinclined to take anyone's opinion without probing their motives.

Charles questioned John closely concerning his attitude towards Sir Robert Holmes.

'Do you consider that Sir Robert's account is untruthful?'

'Not untruthful, but certainly prejudiced. His preconceptions about Smith were unjust and inaccurate – and he wanted the command of *Loyal London* for himself.'

149

'Jealousy as well as prejudice?'

'Yes, and I would add vainglory too. *London* is the newest and one of the most prestigious vessels in your Majesty's fleet. Holmes thought he should have been given its command.'

'I gather you do not care greatly for Sir Robert?'

'Undoubtedly not. He is full of conceit and cruelty.'

'Cruelty? Hmm... I have heard, John, that you too ... can be malicious.'

'Yes, I have malice towards those who would seek to injure me, but I would not seek to ruin a man who had sought me no harm, and who was scarcely known to me.'

'In truth, then, you consider Sir Jeremiah to be slandered?'

'Of course. He is a strong and courageous fighter...' John stopped and smiled, 'however odd his behaviour in the common walks of life.'

'I hear you have studied your ex-commander closely, and that you can give a passable imitation of his after dinner conversation.'

'I rejoice to hear that the imitation is passable.'

'I am told that it also contains a number of untruths.'

'Brought in merely to heighten the comedy, your Majesty.'

'If you lie in certain situations, would you lie to me about Sir Robert's actions?'

'No, I would not give false witness to my King, or lie in a matter of some weight. Telling the truth is both better and safer. A lie is found out sooner or later, and the teller is given no credence by men of sense.'

Charles nodded and was silent. He appeared lost in thought. Eventually he laughed. 'I must hear your imitation of Sir Jeremiah at some later date. If I give ear to it before the court-martial, I might burst into laughter as the poor wight gives his evidence!'

He turned to Clifford. 'But we must now speak of other concerns.'

Clifford drew a chair inviting the King to be seated, and Charles indicated that his host should follow his example. 'I am obliged to you, Sir Thomas, for your hospitality. It is good to be at ease, amongst friends.'

John was motioned to sit opposite the King who regarded him slowly and thoughtfully.

Charles smiled. 'I am told that Lord Hinchingbrooke has withdrawn his suit to Mistress Mallett. They had a tiff when the court was at Tunbridge Wells this summer. The field is now open for you to renew your addresses.'

John raised his brow in surprise. 'I doubt if Mistress Elizabeth would give me a hearing.'

'Your doubts are foolish, boy. She still hearkens intently whenever your name is mentioned.'

'Aye, to gather fuel for ridicule,' said John bitterly. 'In any event I have no money to spend on presents worthy of an heiress.'

Charles looked quizzical. 'No money at all?'

John warmed to his theme. 'I am grateful for the pension your Majesty awarded me at your happy Restoration, but it is paid in arrears, and I am owed two quarters already. I am told there is no money in the Treasury for payment this year.'

Charles turned to Clifford. 'Is the situation as dire as reported?'

Clifford nodded. 'The seamen are like to riot for lack of payment, and court servants and court pensions will have to wait.'

Charles shook his head. 'I must let John have something from the Privy Purse.' He laughed. 'Young Rochester must not be tardy in his wooing!'

* * *

John rowed from Battersea to Putney and secured his uncle's boat to a tree at the bottom of a cottage garden. He walked up the path, with his manservant following. Will held a large box under his arm.

John was about to knock upon the door when it was opened abruptly. Sarah stood on the threshold, a severely aggrieved expression on her face.

'So you have decided to visit me at last!'

John had hoped for a more rapturous welcome, but Sarah was angry.

151

'Are you not glad to see me?'

Sarah burst into tears. 'Where have you been? You returned from the fleet two weeks ago!'

Will took a grave look at the weeping girl. John, not wishing for an audience, told him to set down the box, and to wait in the boat. Will complied reluctantly.

John took Sarah's hands in his. 'My dearest girl, I did indeed return two weeks ago, but I needed money. I could not come empty-handed.'

'I don't want your money. I want your company. I am nearly driven mad here, what with the worry that you might lose your life, and aunt saying what is to become of us if you should not return. The child is due soon, and I feel sick and heavy and like to die.'

She sobbed and John brought out his fine lace handkerchief and wiped her eyes.

Sarah continued. 'For six months I have had no diversion, but for Mr Killigrew who calls here occasionally.'

'So Harry has been here? What has he been telling you?'

'That you have forgotten me, and have been making merry with two women at Portsmouth.'

'The damned snake! How could you believe him?'

'I didn't, but when I cried he said he would take care of me when the child was born.'

'Do you care for him?'

'Of course not, you fool!' She stamped her foot. 'It is you I love.' Her indignation mounted. 'He is short and stupid, and has stubby hands. He handles me roughly if he gets half a chance – I pushed him away and told him to be off.'

John laughed. 'I am glad to hear it.' He went to take her in his arms but she pushed him away. Sarah was prepared to punish him with indifference, but once she had raised her eyes to his, she was lost.

'Let us kiss and be reconciled,' said John tenderly. He knew that Sarah hungered for his mouth, as did he for hers. They embraced passionately and time was eclipsed. Later, they went inside the cottage and closed the door. John murmured, 'I have a present for you.'

152

Sarah's curiosity was aroused. 'What is it?' Her eyes brightened as John opened a velvet box and took out a necklace of pearl. He kissed the back of her neck before fixing the clasp.

Sarah turned. 'Oh John, I have missed you so!'

They again fell into a long embrace, until interrupted by Mrs Cooke who appeared, inopportunely, from the kitchen.

'Well, I am relieved to see you back, my Lord. I have been so worried. We are right out of money.'

'That can soon be remedied, but did you not assure me, when I left in the spring, that you were able to support yourself with dressmaking?'

Mrs Cooke nodded. She was a woman who liked to boast of her financial independence, but the past two months had proved a chastening experience.

'I have had no employment in London because of the fire. There is no money to be had anywhere. We have scarce enough bread to see us through until the morrow.'

'I have brought a hamper of food, and a box of goods necessary for childbed.'

Mrs Cooke bent eagerly over the hamper whilst John and Sarah opened the box. The young girl squealed with delight. 'How did you know what would be required? – so many things, and of the best quality! Where did you get them?'

'At the New Exchange. The shops opened again this week – and the women were most helpful.'

'I'll warrant they were,' said Mrs Cooke with a sniff. 'I hope that is all they sold you.'

John raised his brows. 'I purchased all I had need of.'

Mrs Cooke, irritated at the ambiguity of his reply, returned to her theme.

'Our Sarah needs cheering, and a change of scene, before the child comes.'

John turned to Sarah. 'I am sorry to disappoint you, but I have no home. I am staying with my uncle at Battersea, but I shall visit here as often as I can.'

Sarah turned to her aunt. 'Can you not leave us alone?'

Mrs Cooke frowned. 'Well, your young Lord is here now,

153

which is, I suppose, something to be thankful for – I will leave you together.'

She picked up the hamper and retired to the kitchen. As she unpacked the good food she began to feel a little mollified, yet could not cast off a vague feeling of unease. The young Lord had given Sarah a fine present. It was indeed a beautiful necklace, but she wished it had not been of pearls – for what were pearls but frozen tears?

* * *

When John returned to Sir Allen Apsley's house he found him packing for London.

'The Duke has sent for me. He says there have been disorders at the Navy Treasurer's office and twenty-four guards have been needed to keep the seamen at bay. I have been recalled to supervise the removal of the Duke's gold to a place of greater safety.'

'It would seem that everyone must look to themselves.'

'Aye, I rejoice that the King gave you a present last week; few others will receive payment this year. I thank you for the prompt repayment of your debt.'

''Twas the least I could do, when you offered me a home.'

'Ah, John – that is another subject for discussion. I have visited Sir Walter and he has invited you to stay with him. My lease here runs out shortly and the Bishop is anxious to repossess the property. I must remove my goods to Hampton Court. I shall be in such disorder, travelling from one place to another, that I cannot offer you a settled home.'

John hid his disappointment. 'I am obliged to Sir Walter. Has he any news of my mother?'

'Aye, she rejoices in your safe return from sea and wishes to see you. You are to call upon her in the middle of November, when she returns from Ditchley.'

'I shall certainly do so. Is there any other news?'

'Your friend Killigrew has been banished the court.'

John was surprised. 'How so?'

'Killigrew was drunk the other evening when the King announced that Lady Castlemaine was expecting another child.

154

Killigrew said he congratulated the lady on her fertility, but unfortunately he enlarged upon his theme. He said he had heard she was a little wanton when young and was well practised in slipping her bastards onto parish rates. When her ladyship heard of it, she complained to Charles that she had been slandered, and would not be pacified until he had sworn to ask York to turn Killigrew out of his employment.'

'And it has been done?'

'Aye, he is no more the Duke's Groom of Chamber.

John was quiet as Apsley continued. 'You would do well to drop the idle fellow's acquaintance. His company will do you no good.'

John was a mixture of conflicting emotions; his attitude towards Killigrew veered from exasperation to pity. Since his visit to Sarah, John had had some reservations about Killigrew's friendship, but he was nonetheless indignant to hear of the severe treatment meted out to his erstwhile crony.

'Barbara is a vengeful bitch.'

'We know that, but she has the King's ear, and his favour, and will bear no insult tamely.'

'Caesar's wife must be free of scandal; so must Caesar's whore.'

'Indeed. But I must talk no longer, there is much to be done.'

John went to his room. He remembered the rough treatment he had received at Barbara's hands when they were children. Their first meeting had taken place when he was seven. She was then a precocious fourteen-year-old with an overbearing nature. When they met again he was ten, a bookish lad, with little interest in her tantrums but a lively awareness of the penalties of gainsaying her. They were staying at Lady Winwood's house in Buckinghamshire. Barbara was by then seventeen and sexually experienced. In company with Anne Hamilton and Elizabeth Montagu, she wished to entertain Philip Chesterfield in her bedchamber. She considered that her bookish young cousin should make himself useful by guarding the door. John said he preferred to read, and could not spare the time, but Barbara cuffed him, twisted his arm, and said she would make him agree, or it would be the worse for him. He had been overwhelmingly angry, and had kicked her in an attempt to get free, but had found himself powerless in her grasp. Anne Hamilton had come to the rescue saying it was needless to hurt the lad when he could be bribed instead; fruit and sweetmeats were always more effective than threats. John, grateful to Anne for salvaging his pride, agreed to act as look-out. Barbara, laughing contemptuously, had agreed that he could have the fruit and raisins, but said he would have no books about him until she consented. She had taken them from him, locking them away in the chest by her bed.

John remembered he had told Killigrew of these youthful quarrels with Barbara, when they had both been in drink. He had detailed how Barbara would rub her pubis against the bench end whilst she waited for Chesterfield, the other girls giggling as they followed her example. They despised John as an ignorant child, but Anne had said that no doubt he would surprise them all when he grew up: he had bedchamber eyes and she boasted that she would try his manhood when he reached fourteen. At this sally the three girls had subsided into sniggers, running into the bedchamber and slamming shut the door behind them. Barbara had called out that he was to let them know as soon as he saw Chesterfield enter the courtyard.

John felt uneasy as he remembered his unguarded conversation with Killigrew. The fool's lack of judgement was exasperating, but he had known the fellow to be unreliable, and he castigated himself for revealing so much. Drink had run away with his brain – before he could take stock of the consequences.

* * *

The next day John and Will packed the Earl's trunks and loaded them into his uncle's boat for the short journey to Battersea House. John received a warm welcome from his aunt and uncle. They were kind people but very serious, and strict in their religious observance. Sir Walter kept a chaplain and John knew that he would be expected to attend prayers and discuss the sermon over dinner. Lighter conversation was sometimes indulged when the younger generations were present, but Sir Walter's daughters were away in the country, and his son Henry was staying in town.

Sir Walter urged John to write to his mother. The text in chapel that morning had been *Honour thy father and mother, that thy days may be long upon the land which the Lord thy God giveth thee.* Perhaps his mother would re-grant him his father's estate, it was suggested, if he phrased his letter skillfully.

That evening Sir Walter was in brighter mood. His son Henry had come to pay them a visit. Henry told them of his visit to court and of the fine new playhouse he had seen there. Their cousin Barbara was to grace its opening by viewing the new comedy, *Love in a Tub.*

Sir Walter considered it regrettable that a playhouse should open with a light trivial performance at such a time of tribulation. 'I fear that Barbara puts her soul in jeopardy by entertaining and encouraging such plays.'

John nearly choked over his wine. 'I should imagine the devil has claimed her soul already, and that the encouragement of such a play a mere bagatelle in comparison.'

Sir Walter viewed his nephew sorrowfully.

'God is not mocked. I fear for this generation. Our leading astrologers foretell that the end of the world will occur during the second week in November. It ill behoves the most highly placed in the land to give their attention to any concern but the saving of their souls.'

John tried to move the conversation on.

'I hear Lilly has had to answer to the Privy Council for prophesying the great fire. The King's ministers wish to know how he obtained his information, and whether it was from the Catholics.'

'Aye, 'twas a Catholic plot,' said Sir Walter emphatically.

'That seems to be the consensus of opinion at the present time, but how well-founded is it?'

Silence descended upon the company.

John ventured a new start to the conversation. 'I wonder when the merchants will start to rebuild the City. They will need to raise capital for the outlay, and fee an army of lawyers to establish title to the land.'

Henry said, 'I hear that a special Fire Court is to be set up by Act of Parliament, so that disputes and difficulties about the ownership of land in the City can be quickly resolved, and rebuilding commence.'

Lady St John brightened and ventured a remark. 'My kinsman Lord Justice Hale has been chosen to chair it.'

Her husband smiled. 'He is a good man and will settle all fairly.'

Lady St John continued. 'I saw him last week, at the new Lord Mayor's swearing in – but the procession was a sad sight. No gold maces or fine robes, all the regalia being lost in the fire.'

'And it rained, and there were guards everywhere,' Sir Walter added.

John asked, 'Did you hear any foreign news?'

'Only that peace with Holland is spoken of. We cannot afford to continue the war.'

* * *

After a week of sermons, religious conversation and serious discussion of disasters and politics, John was ready for some diversion. One evening he rowed himself to Putney in the rain. He could stand his uncle's prosing no longer. He was well covered by the tarpaulin cloak he had bought himself in Yarmouth. Sarah was overjoyed to see him and they spent a pleasant hour together. He was a little disappointed that she had neglected learning her lines as Roxalana. The few speeches she could remember she delivered in a monotonous style, but he could not bring himself to scold her. She must be kept cheerful until she was past her ordeal of childbirth. They discussed the arrangements for her confinement.

Sarah said she needed a gold ring to wear on her left hand, otherwise the midwife would ask if she were married. If she could not declare herself so, the woman would have to report the birth of a bastard to the parish authorities.

John said he would provide all that was necessary, but felt

unenthusiastic about supplying the ring. He was on the brink of a reconciliation with his mother and did not wish to complicate matters with rumours that he was married to Sarah.

Mrs Cooke provided a hot supper of boiled mutton, onion and cabbage. She expressed surprise that John had rowed himself from Battersea in the rain. Had he no horse? She hoped he would not take cold on the way back. Her attitude towards the young lovers veered between affection and disapproval. She suspected that her niece was being played with by a feckless young cub. He was pleasant enough, but thoughtless – as was Sarah herself, the foolish young jade.

Mrs Cooke ladled out the dinner, and pricked up her ears when she heard John say that he had written to his mother. She set down her spoon and stood with arms akimbo.

'Tell her we don't need her help,' she said sternly.

John stiffened, and his expression became haughty.

'Why should you think it necessary to tell me so?'

'Because in August your mother sent her maid Woods along to pry into our business. She said her Ladyship would send food, clothes and medicine if we needed it, but no money.'

John remembered Mary Woods. Her name suited her perfectly. She reminded him of a stiff-bristled broomstick. Lady Rochester's maid was a solemn spinster of fifty, who kept her linen spotless and enthusiastically maintained her mistress's finicky standards. It was inevitable that she and Mrs Cooke would ill agree.

Sarah's aunt continued indignantly. 'I said we were managing very well, no thanks to her Ladyship, and that we needed no-one's charity!'

John was a little exasperated. 'That was foolish because it is obvious you would have needed help if I had not returned from sea. I wrote to my mother asking her to assist you.'

Mrs Cooke looked amazed. 'So this is what comes of your fine show of independence – asking your mother to look after your bastard child?'

John was stung to the quick. 'I was expecting to die, Madam, and was thinking of your niece's welfare.' His eyes flashed. 'I was hoping for a kinder reception upon my return from sea.'

Sarah flung her arms round him. 'Do not be angry. You

159

must not mind Aunt. I love you, and we both need you sorely.'

Mrs Cooke saw that Sarah was upset, and relented. She muttered grudgingly. 'All those who know his Lordship are glad to see him back from the war, but everyone has their own troubles, and it sometimes makes them ill-tempered.'

John nodded coldly and finished his meal in silence. He was now eager to be gone. He kissed Sarah and said that his uncle expected him to return soon. 'I will visit you again next week. Pray keep up your spirits and be assured that I will not let you suffer or starve.'

He turned to Mrs Cooke. 'The child will be put into good care when Sarah goes on stage.'

Mrs Cooke nodded and sighed. 'I trust that all will work out as your Lordship intends.'

* * *

The next morning John woke in low spirits, so was pleased to receive a letter from the Duke of Buckingham.

'My dear young Lord,

Hearing from Sir Edward Spragge that Victory is de-commissioned and her company dispersed, I am hoping that we in London can enjoy again your Lordship's most pleasing company.

All the talk here is of the end of the world, which, I am reliably informed by Mr Heydon, Mr Lilly and Mr Evans and several others of their persuasion, will occur tomorrow, the fatal day being the tenth day of the eleventh month of this year of wonders 1666. The numerologists are much excited with the exotic number 10111666.

So be it! However, if the end of the world is to occur I am resolved that a few choice friends will join me in eating a good dinner before we damned are dragged off to the nether regions.

If your Lordship is free, please be so good as to step along to Wallingford House at five of the clock, and we will await the Second Coming together.

I have little other news with which to entertain you – last night there was a fire at Whitehall, but luckily the rain and Duke's guards put it out. This has added to the popular suspicion that the Catholics were responsible for the great fire and that they have plans to massacre us all. Albemarle believes it, and swears he will put all Catholics out of office. This has displeased the Duke (who as you know, has a number of Papists in his regiment), so Albemarle is out of favour too. He has taken to drinking with Troutbeck, whom nobody else will keep company with. He is such a rude lying fellow, as Albemarle has found out to his cost. They were speaking of the Duchess, and Troutbeck says that there really were amours betwixt her and Sidney last winter. Albemarle said it was a great wonder that Nan Hyde should ever have come to be Duchess of York. 'Nay,' says Troutbeck 'ne'er wonder at that, for if you will give me another bottle of wine I'll tell you as great, if not a greater miracle.' 'And what is that?' says his Grace. 'Why, that dirty Bess the washerwoman (meaning his Duchess) should become Duchess of Albemarle.' I hear that her Grace boxed Troutbeck's ears.

Well, my Lord, if the Second Flood has not submerged you at Battersea, I shall expect you tomorrow in company with Shiloe, for the Second Coming.

I do assure your Lordship that I am your Lordship's most humble and faithful servant, Buckingham.'

Another letter, from Henry Savile, told John that Sir Jeremiah Smith had been acquitted. The King had given his opinion that no blame attached to Smith for failing to pursue the Dutch through their own waters, although it had been unfortunate that too much credence had been given to the pilot who had advised that such a pursuit would be unsafe.

There had been a rumour that Smith and Holmes had fought a duel and that Holmes had suffered injury, but the story had been scotched by the sight of Holmes unharmed in Westminster Hall, and Sir Jeremiah being received at court.

Savile surmised that no doubt a garbled report of the doings at Portsmouth had reached the town and that people did not realise it was old news.

Prince Rupert was reported to be much disgusted. He had expected great thanks for his bringing home the fleet in safety, but the Fire of London and the great losses sustained there had deadened all feeling of celebration. He was aggrieved that no glory had been gained by his services. It was said he was to be trepanned by his surgeons, to relieve the pain caused by the wound in his head.

There was to be a Ball at court on the fifteenth of November. Laces and jewels were to be worn, but put off again the next day, in respect of the season of humiliation and mourning declared by the churchmen a month ago.

Lady Denham, the Duke's new mistress, was reported extremely ill. It was said she was like to die, which was strange as she had been in fine health scarcely a week ago.

Savile was staying at his brother's house in Lincoln's Inn Fields. He ended saying that he and Sir George hoped to see John at Wallingford House on the morrow.

11

An Evening at Wallingford House

November 1666

John made the long and cold journey from Battersea in a public wherry, his finery well covered with a large black cloak. The waterman set him down at Whitehall Stairs, where he took a chair for the short distance to Wallingford House. In good weather he would have walked, but the fine mist had turned to drizzling rain, and he did not wish to arrive at Buckingham's house with muddy footwear. His shoes were of the best cordovan leather, and tied with large red ribbons.

Lack of money was preventing him from keeping a coach, and this was proving inconvenient, especially in winter. His uncle did not begrudge him the use of a horse, but tended to ask awkward questions about the arrangements to be made for overnight stabling. Buckingham's men would no doubt have taken good care of the horse, but John considered Sir Walter to be garrulous and tedious where the care of his animals was concerned, and he decided to use a waterman rather than face another interrogation – as if he were a damned ostler! If he could persuade the Treasurer to cash the King's warrant for his pension, he would be in better funds next month. He could feel the document in his pocket: it made a pleasant and reassuring crackle whenever he touched it.

He pondered on the audience his Majesty had granted him two weeks ago. Charles had been well pleased with his service at sea, and with the testimony he had given in support of Sir

Jeremiah Smith. His Majesty had indicated that a vacancy would occur in the Bedchamber within the next month and that he intended John to fill it. His spirits lifted when he thought of the opportunities he was being offered for his worldly advancement. An apartment in Whitehall would solve his accommodation problems and the perquisites of a Gentleman of the Bedchamber would bring him both profit and influence.

The chairmen entered the courtyard of Wallingford House and set the Earl down at the foot of the handsome steps leading into the hall. Buckingham's footmen relieved him of his outer garments and he was ushered into the Duke's presence. Buckingham was a magnificent sight, his tall figure clothed in cloth of gold and silver. He was wearing a large feathered hat. The Duke uncovered to no man except the King. John bowed and Buckingham proferred a ring-covered hand. 'You are welcome, my Lord. Pray wait in the next room. Savile is there, and wishes you to meet his brother, Sir George.'

John was laughing inwardly at his friend's rather formal reception. Buckingham loved the trappings of power and often adopted the air of a monarch. In the past, John's mother had told him that Buckingham had been raised at court in the manner of a prince, and that such privileges had not benefited his character. King Charles the First, devastated at the murder of his great friend, the first Duke, had taken his children into his care, and raised them with his own. George Villiers, tall, healthy and self-confident, had at first been inclined to bully the young Stuart princes, but as they grew older both Charles and James began to hold their own in the nursery quarrels. They were grown men now, but Buckingham's affection for his King was still tinged with a slight contempt. He considered Charles to be easily led. The King could be managed through laughter and pleasure, and he had the necessary powers of invention to keep the monarch amused – whilst he pulled the strings. He considered young Rochester a merry fellow who might prove useful when he was devising schemes for the King's diversion.

John saluted Henry Savile, who introduced him to his brother. Harry was obviously delighted to have his brother in town.

The Saviles were a closely united family. Sir George was a distinguished-looking man of some thirty-three years. He was wealthy and held extensive estates in Yorkshire and Nottinghamshire. He wished for a place in the government of his country, but Lord Clarendon disapproved of the Saviles because of their declared free-thinking in matters of religion. Harry particularly attracted the disapproval of the King's first minister because of his 'frivolity and presumption'. The brothers had little hope of public office as long as Lord Clarendon held the reins of government.

Sir George considered that the present administration made a great waste of public money. He was hoping for a peerage, so that he could take a seat in the House of Lords and make the views of his countrymen known. He was a well-read man, and had spent his early years in France. He and John were discussing the essays of Montaigne, when Buckingham entered the room. His guests were all assembled, and he crossed over to John.

'My Lord, may I introduce John Heydon? He is my "Secretary of Nature", for so his own book describes him.' Buckingham's mouth was twitching at the corners, but he kept a straight face. 'I believe you have expressed a readiness to meet a man who sees visions, converses with angels and visits the celestial regions.'

John suspected he was the subject of banter, and adopted a cool tone. 'I am happy to meet such a well-travelled man.'

He looked at Heydon, but was not impressed with what he saw. The man had a thin, pale face surrounded by straying white hair. He seemed of indeterminate age, perhaps about fifty. His complexion was clear, and his expression pleasant enough, but it was without animation. His grey suit, with its white facings, added to the general impression of bloodlessness. He looked too serious to be a pleasant dinner companion – and was he quite a gentleman? John gave a slight bow, but decided to waste no time on further compliment. He went straight to the point of his enquiry. 'I hear you have the power to converse with the dead. A friend of mine was killed last year at Bergen. Before he died he made a vow to contact me if he discovered a future state. I have not seen his ghost. Would you be able to

165

communicate with his spirit?'

Heydon regarded the young Lord speculatively. Was he serious – or, like so many of his Grace's guests, was he seeking to ridicule him?'

'Yes, it is possible, but the success of the communication depends upon the sincerity and the motive of the seeker, and the quality of his relationship with the dead person. I recommend that you read my recently published pamphlet, *The Way to Converse with Angels*.'

John smiled. 'My friend was a good fellow, but I would not describe him as an angel.'

'Your Lordship mistakes me. The help of an angel is necessary to effect a communication betwixt the living and the dead.'

Buckingham intervened, seeking to make mischief. 'The Church would say it was the help of the Devil which was necessary.'

Heydon regarded the Duke apprehensively. 'Your Grace knows that I have no truck with the black arts, only with the Holy Guide, the Complete Physician and the Holy Household of Rosicrucian Philosophers. They have opened to me all their doctrines and secrets, which I would guard with my life.'

'Oh come, my dear Heydon, stop romancing.' Buckingham was quite openly laughing. 'I have found it superfluous to guard the secrets of the Rosicrucians, for the simple reason that they never possessed any.'

Heydon was evidently used to such comments. 'Your Grace finds sport in all things, even the most serious, and the most holy.' He paused. 'But you have a generous heart, and the Queen of Heaven sees it and loves you for it.'

'I rejoice to hear it. Where does she lodge – and when may I come at her?'

'Nay your Grace, I cannot allow you to jest of my Beata. She is all spirit, and a virgin, although a mother of children. She cannot be looked upon with adulterate eyes.'

Buckingham sighed and took John's arm. 'I suggest we go in to dinner, before I lose my appetite.'

They entered a richly appointed dining hall. The table was

laid with gold and silver vessels, and decorated Venetian glass. Liveried servants stood behind each chair, ready to attend to every need of their master's guests.

'Your Grace has known Mr Heydon long?' queried John.

'Oh, about three years,' said Buckingham airily. 'Arran told me the poor wight was in prison for calling Clarendon a tyrant. I thought his comment showed a deal of discernment, and that he had great courage to express it. I had a word with his Majesty, and obtained his freedom, but on closer acquaintance have discovered him to be a most foolish fellow. Yet he has his uses. He has great knowledge of herbs and medicines. I took him into my household as a servant, and found he could cast horoscopes. I have since set him up in lodgings at Tower Hill, where he has developed a quite considerable astrological practice. He is a good fellow but I have advised him to curb his lust for politics.'

'I take it as an ill office in your Grace to make him my dinner companion – when you yourself admit he is a fool.'

'Do not fret, my dear young Lord. I shall be on the other side, and hope to derive much amusement from your conversation – the juxtaposition of the wittiest young man in town with this most foolish of prophets.'

'It would seem that your Grace regards me as a performing dog – to nip your house spaniel for your sport.'

There was a slight annoyance in John's tone, and Buckingham looked intently at his face.

'You mistake me, my Lord. I value your company highly. Not only for your wit … but for your decorative qualities too.' He gestured towards John's suit of rich plum-coloured velvet, and stroked his hand along the sleeve. He smiled and squeezed John's wrist before his hand dropped away.

John, a little disconcerted at the deliberation of Buckingham's gaze, said that he found dressing well advanced him in the favour of women, but that he did not regard apparel as the main business of living.

'And what do you consider the main business of living?'

'Acquiring a good estate.'

Buckingham laughed. 'Aye, nothing is done without money.

167

You must marry an heiress, sensible but plain. Plain enough to be grateful for your attentions, but sensible enough to know that she cannot monopolise them.'

'Does love have no part in the transaction?'

'Perhaps at the outset, but it must be underpinned by understanding. Love is too transient a feeling to form the foundation of marriage.'

'But is not love a divine inspiration?'

'It is, most truly, but as Walter Raleigh once said," Know that love is a careless child, and forgets promise past."'

John felt he was being patronised. He was no greenhorn in matters of love. He said, somewhat vehemently, 'If I recall rightly the poem ends, "But true love is a durable fire, In the mind ever burning. Never sick, never old, never dead, From itself never turning."'

Buckingham raised a brow. 'I see you know the poem well. If poetry and love are to be your themes, then we must have Mr Cowley with us.' He looked around and called out.

'Cowley, you are to sit on my right-hand side.' He turned to John. 'He has left his country retreat to visit me today.'

John looked up as the man approached. He had admired Cowley's poetry for years, and had often wished to meet him. 'Mr Cowley, I am delighted to make your acquaintance. I hear you have renounced poetry for farming, but I am hoping you will be kind enough to look over some of my verses when you are at leisure.'

Cowley bowed, then looked closely at Buckingham. 'You did not warn me I was to meet your new young Apollo.'

Buckingham laughed, and spoke to John. 'You see the fame of your verse has already reached Chertsey.'

Cowley turned to John. 'I am flattered that you should seek my opinion, and will be happy to read whatever you send me, but your Lordship will I hope pardon me if I take several months before I give you my opinion. My small farm takes all my attention, and I am not often in London.'

Buckingham motioned Cowley to a chair. As his guest seated himself he was taken with a violent fit of coughing, and found it hard to recover his breath. Eventually he was able to turn again to John. 'I find the London fogs unbearable, so I leave for Chertsey tomorrow. However, if your Lordship will trust me with an example of your work I will take it with me.'

John brightened. 'I have written a rhymed debate on the conflict between faith and reason and would be glad of the opinion of 'the Muse's Hannibal.'

Cowley smiled deprecatingly. 'I gave up writing on philosophical themes many years ago, and now find the natural sciences a far more rewarding study. In fact I seldom come to London except for meetings of the Royal Society – but I anticipate great pleasure from reading your verse, and will give it close attention. Have you met Sir William Davenant? He too is writing upon the theme of faith.'

'What is this?' said Buckingham. 'Conversation on serious themes? I will not have it – no epics on King David, no Pindaric odes or Hymns to Light! Cowley you must let us have your verses *To the Mistress* and *To Drinking.*'

'Your Grace has a good memory. Those were the verses of my youth.'

'And they are still appropriate for merry occasions.

> *Fill up the Bowl, Oh fill it high*
> *Fill all the Glasses there, for why*
> *Should every creature drink but I?*
> *Why Man of Morals, tell me why?*

Buckingham motioned to the lackeys to start serving, and his butler poured a superb claret into the glasses on the high table. The Duke stood up and raised his glass.

'To all my friends gathered here tonight, to his Majesty who was to have been present, but who unfortunately has been detained at Windsor, to my Lord Rochester, one of our young heroes back from victories at sea, to my old friend Abe Cowley who shared many dangers with me during the late Civil Wars, to all gentlemen of the Parliament anxious to promote the good government of this country, I give you my toast: "Success and good fortune to all present!"' The Duke swept off his great feathered hat and bowed to the company. As his eyes fell upon his chaplain, he laughed, and threw his hat at him. 'Come Tom, say a few kind words to the Lord and free us to commence the pleasurable part of the evening.'

Thomas Sprat seemed unconcerned at the Duke's informal approach to prayer. Smiling, he shook his head at Buckingham in mock reproof, and placed the hat upon the table. Placing his hands together, he offered a short grace. As soon as it was done, Buckingham signalled to his musicians to commence playing.

'Sit next to Cowley, Tom, but don't monopolise the conversation. It is not often I get a chance to see my old friend.'

'I hear you spoke against the amendment to the Irish Cattle Bill last month,' said Cowley, addressing the Duke.

'Yes, that damned family of Butler hope to flood the country with their produce, and leave the Englishman without the wherewithal to pay his taxes.'

'My Lord Ossory is in some choler against you for slighting his father.'

Buckingham laughed. 'Yes, I declared publicly that all those who favoured the amendment must have an Irish interest or an Irish understanding.'

'My Lord Clarendon is displeased that you should offend the Duke of Ormond and his sons.'

'A fig for that!' Buckingham scoffed. 'It is my intention to rid the country of that troupe of self-important prigs.' He cast his eye around the company and added, 'I am hoping that several of the capable and patriotic gentlemen here tonight will assist me in the project.' His eye fell upon the Savile brothers seated a few places away.

Buckingham admired Sir George's ability for political argument and considered he would be a useful man to have at his side when plaguing his enemy Clarendon. Sir George disapproved of any monarch or minister having absolute power. He had been heard to declare that he could not contemplate living under a ruler who had the power to take money from his pocket whenever he chose, without the consent of parliament. He had a great respect for the restored constitution but did not consider it sacrosanct. A constitution should always be subject to reform, he maintained; without suiting itself to differing times and circumstances it could not live.

Buckingham remembered their past conversations and raised his glass.

'Sir George, to your health – and a new constitution!'

Sir George rose and bowed, but resumed his seat without comment. He was known as a man of reserve.

Further toasts followed and the company enjoyed the fine fare set before them. When fruits and sweetmeats were served, jugglers and fire-eaters entered the room and displayed their talents. Buckingham had learnt juggling in his childhood, from Charles the First's court jester, so he beckoned the performer and borrowed his clubs. He gave a creditable performance, declaring that he had once saved his life by disguising himself as a juggler, when Oliver's men were hunting for him after the Battle of Kingston Common. Conversation, music and laughter were the pleasures enjoyed at Buckingham's table. Time passed quickly and it was midnight before the more sober of Buckingham's guests began to depart. Sir George made his adieus and said he would be pleased if John would care to visit him, either at Queen Square or at Rufford if he was ever in Nottinghamshire. When Buckingham returned to the dining hall he suggested that the remaining guests should retire to his study for verse-making and serious drinking. John, Henry Savile, Harry Killigrew, George Jefferies, Ellis Leighton and Samuel Butler agreed readily, and began to stagger up the stairs. Further supplies of Buckingham's claret would be too good to miss. It had been agreed that they should concoct a satire upon Buckingham's arch-enemy and rival, Lord Arlington. They were released from adult judgement by the power of wine. Now, full of high spirits, their behaviour deteriorated into that of senseless schoolboys, but no-one cared, least of all their host. The company completed a set of verses detailing Arlington's defects of character and appearance, and Buckingham pronounced himself well satisfied with the result.

Buckingham asked John to produce a verse in praise of drinking. In his fuddled state, John endeavoured manfully to comply, but the squib was not one of his best creations.

'Is that all?' queried Buckingham. His sensuous mouth

171

drooped at the corners. 'The final couplet, John – you must let us have that. No poem is complete without a rhyming conclusion...'

'Which must pithily summarise the argument of the whole poem,' put in Henry Savile. 'You will lose your forfeit, Jack, unless you produce two more lines...'

'Which must be pithy,' repeated Killigrew drunkenly. 'Pithiness is all ... in a witty poem ... as I always say...'

'For God's sake, John, shut him up!' interposed Buckingham. 'A witty line, immediately, for all our sakes!'

John took one look at Killigrew... 'Everything fuddles, then that I ... Is't any reason should be dry?'

Buckingham lead a cheer.

'Congratulations to my young friend here! John Wilmot, a prince amongst good fellows ... as was his father, in days long past. Ah, I remember him well.'

Buckingham, now a man of thirty-eight, recalled how as a lad of fifteen he had fought in the company of Lord Wilmot at the commencement of the Civil Wars.

'We shared many other misfortunes together,' he reminisced. 'Scottish hospitality being one!'

'And sermons,' added John. 'His Majesty tells me that but for your jests and those of my father, he would have despaired when in the hands of the Covenanters.'

'Aye, they were a set of plaguey dull rascals ... it fills me with ennui to remember them.' Buckingham gestured to the bottle. 'Fill your glass again, John, and think of another verse.'

John realised that he was drunk: thoroughly, gloriously, ridiculously drunk. The crazy piece of doggerel he had just invented seemed the equal, to his mind, of a verse by Catullus. He wrapped his tongue around the words with heightened pleasure.

Buckingham grimaced. 'A good artist never repeats himself, Jack.' The Duke called for his page. 'Drink, while Jean-Paul sings!'

The graceful stripling sang a light French air, whilst a fresh bottle was opened and glasses re-filled to the brim. John felt supremely happy; that last bottle had made him the inhabitant of a new world, a world charged with light and beauty. The candles burning softly seemed somehow the material embodiment of love. The grapes piled high in the silver bowl in front of him seemed as miniature spheres of amethyst, glowing with an internal light of their own. Everything was spinning in a universe of sparkling lustre.

Buckingham clapped his hands, rose, and thanked the boy for singing. The Duke enslaved all his servants with his courtesy and openness of manner. He also moved superbly, dressed magnificently and entertained handsomely. No wonder, thought John, that the French King considered him 'the most perfect gentleman of his age'. Of course, it was obvious that Buckingham thought so too... In the pleasant state induced by his host's wine, John felt removed from any state of criticism. Everything was supernaturally brilliant and distinct, yet at the same time remote. Strangely remote, he thought, as he looked around at his laughing friends. Their figures and attitudes were suddenly reminiscent of a group of Italian statuary ... seen under water ... in some Mediterranean bay ... or in a still pond. Yes, a still pond ... and he was a fish ... a fish of genius ... a carp which was also a god.

'I am a carp' he announced. 'A divine carp.'

His statement was greeted with gales of laughter.

'Exactly so,' said Buckingham, 'staring at the world with great goggle eyes. I have been puzzled to know where I have seen the like. 'Twas in my pond at Clifden.'

The rest of the company watched closely, not wishing to miss an exchange between their jester host and his extraordinary young companion.

'Tell us more, Jack.' prodded Henry Savile. 'Oh thou most excellent carp!'

Buckingham spluttered over his wine. 'My Steward tells me they, too, are most infinite breeders!'

Hearty guffaws ensued as Savile enquired, 'Has pretty Sarah been delivered yet?'

'Of her fish-offspring!' choked Killigrew.

'The child of the Divine Carp,' added Buckingham, his hands placed together in the attitude of prayer.

Mention of Sarah brought several unwelcome thoughts to

John's mind, but he pushed them resolutely aside. He smiled at Harry with a look of forgiving indulgence. 'The fruit of rapture awaits the propitious hour.'

Once again, howls of laughter emanated from the company.

'And was it rapture?' queried Bucks. 'You gave us an amusing account of how you warmed each other in that freezing garret of hers, but now I hear she is becoming a drain upon your pocket.'

John sighed. 'True alas, 'tis love alone exalts ... but such is love's exalted power that were she the meanest upon earth ... when loved by me she becomes princess ... goddess ... houri ... saint.'

'My Lord soars aloft; he is upon another of his flights of eloquence,' teased Henry Savile. 'But I am delighted to hear of Sarah's canonisation.'

John warmed to his theme. 'St Thomas Acquinas was forced to admit that no mind can see the Divine substance unless it is divorced from the bodily senses...'

Buckingham choked. 'So you got the young carp whilst divorced from your bodily senses? A new Immaculate Conception by God. A miracle wrought upon the Thames! You tell me one occasion was upon the Thames, was it not?'

'It was upon the Thames,' repeated John gravely 'but you interrupt me. I was about to say divorced from the bodily senses either by death or some rapture – some rapture, mark you, ... and rapture is always a rapture whatever induces it ... claret, Euclid, poetry...'

'Or fucking a wench in a boat,' put in Bucks.

'Preferably in a boat, dear George,' said John, quite unruffled, 'for what does water say but rapture, ecstasy, divorcement from earthly care until the breath of our bodily frame, and the motion of our blood is suspended...'

For Savile this was becoming too much to stomach. 'You grow too philosophical, my Lord. You must listen to this:

> *In Milford Lane near to St Clement's Steeple*
> *There lived a nymph kind to all Christian people...*

John frowned. 'Spare us your rhyming squibs, Harry. What

have we done to deserve such a penance.'

'You must excuse it, my dear fellow, but I was inspired by the power of your words.'

'Pray continue then.'

> *A nymph she was, whose comely mien and feature*
> *Did wound the heart of every man-like creature...*

'If you are in the mood for poetry, you oaf' said John, 'get these lines into your fat head:

> *Go, Love, thy banners round the world display*
> *And teach rebellious mortals to obey.*

'Pshaw!' said Harry. 'I know a better verse than that –'

> *Jack drink away, thou'st lost a whole minute.*
> *Hang wenches and play, there's no pleasure in it!*

'Sacrilege!' shouted John in mock horror. 'The contention that pleasure lies in wenches and play is one of the most sacredly-held beliefs of our newly composed company of The Ballers. As General-in-Chief I intend to have you expelled at our next meeting!'

'Aye, but I shall defend him,' put in Killigrew, 'for 'twas only to praise drink that he did it, and drink is the salver of all ills – which is another of the rules in our catechism.'

'We have a problem here,' said John gravely, 'which can only be solved by a lawyer. Gentlemen, I put it to you, how far is it justifiable to deny one law in the active pursuit of another? May we have the opinion of any legal gentleman here?' Mr Jefferies, what is your view?'

The young barrister joined in the banter. 'We must debate the matter, and my Lord Buckingham here shall be our Lord Chancellor.'

Buckingham was about to make use of the fire-irons for his insignia of office, when there came a loud knock upon the door. It was Richard Braithwaite, Buckingham's chief agent and man of business.

'Mr John Heydon wishes to speak with you, my Lord. He is

most insistent, although I told him you were engaged. A matter of life and death, he said.'

'Indeed? Show the good man in.' Buckingham grimaced. 'How apt a re-appearance he makes,' he murmured. 'We were about to discuss a question of conscience.'

Heydon entered in a profoundly dishevelled state, his collar torn and dirty, his shoes and stockings splashed with mud.

'My Lord, I come to you in some distress. I cannot reach my house because the way is blocked by a vast crowd of discharged seamen assembled on Tower Hill. They would not let me pass until I had given them all my money. When they learned I was the Duke of Buckingham's astrologer they grasped my footboy and said they would string him up unless I did their bidding.'

'This is scandalous!' roared Buckingham. 'But my poor fellow, pray sit down. How did you escape them?'

'I did not,' said Heydon. 'They demanded that I should seek you out immediately and bring their wrongs to your attention.'

'How do they think I am involved? I do not sit at the Navy Board.'

'They believe you have access to the King and that you would give them a generous and sympathetic hearing. They have been discharged without their pay, no-one will give credit on their tickets and they and their families are like to starve. They declare no-one will be allowed to enter the Tower until a person of note gives ear to their grievances.'

'And they have chosen me?' queried Buckingham. His eyes narrowed speculatively.

'Yes,' said Heydon, 'they will keep my boy until an hour after light, and if your Grace has not appeared by then, they swear I shall not see him again.'

'Never fear, I shall be there.' Buckingham had sobered quickly. 'If I can persuade them to disperse peaceably I shall be in good stead with the King tomorrow.'

He turned to Braithwaite, a stiff reserved man who had served on Oliver's council.

'Go tonight to the bakers in Moorfields, and order as much bread as can be supplied – sufficient to feed a thousand men. See it is transported to Tower Hill at my expense. It must be made clear to the men that it comes from my bounty, and perhaps they will be in a comparatively amiable mood by the time I arrive.' He paused, thinking of his next move. 'I should be there by nine in the morning. His eyes fell upon Heydon. 'My dear fellow, you are exhausted. Find yourself a bed and sleep till morning. Nothing more can be done now.'

'My Lord, I could not sleep, I must busy myself in some way.'

Buckingham shrugged. 'Cast the King's horoscope, and see what it has to say about today. Is it not known as "the fatal day of the year of the beast" – the tenth day of the eleventh month of the year 1666?'

'Lilly has forecast it as such, but he is not to be trusted,' said Heydon frowning.

'Did he not forecast the Plague and the Fire many years ago, and have not all these disasters come about? Has not London suffered dreadfully during this same year, in spite of our victories at sea?'

Braithwaite listened closely to this exchange. 'Many more disasters must be expected, before England finds herself again,' he contributed gloomily.

'Faith, then I must do my best to divert rebellion, before a massacre tops previous disasters.' Buckingham was a changed man, his amused bantering tone of earlier now gone. He was busy making plans for the morrow. His eyes fell upon his guests – he had almost forgotten them.

'Gentlemen, forgive me but I must leave you. My servants will show you to your chambers. I thank you for your good company, but business presses. Fare ye well.' He grasped Braithwaite and Heydon by the arm and propelled them hastily out of the room.

Buckingham's guests looked at each other dumbfoundedly.

'Well, that is the last we shall see of our host tonight,' said Savile with a grin. 'The political animal has taken over from the genial host, though I doubt if anything momentous will come of this. Our George is everything by starts, but nothing long.'

The rest of the company laughed in agreement, and made their unsteady way to bed, though not before finishing the last of the claret.

12

Tower Hill and Other Encounters

John did not sleep well that night, tossing and turning restlessly. He dreamt he was once more aboard *Success* and that Frank Jones was giving succour to a dying woman whose face, as she fell back, was that of Wyndham ... his friend Wyndham who had died on *Revenge* ... some fourteen months ago now. John awoke sweating, with a dry mouth and heavy head. When tomorrow's trouble was over he would seek out Heydon and engage his services. He was said to use a scrying ball. If spirits did exist, perhaps they could give some sign, even if the means used were imperfect and incompetent...

However, John had no great confidence in Heydon's ability to harness magical powers. If so, the man would surely have tricked his way out of the danger in which he had found himself with the seamen ... The world was full of tricksters ... and incompetents, and poor deluded fools ... Why could he not sleep...! He would have to see Sarah tomorrow and reassure her of his love. At length he fell into an uneasy sleep and did not wake until he felt Buckingham's valet shaking him, asking if he would care for hot chocolate and whether he wished to accompany his Grace when he rode to Tower Hill.

'If his Grace can lend me some boots, and a horse, I shall be happy to accompany him – I came here last night ill-equipped for such an expedition.'

Buckingham's valet assured John that all he required would be supplied, and by eight in the morning the party was on its way to Tower Hill.

Buckingham was accompanied by Heydon, Braithwaite, Killigrew and Savile, and several strong fellows from his household, including his drummer. A watery sun was just beginning to lighten the sky as they made their way along the Strand.

'Well, the world is still here, and so are we,' laughed Buckingham. 'I suspect that yet again the astrologers have mis-read their signs.'

'Aye, one listens to their forecast but for diversion,' agreed Killigrew. He looked about him. There were very few people on the streets. 'Today is the Sabbath. Did your baker supply your loaves before midnight? He can make no bread today or he will be in trouble with the parish authorities.'

'Braithwaite tells me all was done during the night. The baker was told that if any sneaking neighbour betrayed him to the Constable my servants would ensure that he changed his evidence before the case got to Sessions.'

'It must be pleasant to have such influence,' bantered John.

'Undoubtedly so, but your Lordship does not lack it – at least with the fair sex.'

'Except in the case of my mother,' John replied laughingly. 'However, she has sent me a message to wait upon her shortly, so I have hopes she will restore my allowance.'

'No doubt she relents of her severity and wishes to reward the hero returned from the wars.'

They had by now reached Temple Bar, and the devastation wrought by the Great Fire came into view. Temple Church still stood, but all the surrounding houses had been pulled down to stop the passage of the flames. The conflagration had swept up Fleet Street in spite of the obstacle of the Fleet River. The wind had been so high that the burning sparks had fallen on the Temple, St Dunstan's Church, and even upon Temple Bar Gate itself. Killigrew had been present in the Duke of York's party, fighting the fire on those terrible nights in September. He had many anecdotes to tell, and seemed quite unabashed over his banishment from the Duke's court.

Savile said that his brother knew of many lawyers' chambers in Whitefriars, Serjeants' Inn and part of the Inner Temple which were completely destroyed and their contents lost.

Money, law books and deeds had gone up in the flames and evidences of many men's estates had been burnt.

As they rode up Ludgate Hill, the site of the former City revealed itself as a dismal desert. Often they could not tell where they were until the sight of a distinctive tower or shell of a well-known building enabled them to take their bearings. Killigrew said that since September much clearing work had been done, the passage of the major roads had been marked out, but that many of their surfaces were still treacherous. Five-sixths of the area within the walls had been destroyed and nearly two hundred thousand people left homeless.

Among the ruins of one of the churches a stone was revealed bearing a Latin inscription which read *When these letters shall be read, woe unto London, for they shall be read by the light of a fire.*

'One of your Roman predecessors was at work here, Heydon,' said Buckingham with a smile. Heydon did not respond. He was worried about the fate of his boy and was anxious to arrive at Tower Hill.

Braithwaite looked about him gloomily. 'All the finest of the City's public buildings have been destroyed. Of the great City halls, only eight remain undamaged, and many people whose fortune depends on rent from properties are ruined.'

'Thou'rt a dumpish Jeremiah, Braithwaite,' laughed Buckingham. 'I prophesy that within two years these people will recover their fortunes. Look at those fellows over there. The unquenchable optimism of the people of London has been underrated. Those men are constructing a timber cover for their cellar where they have found many of their goods, deep in their vaults, quite undamaged. As soon as they have made a counter with a tarpaulin cover, they will be opening for business again.'

'Aye, if the parish authorities do not stop them,' said John 'It is Sunday, and if an officious prodnose sees them on his way to church, they will be prosecuted.'

Braithwaite turned and looked at John disapprovingly. 'The Lord's Day should be kept holy. It is the disregard of God' word which has led to this devastation.' He warmed to hi theme. 'What a ruinous confused place this city is, only chim

180

neys and steeples standing in the midst of cellars and heaps of rubbish. No one who has not seen it can have a right apprehension of its dreadfulness.'

John thought that Braithwaite's severe expression betrayed an almost gloating pleasure. He did not like the man and was surprised that Buckingham kept him in his confidential employment.

By the time they arrived at Tower Hill dawn had broken and a chilly wind was beginning to blow. The scene before them was quite amazing. Tower Hill was full of men, as far as the eye could see. Some of them were accompanied by women and crying children. Angry and haggard faces were raised to the gentlemen on horseback.

'Make way for my Lord of Buckingham!' roared his Grace's servants. Respect for authority was still strong amongst the seamen, and they broke their ranks to give the party passage to the highest part of Tower Hill. Once arrived, Heydon came forward, raising his hands for silence.

'According to my promise, I bring you my Lord of Buckingham. Now fulfil yours to me, and bring my boy to my side.'

An old seaman came forward bringing with him a pretty fair-haired child who straightway ran to Heydon and hid his face under his master's cloak. John looked at the seaman, and recognised his gait and face. 'Why, Frank Jones, I did not think to see you here! How are you?'

'Starving, my Lord, as are most of my fellows. His Grace's bread did not reach as far as my party. Can you spare a crown for an old man?'

John searched his pockets for some silver and gave him what he found. Their interchange was silenced by Buckingham's servant beating his drum.

Buckingham bowed to the crowd and stepped forward. He said he was there to hear their grievances, but they would have to elect a spokesman. 'If I stay to hear all of you, I shall be here till Domesday,' he quipped. 'I am aware of your desperate state, and will do all in my power to put it right.'

A growl of approval went up. Buckingham swept off his hat, and bowed to the crowd again. 'I will retire to my friend

Heydon's house, and will await your spokesman there.' He motioned his party to a three-storey timber-framed house, where Heydon proceeded to open the door and bow them in. John stepped into the hall, and was intrigued to find it luxuriously furnished. A strange sweet smell of incense pervaded the house, the floor was polished and shining and many thick velvet curtains covered the walls. The curtains were covered with embroidered emblems worked in gold and silver thread. It was evident that the practice of astrology paid well.

Buckingham seated himself at the fire and turned to Heydon. 'Pray bring up some of your wine. I do not know how long we shall have to wait for these fellows, but good wine will loosen their tongues. I hope it will also incline them to be agreeable when I suggest that they should all repair to Wapping.'

'Why Wapping?' questioned John.

'Because the Navy Office store their ships biscuits there, and I am hoping the Commissioners will release them to save the men from starving.' Buckingham laughed. 'After the fire the King offered ships biscuits to the homeless Londoners as they camped in Moorfields, but their stomachs were too dainty. They thanked the King for his kindness but they did not eat them, and eventually they were returned to the Navy stores. These poor seamen are desperate and in any case are used to such fare, so I have no doubt they will consume the biscuits in default of better supplies. If I can persuade them to go to Wapping they will at least be out of the way whilst I try to get their tickets paid.'

'I hear my Lord Treasurer is sick, and that his officials are in sad array. I doubt if you will have much success.'

'Then I shall approach the King himself.'

While they were waiting for the seamen's representatives, the company amused themselves by looking around Heydon's residence. John was intrigued by the strange banners and diagrams which hung upon the wall. One was a full-length diagram of the human body with anatomical details fully shown. Another gave a list of planets and signs of the zodiac. Heydon suggested they should view his consultation room and they were taken down stone stairs to a comfortably furnished room below ground.

'This,' he said, 'is where I prepare a fitting temple for the Goddess of Light and her Servants.'

'When can I meet this illustrious personage?' asked Buckingham. 'She may perhaps advise me on how to move the heart of the obdurate but enchanting Mistress Stewart.'

'For the King's advantage, or for your own?' questioned Savile. 'I hear she boxed your ears last week for proving too bold a suitor!'

'I fear I misjudged the happy minute,' agreed Buckingham, ruefully. 'But 'tis persistence wins a woman in the end.'

Their light-hearted banter was interrupted by a knock upon the door. A startlingly ugly man entered the room with a sheaf of papers in his hands. He broke into the conversation abruptly. 'Heydon, here are Lilly's forecasts for the next year. I hear he is much in Ashmole's pocket of late and is tailoring his predictions to suit his court masters. He is up to his old tricks again.'

Heydon looked embarrassed and took his acquaintance aside. 'It is indeed regrettable that one of our brotherhood should prostitute his Art for political purposes, but that has been Lilly's way since the late King's time.'

Heydon recollected that the Duke was not acquainted with the new arrival and introduced Mr Arise Evans. He said that Mr Evans had taught him all he knew of astrology, numerology, geomancy and the raising of spirits.

The Duke bowed with exaggerated courtesy. 'I am pleased to meet such a learned man – one, I hear, who has been cured of the Kings' Evil by our present sovereign.'

'Aye, I was touched by his Majesty and cured of the disease.'

'You have reason to be thankful for the happy Restoration of the Stuarts then?' enquired Buckingham.

Evans viewed the Duke suspiciously. The astrologer had sought the patronage of eminent Parliamentarians in Oliver's day, and Buckingham's mocking tone annoyed him. He made no rejoinder, but bowed briefly and left the room. Heydon's servant appeared and on hearing that the seamen's representatives were ready to talk, the company returned to the upper floor, forgetting the strange intruder.

Buckingham persuaded the seamen to comply with his advice, promising that he would take the matter of their wages to the King himself if he could get no compliance from the Navy Office or the Treasurer. Will Long, the seamen's leader, said that the men would be back and invade Whitehall itself if they received no message from his Grace within three days.

John stood outside Heydon's house and watched the seamen disperse. Slowly they took the eastern road. John doubted if they would find much cheer at Wapping, in spite of Buckingham's promises. He caught sight of Frank Jones hobbling along on his stick, and his heart was moved with pity. He hastened after him and caught him up.

'Frank you cannot walk to Wapping today. The weather is foul and you are an old man.'

Frank looked angry. 'Not so old, my young Lord, that I cannot look to myself in all weathers.' He looked at John speculatively. 'Have you more money about you, Sir? That would be a sovereign remedy against all ills.'

'How much money is owed to you by the Exchequer?'

'A year's wages, my Lord, at two pounds per month. It comes to about twenty-two pound, taking into consideration the lower rate we was paid for being laid up last winter.'

'I can give you ten pounds now, if that would help. You can repay me in better times. You will find me at Sir Walter St John's house at Battersea, should fate take you that way.'

Frank was touched in spite of himself. He put the gold into a battered leather pouch, looking about him as he did so. 'Last year we received our pay at the autumn lay-off. The good Lord Sandwich saw that we received our due, but this year,' he paused and spat before recommencing, 'those court princes and dukes care not for their men once the heat of battle is over.'

John was inclined to agree, but considered it would be impolitic, and bad for discipline, to give voice to such a sentiment. He decided to change the subject.

'Were you successful in obtaining the wages of the young man who died after Bergen? I believe you said you would seek out his dependents?'

'Aye, I got to his village, but his babe had died, and his

184

young woman on her death bed, through ill-treatment. I guess I came too late to help. The money paid for her burial.'

'A sad story.'

'Aye, but there be many such. My thanks to your Lordship. I wish you good fortune.' The old man seemed anxious to end the conversation. John watched him as he plodded down the road in determined fashion. John doubted if he would ever see his ten pounds again, but felt he could better spare it out of his plenty, than that the old man should starve after a lifetime in a hard calling.

He rejoined Buckingham's party outside Heydon's house, and they were just about to mount horse when Arise Evans appeared again. He was short of stature, and had a slight limp. Evans made straight for John and spoke with a thick tongue. 'I see a slender youth standing beside you. His head is wrapped in a red scarf.'

John looked round. There was no-one there. He was repelled by Evans' presence – not only because he exuded a smell of unwashed linen and stale tobacco, but because he inspired a feeling of horror and unease. Yet the man's remark brought back a flood of painful memories, memories which John had firmly suppressed for nigh on fourteen months. He remembered unravelling a red sash from a corpse as it lay upon the deck of *Revenge*.

John shuddered, but was determined to show no emotion. He said coolly, 'How surprising, Sir. I see no man myself.'

Savile and Killigrew decided, mischievously, to join in the conversation. They walked round John's back, pretending to look for a phantom. They bantered Evans mercilessly, declaring that he had supped too deeply on Heydon's wine.

Evans flushed and turned angrily on his heel. 'You will wish to know more of this matter ere long, Sirs. Tell Mr Heydon if you wish to reach me.' He replaced his high crowned hat firmly upon his head, and limped away across Tower Hill.

The gentlemen laughed as they mounted their horses. Many came forward with stories of apparitions sighted by members of the Royal Society. The Reverend John Glanvill had written a book on the strange hauntings at Tedworth, where the inhabitants were prevented from sleeping by the drumming of a demon in the middle of the night. John returned with Buckingham to Wallingford House, where they ate a good meal. After thanking his host John returned to Battersea by water.

His aunt came to greet him in the hall and delivered a mild lecture. He had not said that he was to stay in London the previous night. Will had sat up for him. John apologised and quickly retired. He was disinclined for conversation. It had been an eventful day and he felt exhausted. He found it hard to settle. Eventually he lost consciousness, but tossed and turned in his sleep. In the middle of the night he awoke, sweating with fear. He had dreamt he was being throttled with a red silk scarf.

He lay in his bed and tried to rationalise his thoughts. He was in no danger, but he remembered Wyndham's death with remarkable clarity – something he had pushed from his consciousness as being too painful to recall. When the seamen had endeavoured to remove Wyndham's body from the deck they had asked for his assistance in removing the red silk sash from Wyndham's waist. The sash had been bound about the remnants of his friend's head, so that the corpse could be prepared for burial with some decency. Blood, brains, bone and hair had littered the deck on that dreadful day in Bergen. The details had been too horrible to talk about.

John could not forget Evans' words. How had he known about the red scarf? He had not mentioned that detail to anyone. The man was probably a clever charlatan who had perhaps heard from Heydon of his wish to contact the spirit of his friend. He would think no more about it ... he had no wish to see the unpleasant man again. And yet ... how had Evans known about the scarf? John was intrigued in spite of himself.

The next day Harry Killigrew called to see him. There had been high words between Buckingham, Lord Arlington and Sir Robert Howard in the Council Chamber. Howard had declared there was no money in the Receipt to pay the seamen. Bucks had made a swift rejoinder that there appeared to be enough money to pay Howard's salary and those of his cronies. The meeting had ended in acrimony. Later Bucks had visited Sir Robert Vyner, a rich city merchant. 'Though I doubt if he obtained any money there,' said Killigrew. 'Sir Robert has suffered in his business as much as any man of London, because of the fire.'

John was bored staying at Battersea and asked Harry if he knew of a room to let in the Covent Garden area.

'Come and stay with me for a few days,' said Harry. 'I have a lodging in Drury Lane, next to the Theatre. My father let it to me, when I had to leave the Duke's Court.'

'Is the Duke like to relent of your dismissal?'

'My father tells me that I shall be reinstated as soon as Barbara has forgotten my foolish words. The Duke is annoyed that Lady Castlemaine has presumed to meddle in the staffing of his household.'

John moved to Drury Lane during the next day and was told by Killigrew that plans had been made with Savile to meet at Tower Hill, where, with the aid of Mr Heydon and Mr Evans, they were to raise prophesying spirits.

'If the jape proves disappointing,' laughed Killigrew, 'we shall repair to "The Bear" and try spirits of another sort! Have you tasted usquebaugh? Lauderdale served it when I dined at his table. He says they drink much of it in Scotland.'

That evening when John, Savile, Killigrew and Heydon were seated at a polished table in the basement room, Arise Evans entered dressed in a long purple gown. His ugly pitted face drew and yet repelled the eyes of his audience, whilst his own sharp eyes darted from one to the other of the young men, taking in every detail of their appearance.

Evans took charge. 'Let us sit in quiet and still our thoughts. The spirits wish to draw upon our energies. They will then speak through the mouth of our friend, Heydon.'

Silence descended upon the room. The single candle wavered, the light waxing and waning, seemingly without cause. It was uncommonly cold and John felt a slight draught blowing about his legs.

Suddenly Heydon leapt to his feet, opened his arms above his head, and began to speak in a deep voice, quite unlike his usual honeyed tones. He pointed to John. 'Fair son of Astarte. I rejoice to see thee here. The spirits of Babylon intend to use thy talents in London.' He took a deep breath. 'I have a message for thee. "Win thy dam, lest the lion rend thy vital parts and destroy thee."'

Killigrew smothered a laugh. John was puzzled. The message seemed meaningless. Further utterances were addressed to Savile and Killigrew – to the effect that they would never enjoy great riches, but would have many friends, and live their lives to the full.

Silence fell upon the group again. Arise Evans shifted in his chair. They heard a faint tinkling of bells, but no-one could detect from whence the noise came. Heydon recommenced his peroration, but this time his voice was extremely high. 'I am Mab, Queen of the Fairies, and will confer many gifts on those present.'

Savile and Killigrew burst into uncontrollable laughter, whilst John turned to his right and looked at Evans. He detected a silken ribbon strung with small bells trailing from Evans' pocket.

'What are these blessings?' John ventured, stifling his laughter.

'The favour of princes, of bards and of fair women,' replied Heydon.

'What of rich ugly women?' joked Killigrew.

'They too will have their uses,' boomed Heydon. He was speaking in deep tones again. The Queen of the Fairies had evidently taken her departure.

Heydon seemed unaware of the amusement his utterances were inspiring amongst his audience, but Evans knew the gentlemen were not gulled and decided to bring the sitting to a close.

'Queen Mab, we thank thee for the inexpressible honour of thy visit. Pray release thy servant Heydon from thy presence.'

Heydon sat down, and began to moan. Evans rose and went over to him. He made a number of passes in front of Heydon's face, and then laid his hands on the top of his head as if in blessing.

'The spirits have departed, dear Sirs. There will be no further messages tonight.'

'Ballocks,' said Killigrew in mock dismay. 'I wanted to lay my hands on fairy gold.'

'Such gifts must not be spoken of,' said Evans disapprovingly. He lit a new candle from the single one burning in the room. He bowed, then went over to the door. 'I bid you good night, gentlemen. If you wish to consult the spirits on a further occasion, inform Mr Heydon, and I will meet you here.'

He closed the door and they heard his halting footsteps mount the stairs.

Savile shuddered. 'I am glad that unpleasant fellow has gone. Let us make our way to "The Bear" and savour the earthly delights provided. The utterances of spirits do not attract me greatly.'

Heydon's moaning ceased abruptly. He recovered his senses sufficiently to say that they owed him five guineas. The gentlemen laughingly paid him the agreed amount and departed into the cold night air.

John, Savile and Killigrew spent a hilarious evening at the tavern, imitating Heydon and Evans. They became extremely drunk. John decided he would buy a long purple gown and wear it at court. He would disguise his face with a long black beard, and persuade Progers, Groom of the back stairs, to announce him as an eminent Armenian astrologer sent by the Tsar of Russia to tell the King's fortune. It might amuse his Majesty after a dull session in Council Chamber listening to Arlington, Clarendon, Coventry and York.

John found it hard to settle that night. His spirits were too excited by laughter and by wine. He rose from his bed and spent an hour devising a speech for his Armenian astrologer. The farcical proceedings in the earlier part of the evening had relieved him of any need to believe in an afterlife, but at the same time the experience had left him feeling vaguely angry and disappointed.

It was evident that Evans was a clever charlatan, with sharp ears and a vivid imagination. His hitting upon the image of a red scarf had been the merest chance, John decided. He no longer believed that Evans had really seen a phantom beside him...and yet part of him had wanted to believe that Wyndham's spirit was indeed returning with a message for him. Why had Evans not developed his clever invention at the séance? There was no mention of a dead friend there. The

Queen of the Fairies' flattering address and her vague promises of good fortune in the future were no recompense for the failed hopes of finding a reason for Wyndham's death.

He returned to bed thinking of the morrow. Killigrew had told him that Bess Mallett was to be at the Queen's Birthday Ball and that the King was expecting John to attend, and to renew his addresses to the heiress...

He anticipated the encounter with some trepidation. He wondered if Elizabeth had changed her mind. It was nearly a year since he had last seen her, at Lord Sandwich's house. Had she refused Hinchingbrooke for his sake – perhaps in the hope that they could renew their relationship? Or did she play with the emotions of all men, leading them to expect favours, when she was inclined to give none? He sometimes wondered if she wished for marriage at all. She gave no hint of possessing natural desires during the brief occasions when they had been allowed to be together... Of course he had never been completely alone with her, heiresses being always well-chaperoned.

He thought of a pleasant May evening two years ago, when the Duke and Duchess of Ormonde had taken a party on an excursion in the ducal barge. Their servants had rowed the party to Battersea, to view the fine cedars in the garden of John's uncle. Lord Arran and his sister had brought their guitars and they had entertained the company with fine playing and singing. The talk had been easy and amusing. Enjoying the good fortune of being placed next to Elizabeth, John had taken advantage of all the opportunities offered for closer acquaintance. He had clasped her hand and had been overjoyed to feel pressure from her fingers as he held them in his.

Under the vigilant eye of the Duchess of Ormonde, there had been little opportunity for bolder behaviour, but upon one occasion he had succeeded in placing his foot against Elizabeth's, only to have her turn from him when she wished to view the riverside village of Chelsea. She had laughed with Arran when that young man had told her of the hopeless passion nurtured for her by one called John.

She had mischievously pretended to misunderstand Arran, saying that she was acquainted with his brother, Lord John

Butler, but considered him too young to take his suit seriously. In any case she expected those who wished to win her to speak for themselves. Turning to John, and delivering a challenging look, she had removed her hand from his grasp. John, denied the opportunity of pleasant embraces, had to content himself with conversation. Nevertheless, he had found a most enjoyable companionship of the mind. Elizabeth, he discovered, was one of the few young women with whom he could spend long periods in conversation. During his years abroad, he had found great pleasure in discourse with intelligent well-read French and Italian noblewomen. In their salons these women would discuss religion and philosophy. They criticised poetry, and wrote it with ease. If they found a man agreeable, they would bestow many favours upon him. He remembered the good fortune he had found in friendship with the Marchesa dell'Oro. She had initiated him into the arts of love, and he remembered her with gratitude and affection.

He sighed with regret for lost pleasures. Love was indeed considered an art in the warm countries of the Mediterranean. It seemed to him that Englishwomen were bred in fear of their bodies, and fear prevented them giving a generous response to the advances of any suitor. Elizabeth's interested manner and intelligent questions had attracted him and had reminded him of the women of Italy; she too had dark hair and flashing eyes. Would that she had the same appreciation of the delights of love, – and resolution to elude the control of her guardians!

Memories continued to flood back. On one occasion he had ridden with her to Clifden, in the company of the King and the Duke and Duchess of Buckingham. The Duke had conceived the idea of building a great house there. It would have a magnificent view of the Thames. His plan was to build riverside terraces and to plant woodland walks on the wild heathland of the hillside. While the King and Duke had wandered over the site, discussing the problems of construction, John and the ladies had sat upon the grass admiring the view.

The conversation turned to the proceedings of the Royal Society. Many promising young architects were members, and it was thought that the Duke might ask Mr Christopher Wren to design his house. John mentioned that he had attended a lecture at the Society during the previous week. It had been given by Robert Boyle, on the qualities of gases. John was entering into a detailed analysis of Boyle's theories, when the Duchess of Buckingham had risen from the ground explaining that she had something to say to her husband. Smiling, she took her departure and for a delightful half-hour he and Elizabeth had been left alone.

They had talked animatedly of the experiments of the Royal Society, of the varieties of metals, of the medicinal qualities of plants, and of the ludicrous nature of some of the Society's experiments. They had conversed until the sun began to set, turning the river to rippling gold. The Duchess had returned to say that it was time for the party to return to Windsor. She gave a knowing smile saying, 'No doubt your friends will soon be calling for lawyers to draw up marriage settlements.'

They had looked at her in astonishment, and Elizabeth had burst out laughing.

'Lord Rochester knows better than to tease me upon so tedious a subject. We have been discussing chemistry, something of much greater interest.'

The King and Buckingham overheard her remark and it had inspired them with great amusement. Guessing their thoughts, all John could do was mutter briefly that Mistress Mallett had a most surprising knowledge of the subject.

'Then,' said the King, 'she must converse with me upon the way back to Windsor. I have a great curiosity to hear Beauty discourse upon the Natural Sciences!' John was left to accompany the Duchess.

Although deprived of Elizabeth's company, he reflected philosophically that every situation can be found to have its compensations. From his position at the rear of the party he was able to admire the turn of Elizabeth's body as she applied herself to the management of her horse.

The Duchess of Buckingham addressed him. 'I fear I cannot rival the attractions of Mistress Elizabeth, but perhaps we may pass the time pleasantly enough, conversing of poetry. I hear you greatly admire the Latin poets, especially Lucretius.'

John considered the Duchess a plain woman, but she was obviously sensible and well educated. He learned with surprise that Andrew Marvell had been her tutor at her father's house in Yorkshire, and that they had written poetry together. Marvell was now opposed to the present government, and had turned his talents to politics and satire, but the Duchess said she would never forget the kindness he had shown her when he had dwelt with her family.

As they entered Windsor, Buckingham had taken pity upon John, and had ridden up to his wife. 'I think Mistress Mallet would be glad of my Lord's assistance in finding Lord Hawley's lodgings.'

Leaving the smiling pair, John spurred his horse and caught up with Elizabeth at the Castle Gate, just before she dismounted. He helped her down and tried to retain her hand, but she would not permit it. Charles had laughed, 'You must address Lord Hawley, John, if you wish to gain the lady's hand! See her safely into her grandfather's care.'

John accompanied her to her guardian's lodgings, but she seemed disinclined for conversation and would not raise her face to his. When they reached the door she had quickly lifted latch and run inside. 'I bid ye goodnight, my Lord.'

He remembered viewing the shut door with some exasperation. She was truly a most teasing and puzzling young woman. He was not at all sure that he wished to return to the courtship.

13

Elizabeth

The Ball given in honour of the Queen's birthday was proving
a great success, in spite of the general air of gloom pervading
London. The merry air of a gigue invaded John's ears as he
crossed the outer court of Whitehall Palace and entered the
Banqueting House. A brilliant sight met his eyes: the graceful
proportions of Inigo Jones's design were revealed by the light
of a thousand candles. The light of the flames was enhanced by
reflection from mirrors upon the walls. Richly-dressed men and
women crowded the room and their jewels sparkled and
gleamed in the light. The King, attired in a suit of silk trimmed
with silver, smiled benignly upon his wife as he led her out for
the next dance. Catherine, used to the formality of the Portuguese
court, found it difficult to relax, and her husband was leaning
forward to tell her something amusing. John noticed that
although the King was paying attention to his short dumpy
wife, his eyes were following the movements of Frances Stewart.
The fair beauty was a dazzling sight in black and white lace
with her head and shoulders decked with diamonds.

John moved across the room in her direction, and saw
Elizabeth Mallet in her company. During all the stirring and
terrible experiences he had known at sea, she had remained in
the background of his mind, a source both of pain and fascina-
tion. At sight of Elizabeth, his heart fell like a stone and all
resolutions of giving up the pursuit vanished. She was dressed
in yellow satin trimmed with gold, and her hair was threaded
through with pearls. The contrast of the yellow satin with

Elizabeth's dark brown hair and clear complexion was excessively pleasing. She was standing next to Frances in a group of young men and women engaged in animated conversation.

As John drew near the charmed circle he heard Elizabeth say, 'And as for Sir Francis Popham – he would kiss my breach to have me – or, perhaps it would be truer to say, my fortune!'

Frances, amused, enquired whether Lord Hinchingbrooke was still her suitor. Elizabeth replied that all was now over between them. She rolled her eyes and, placing her hands demurely together, said, 'I fear he was not pleased with the liberty and vanity of my carriage.'

John pushed past young Anthony Hamilton and interjected, 'And you – what reason gave you for refusing Lord Hinchingbrooke?'

Elizabeth, astonished at the sight of him, and startled at the sudden interruption, felt the colour rush to her cheeks.

They became the focus of all attention.

'Why, my Lord, what any maid would say when she wishes to be rid of an unwelcome suitor. I declared my affections to be fixed elsewhere.'

'And are they?' John persisted.

'No,' she replied. 'I am still free.'

The whole group fell silent and John was thankful when the musicians struck up a tune.

'Will you dance?'

'Yes.' She recovered her poise and smiled at him mockingly. 'How I could refuse to dance with a returning Alexander, one so high in the King's favour?'

'I would prefer you to dance with me because you wished it, not because the King advised it.'

Seeing his tense expression, she relented. 'I shall be very happy to dance with you, and to hear of your adventures since last we met. I am sorry you have been away so long.'

Her words elated him, and all past resentments were forgotten. Elizabeth, looking up at him, thought how different he appeared after his two years at sea. He carried himself with authority, like a man, and was a great improvement upon the graceful but somewhat effeminate-looking youth she had remembered. His face had matured in some undefinable way, the mouth now strong as well as sweet. She risked a gaze into his glittering and compelling eyes, and it was some time before she realised that he was enquiring after the health of her parents.

'They are well enough to plague me,' she laughed.

'And your grandfather?'

'Still boring Frances with his attentions.'

Lord Hawley's hopeless passion for Mistress Stewart, some forty years his junior, was the subject of an old jest between them. They were laughing heartily when John swept her into a country dance.

* * *

The next day John went to pay his respects to the Queen and looked eagerly about the antechamber, hoping to see Elizabeth. She had told him she would be there. Arran came up to him.

'Shall we attend my sister and Bess Mallet? They are about to sing.'

They strolled over to the corner of the room where the two girls were playing their guitars. Lady Mary Butler suggested that her friend should sing the old North-country song taught her by Lady Buckingham. Elizabeth agreed, but announced that she would give it a personal application by singing of her own home country.

A West-country maid up to London had strayed
Although with her wishes it did not agree
For she wept, and she sighed, and so bitterly she cried
How I wish once again in the West I could be.

John watched her closely and observed the feeling she put into the words of the song.

For he that I wed, must be West-country bred
And carry me back to my West-country home.

Elizabeth acknowledged the applause of the onlookers but noticed that John was unmoved.

'Sir, how you stare at me!' she said. 'Of what are you thinking?'

196

'Where I might find two ancient rustics who, for a trifling sum, would swear that I first saw the light of day in Somerset.'

'You are quite ridiculous!' Elizabeth cried with a scornful pout.

'Your tongue is cruel, but your eyes tell me you find me not displeasing.'

'I find you amusing.'

'Would not an amusing husband be better than a dull one?'

'Would not a faithful husband be better than a neglectful one?' countered Elizabeth, mindful of the rumour that a maid-servant was to bear Lord Rochester a child.

'Agreed,' said John, 'but to my observation the one quality does not necessarily exclude the other.'

'How so?'

'You may perhaps have observed that the Duke of Buckingham is most courteous and attentive to his wife, but is he what the world would call a faithful husband?'

'No, indeed.'

'The gossips of the town cannot but acknowledge that Sir Bayham Throckmorton, for all his faults, is faithful to his wife?'

'It would seem to me that women do not interest him.'

'Is he attentive to his wife?'

Elizabeth, wondering where the conversation was leading, replied, 'No, horses and cattle claim more of his attention.'

John smiled triumphantly. 'Now, which of these ladies do you think is the happier wife?'

'Neither, it would seem to me, is perfectly happy.'

'Perfect happiness is for the angels,' John replied. 'We poor mortals must content ourselves with something less.'

He watched the colour rise in her face, but she met the compelling stare of his eyes boldly.

He pursued his point relentlessly. 'Would you not agree that the Duchess of Buckingham is the happier woman?'

'Perhaps,' admitted Elizabeth, lowering her lashes over her eyes. 'It can be imagined that her husband brings her greater joy than does Sir Bayham his lady. But,' and here she pointedly stared John straight in the face, 'he most probably brings her greater pain as well.'

'Is not the pleasure worth the pain?'

'That is a question every woman would have to answer for herself.'

'How would you answer it?' John came nearer and placed his arm along the high back of her chair.

'I do not know. Why do you question me so closely?'

John noted the quick rise and fall of the lace at her breasts.

'I think you should consider the matter seriously.'

She said quickly, 'I could perhaps love a man if he vowed to be always my friend, as well as my lover.'

'I wish I could have the happiness of believing you, and of being that man.'

'Why not?' Elizabeth smiled, recovering her self-possession. She spoke mockingly. 'Believe that I love you if it ministers to your pleasure.'

'I may be a conceited coxcomb,' said John, 'but not so great a one as to be oblivious of the fact that you are making game of me.'

'La! Would an ignorant country girl dare to make game of that awesome wit, the Earl of Rochester?'

'Mistress Mallet would dare anything, and that is why I love her.'

'I wish I could believe that,' she answered defiantly.

'Why not, if it ministers to your pleasure?'

'If we converse in circles we shall never reach our destination.'

'If the destination be agreed upon, conversational circles may be bisected with ease,' John quipped.

'Your arguments are too Euclidean for me to follow,' she said, with a glimmer of a smile. 'What destination had you in mind for us?'

'The third curtained alcove in the Banqueting House, at ten o'clock tonight.'

Elizabeth opened her eyes wide. 'You are very precipitate, Sir. My guardians would not approve of my making assignations with you.'

'Guardians never do. They are obstacles which need to be circumvented. Do not keep me waiting long.'

'You may wait all night, for all the sight you will have of me.'

'You are cruel.'

'No, indeed I am not.' She picked up her guitar and cast a mocking glance at him as she left the antechamber. 'I am so kind as to wish you will not take cold upon your lonely vigil. Farewell.'

* * *

John walked along the Mall through the gathering dusk. His mother had returned to town and had requested John to call upon her at her lodgings in St James's Palace. He felt happy that they were to be reconciled, but was determined to take no direction as to how or with whom he would live. He knew that he wanted to marry Elizabeth. He had just had a discouraging conversation with Arran, but it had not shaken his belief that he could win her.

Arran thought Elizabeth one of the most accomplished jilts in London. He assured John that she was certainly not without malice, and that she often recounted to her female friends the details of a man's behaviour towards her. He said that his own brother, Lord John Butler, had experience of her cruelty, and that Hinchingbrooke considered her a bundle of affectation and self-will.

John considered Arran's opinion a little unfair. Elizabeth could not be blamed if presumptuous fools mistook her free conversation for a greater invitation, or for laughing at the extravagances of his own sex in matters of love. Had not Arran often boasted to him of his accomplishments in love-making, and had they not both been free with the names and reputations of many of the women at the court? As for Lord John Butler, had she favoured the idiotic young puppy, it would have dampened his own ardour, to think her guilty of such bad taste.

He could not be sure of Elizabeth; she was undoubtedly a tease, but he sensed that if he succeeded in embracing her, he would find a warm and generous response. It was this belief which had encouraged him to attempt her abduction two years ago. Having met with frustration in all his efforts to meet her alone, he had been compelled to act boldly. God knows he had intended her no harm.

He remembered her confidences at the Queen's Birthday Ball. They had danced together for most of the evening, and she had told him that she had quarrelled with her step-father, Sir John de Warr. Her guardian had chopped down all the fine trees upon her estates, to take advantage of the high prices offered for wood during time of war. She thought his policy short-sighted and considered the value of her estates much lessened. She suspected that most of the capital derived from the sale of the wood would be spent on Sir John's own land. In the atmosphere of John's ready sympathy, she became even more expansive, and told him that her mother gravely spoiled young Francis, her step-brother, and that she was extremely unhappy at home. Although she loved her mother, and appreciated her care, she considered her to be a doting fool in any matter where her step-father was concerned.

Last night Elizabeth seemed to be seeking his support and advice. Today she had seemed challenging and dismissive. John wondered how long he should wait at the Banqueting House. She would most probably not come, but the possibility that she might do so, would draw him there at the appointed hour. In the meantime, he was to visit his mother.

* * *

Lady Rochester greeted her son with genuine affection. His brave actions at sea had proved him a worthy son of his father. She was pleased he had written to her. She reflected upon his redeeming qualities. He seemed anxious to act responsibly in the matter of the young woman and her expected child, so she was prepared to admit him once more to her good graces. It was unfortunate that he was lodging with the objectionable young man, Killigrew, but she had no doubt that she would be able to persuade her son to live with her at Chelsea, once she had completed her arrangements for the lease of the Duke of Ormonde's house there.

John was eager to tell his mother the news of his good

fortune at court, and how he had regained the King's favour, but Lady Rochester had recently returned from her first husband's Oxfordshire home and had much news to tell John of his step-brother's family at Ditchley.

Her son, Sir Francis Lee, was married to Elizabeth Downe, the heiress of Wroxham. It was an advantageous match, but unfortunately, the bride's family were Roman Catholic. Lady Rochester had experienced a stormy interview with her daughter-in-law, when she had indicated that it would be extremely unfortunate for Sir Francis, who had ambitions to become Lord Lieutenant of Oxfordshire, to have his young son raised as a papist.

Lady Lee had been insistent that the soul of her young son was in her care, and that he should be instructed in the true religion. Lady Rochester had said that truth in matters of religion was debatable, but the law of the land, preventing Roman Catholics from holding responsible office, was a fact, and that Lady Lee should reflect upon the matter. Sir Francis had supported his wife, so Lady Rochester had departed in high dudgeon for Adderbury, the home of her second husband.

While there she had decided to remove her two young grandchildren, the daughters of her deceased eldest son, Sir Henry Lee, from the unfortunate influences in the Lee household. As their guardian, she had the right to take them from their uncle's care, and she had brought them to London to be educated with the children of the Duchess of York.

'Are not papist influences strong in the Duke's court too?' asked John.

'The Duke is a foolish fellow, but his wife is a worthy daughter of Lord Clarendon. She would never forget her duty towards the Church of England.'

John considered that his mother's partiality for the Duchess blinded her to a number of facts about her mistress, but he held his tongue. Lady Rochester expanded at length upon the Duchess's forgiving nature. In spite of the sorrow caused to the Duchess by her husband's unwarranted suspicions of her conduct with Mr Sidney, she was prepared to overlook the Duke's interest in many of the young women at court. The brazen behaviour of Lady Denham was a case in point. Despite the Duke's public acknowledgement of his immoral interest in another man's wife, the Duchess was disposed to forgive him, and the woman too. When she heard of Lady Denham's illness, the Duchess was ready to believe her innocent of adultery, and was about to send a present of chocolate to cheer her.

John raised his brows, but made no comment. He had no wish to argue a point which did not affect him personally, especially when he and his mother had just made peace with each other.

The conversation turned to the King's wish for John to renew his suit to Mistress Mallet. His mother was aware of the material advantages of the match, but had severe reservations about Mistress Mallet's disposition.

'She is immodest and self-willed, and I do not care for the way her mouth turns down at the corners.'

Lady Rochester had great confidence in her ability to judge character, upon even the slightest acquaintance. When John repeated the unhappy story of Elizabeth's family life, his mother sniffed.

'A young woman who has every advantage in life, and is yet displeased with her friends and relations, has most probably a discontented temperament, and would perhaps be unhappy and displeased in any situation. I hope that you will cease all thought of approaching this young woman. I have several other advantageous matches in mind for you.'

John decided to change the subject, and asked after his young nieces, Elinor and Anne. They were now seven and eight years old respectively, and were looking forward to joining the Duke's daughters for their lessons. The Princesses Mary and Anne were younger than Lady Rochester's grandchildren, but they agreed famously. Lady Rochester thought it would be a splendid opportunity for her charges to learn the ways of a court. Their fortunes were such that they could marry into the best families in the land. Now that her dear friend Sir Ralph Verney had negotiated a settlement with the law courts and had cleared up the unfortunate misunderstanding about their late grandfather Sir John Danvers having signed the late King's death warrant, the estates were safe and were to be divided between the girls. The State would have no claim upon their money.

John congratulated his mother on the successful outcome of her endeavours. She was indeed a good business woman. However, time was pressing, and he would have to leave: he had been promised an audience with the King.

* * *

Elizabeth went to the alcove that evening, partly out of curiosity – how would that experienced young man behave?, and partly out of daring – she could play with fire and not get burnt. But principally she went because she wanted to; she had felt the force of his attraction. She dressed with special care but had no premonition that this evening would see the end of her freedom. It was the last hour in which she possessed that enviable state, independence of mind.

Elizabeth had resided in London for three years and had often been at court. Although chaste and sensible, she was not entirely ignorant of the ways of young men. She had coolly doused the indisciplined ardours of Lord John Butler, she had skillfully avoided the fumbling hands of Sir Frances Popham (he being the suitor greatly favoured by her grandfather), and she had received a number of disappointing kisses from Lord Hinchingbrooke. Why a young man, to convince a woman of his passion, felt it necessary to hug her like a bear and practically knock her teeth into her mouth with his own, she really could not imagine. Surely love was a softer, gentler joy? When would she discover a man who shared her feelings? She had found men at close quarters very disappointing; perhaps Lord Rochester would be no different.

When Elizabeth slipped through the curtain later that evening, John was so amazed that for several minutes he could say nothing. Elizabeth stared at him apprehensively. The Banqueting House was empty as most of the court were attending a play. The vast room was lit by a single candelabra, but there was light enough to observe his astounded expression. She realised that he had not been sure of his conquest, and that she had hidden her feelings better than she had imagined. She was touched by his unexpected modesty.

When John found his voice, he was surprised at its strangled tone. 'I am so glad you have come.'

There was another lengthy silence. At last Elizabeth broke it, saying, 'You are not often at such loss for words. Have I struck you dumb?'

'Yes, dumb with awe – at your beauty and kindness,' he stammered. Elizabeth smiled at this unfamiliar lack of self-possession. He, taking courage from the kind look in her eyes, ventured to touch a curl at the side of her face. Feeling its silken texture, he was filled with delight.

'Yes, it is real,' he murmured. 'Is the rest of the goddess real as well?'

'Why don't you find out?' she said, lifting her mouth to his.

He was overcome by the warmth and perfume of her body and the nearness of her mouth. Yes, he thought inconsequently, it may turn down at the corners, but only a fool would care!

Elizabeth need not have doubted his reputation of success with women: John's kiss transported her to a melting state of bliss where tenderness and passion fused to produce a paradise. She recalled afterwards that he had held her with firm gentleness, that following that first kiss his searching lingering mouth had been telling her that she was infinitely precious and pleasant to be near. How long he held her in his arms she did not know.

John laid his cheek against hers; now that he had known her rapturous response, a feeling of great tenderness and elation spread through him. He wanted to hold and touch her, not only for his own pleasure, but to assure her of his love and regard.

To cover the depth of her emotion Elizabeth asked him lightly where he had learned to kiss so well.

'It is an inborn ability,' he murmured, 'improved and developed by practice in Italy.'

Elizabeth laughed. 'Did I not know of your self-mocking humour, what an unsufferable coxcomb that speech would make you!'

'But I have in truth an insufferable conceit,' said John. 'It is only the realisation of this truth which distinguishes me from the other fools who swarm about the town. I no longer labour under the delusion that I am perfect, modest and sinless.'

He put his hand about her neck, his long fingers stroking her perfumed skin. 'But I am an even greater fool than I thought. Why am I wasting this delightful opportunity in mere talk?' He found her mouth and knew his paradise again.

Elizabeth clung to him in rapture, and he, feeling her response, felt a new excitement engendered within him. He kissed her eyes, her ears and her hair saying, 'Oh my love, my love.' He whispered many tender and intimate endearments, and Elizabeth knew that her future was now committed, irretrievably, to him.

14

A Son, and A Betrothal

At the beginning of December Sarah gave birth to a male child. Mrs Cooke and Mrs Joyner assisted the midwife at the birth, which was protracted. The baby was perfectly formed but had some difficulty in breathing. After he was washed his breathing became more regular, and Mrs Cooke wrapped him securely in linen and wool and gave him to Sarah. He had his mother's blue eyes. Sarah and the babe were made much of by the two aunts. Sarah was exhausted but in a day or two she made a good recovery, and began to ask if John had been informed. They had not heard from him for over three weeks, though Sarah had not lost hope that he would visit, once he heard of the child's birth. She begged her aunt to send a message to Battersea House, so Mrs Joyner made a journey there the next morning. She asked to see Lord Rochester, but Sir Walter's porter said the young Lord had returned to London more than two weeks ago, to stay with a Mr Killigrew. He suggested that Mrs Joyner ask for him at the King's playhouse. He had heard that his lodgings were to be at the next door.

Mrs Joyner returned to the cottage, packed her bundle, and walked to Putney ferry. She called for a waterman to take her to Temple Stairs, but had to wait in the cold and sleet, as none of the watermen wished to travel that far with a single passenger. After an hour's wait the wherry was full and the journey was made, in the foulest of weather. By the time they arrived at the Temple, dusk was falling, so Mrs Joyner straightway decided to make for her lodgings and the warmth of a fire. She would call at the theatre early the following morning, and while there would ask if the company needed a fine washerwoman. She was determined that her journey would not be spent entirely upon her niece's business.

* * *

John and Killigrew, having spent the previous evening talking of politics, plays and lampoons, slept late the following morning. They were woken by a loud knocking at the outer door. John heard Harry's servant reply to a loud-voiced woman, 'Lord Rochester does indeed lodge here with Mr Killigrew, but he cannot be disturbed at present.'

Mrs Joyner was not to be fobbed off. 'Tell him I have a message of the greatest importance, and I must deliver it to him myself.'

Harry woke and yawned. 'Devil take the jade – she will wake the neighbourhood!' He shook John. 'Is she a bawd dunning for your money, or the washerwoman you were saying you needed?'

John raised himself, yawned, and wrapped a gown of Turkish silk about his slender body. He could not imagine what the commotion was about. He entered the day room.

'Well, woman, I am Lord Rochester. What is your business with me?'

Mrs Joyner looked at him critically. A handsome enough fellow – she could understand why a young chit like Sarah was taken with him. 'I have come to tell you that my niece Sarah has given birth to your son, a healthy babe, and that she would be glad to see you.'

John, surprised and half-asleep, nevertheless managed to gather his thoughts. He realised that he had not been to Putney for some weeks. 'Has Sarah been delivered before her time?'

'That I cannot say. I believe the child was expected in December.'

Harry appeared at the door laughing. 'So the young fish-god has made his appearance!' He came over and pushed John with his fist. He turned to Mrs Joyner. 'And how is little Sarah?'

'Well enough, but she keeps asking for my Lord, and will fret until she sees him.'

'Keen for another already, is she?' chuckled Harry.

John, irritated at his friend's jocularity, turned away and went over to the window. He was filled with remorse. Was it really three weeks since he had last been at Putney? Since his evening meeting with Elizabeth, life had been an exciting, exquisite, almost unbelievable dream. She had promised to marry him, but it would have to be without her step-father's or Lord Hawley's knowledge. Most of their time had been taken up with brief stolen meetings, and hectic arrangements with friends to make those meetings possible. He had forgotten all about Sarah, he realised, and now Sarah had born his child. He must go to see her, but it was going to be difficult to arrange.

Mrs Joyner cast sharp eyes about the room. It was furnished sparsely, and was disgustingly untidy: a pile of tumbled linen lay in one corner, a mound of books in another. Wine bottles, pewter mugs and dirty plates filled the table.

Harry yawned and addressed his man. 'For God's sake, Jenkins, get me some ale. I have a mouth like an ash-pit.'

'There is none in the house, Sir.'

'Then go out and buy some, before I give you a kick!'

Jenkins made hastily for the door and bawled from outside 'They won't give you credit, Mr Killigrew.'

'Get going, you blockhead, and tell them they will be paid tonight. I will have my ale, or 'twill be the worse for them – and for you.'

Harry turned to John. 'Will you be seeing Sarah?'

'I shall be at Whitehall most of the day. I have an audience with the King.' John addressed Mrs Joyner. 'Will you be returning to Putney? I wish to send Sarah a note.'

'I have a living to get,' Mrs Joyner sniffed, 'and cannot be junketing all day on the Thames, delivering notes. Cannot your man take one?'

'Perhaps.' He looked at her quizzically. 'What is your calling?'

'Washerwoman.' She looked about the room, fixing her eyes upon the pile of dirty linen. 'It looks as if you are in need of one here.'

John heaved a sigh of relief. 'You must have been sent by beneficent gods! You bring me good news of Sarah's safe delivery – and you wash clothes. Will you take me as a customer?'

Mrs Joyner nodded her assent, and John turned to Killigrew. 'Do you wish your shirts to go as well?'

'Yes, if the woman can wait a while for her money.' Killigrew shrugged. 'I cannot understand Jack, why you are always changing your shirt. I keep mine until it is really soiled.'

John grimaced. 'So I observe, and when you discard it Jenkins uses it as a dish-rag.'

Killigrew laughed harshly. 'Does he indeed? I must give the fellow a kick!'

Mrs Joyner sighed and gathered up the washing. She said it would be done within the week, and hurried away.

When Jenkins returned with a jug of ale, Killigrew took a deep draught, and asked if a clean shirt could be found in the house. When his manservant discovered a torn one Killigrew struck him: it should have been repaired in readiness for his use.

John was heartily relieved when Harry departed on a mysterious errand, in company with his man. Killigrew was evasive about his destination – that it was to do with a woman was all he would divulge.

John returned to the window and observed a crowd of players assembling outside the theatre door. They were gathering for the morning rehearsal: Sir Thomas Killigrew insisted upon prompt attendance. He must seek out Harry's father, with regard to a part for Sarah. It was now more than ever necessary to think of her future. Their affair was at an end, John knew, but he must aid her into a new and independent life.

He turned and looked at the disordered room with some disfavour. He was grateful to Harry for offering to share his lodging, but the arrangement was not proving suitable. The rooms were too small, and Harry's standard of behaviour was appalling. John longed for comfortable quarters in a civilised, well-ordered household, where he would be able to lodge a manservant of his own. When he had left for sea, two years ago, his uncle had agreed to employ his man at Battersea House. He had not yet had the opportunity to take Will back into his service.

He had become accustomed to shaving himself and caring

for his own clothes, but court attendance required higher standards of presentation. He felt the need of a valet this morning. He also needed a messenger; he would have to find a porter, and pay him to take a message to Putney.

John dressed with care, donning his new black and white suit. The King was pleased when courtiers followed the royal fashion. When he had completed his attire with a cloak and large feathered hat, he felt reasonably satisfied with his appearance. He went to the door and called for a chair. A group of chairmen could always be found gathered outside the King's Theatre. He was answered swiftly, and was soon upon his way to the Palace.

At the first Audience Chamber, he heard that Buckingham was in waiting, and sent in his name. His friend came to greet him and gave him advice on the King's disposition.

'He is damned tetchy this morning,' warned Buckingham. 'He had a lecture from Clarendon yesterday about extravagance. He is embarrassed at the lack of money to pay off the seamen, and is worried that there will be no money to equip a fleet next year. I got my head bitten off when I suggested that Lady Castlemaine should wait before he paid off her debts. It would appear I touched upon a raw nerve. Clarendon had drawn his attention to a list of "unworthy persons" who were petitioning the Exchequer for payment of their pensions and allowances.'

'I suppose Barbara was one, and I another,' said John with a laugh.

Buckingham smiled. 'I don't think your name was mentioned, but I doubt if you will get any further payments for some time.'

As he waited for his audience John reflected upon his financial affairs. He was thankful that he had persuaded Sir Robert Howard to honour his King's warrant during the previous week. He had lodged his money with Child the goldsmith, so that at least he would have enough money to see him through till Lady Day. His mother had promised him the rents from Adderbury, due in March, and by then he and Elizabeth would be wed. His mother did not know of his intended marriage. It was essential to keep their plans as secret as possible.

In spite of Buckingham's warning that the King was in a

dour mood, Charles seemed genuinely pleased to see young Lord Rochester. 'I hear you have important news for me. I observed a rapturous expression on Mistress Mallet's face last evening, and imagine you have had some success with her.'

'We are to be married, if we have your Majesty's approval.'

Charles beamed. 'That is capital news!'

He bore John much affection, and had been persistent in persuasions to Lord Hawley to allow Lord Rochester to renew his suit, thus far without success. Lord Hawley had excused his refusal, saying that negotiations had progressed so far with Sir Frances Popham that family honour would not allow the alliance to be dropped in favour of another suitor.

'So the family has relented?'

'No, Elizabeth cannot obtain their consent for me to visit, let alone to renew my suit. We shall have to marry secretly, and I have come to seek your Majesty's advice.'

'Mindful of the dire consequences of neglecting to seek it on a previous occasion,' murmured Charles. He turned, and went over to the window. After some minutes he beckoned John to him, and said softly, 'The marriage, when it takes place, must be witnessed by persons of such consequence that its validity could not be disputed at a later date. You will be married in the chapel here. I shall be present, and the Queen and three persons of known integrity will attend. You have the maid's consent, so the family will have to go whistle with their objections.'

John felt overcome with gratitude. His King was proving an indulgent guardian and very good friend. John outlined the difficulties Elizabeth was experiencing.

'Secrecy will be essential. If the family obtain an inkling of Elizabeth's promise to me, they will restrict her movements, and may even return her to Somerset.'

'I have no doubt of Mistress Mallet's discretion or of her ability for intrigue,' reassured the King. 'All will be well. Lord Clifford will inform you when arrangements have been made for the ceremony. It may take some weeks to bring it about, but I hope to see you married in January. Behave discreetly until then.'

Charles extended his hand for John to kiss, an indication that the interview was at an end. 'I have much business to

211

attend to this morning, otherwise I would have been happy to extend my time with you. Buckingham tells me you have some jape in mind for our entertainment at Christmas.'

John was a little irritated to hear that Buckingham had given advance notice of his intention. 'I trust his Grace has not given details, or the element of surprise will be lost, and my poor efforts to entertain your Majesty will be spoiled.'

Charles smiled indulgently. I know none of the details – and in any case your company is always pleasant to me, as was your father's. I hope to see more of you when your appointment to the Bedchamber can be effected.'

John expressed his thanks and withdrew, feeling happy that he had secured the King's approval, and that most of the problems associated with his proposed marriage were now likely to be resolved.

* * *

John made a visit to Putney the following week. Mrs Cooke handed him a heavily-wrapped bundle, saying, 'He will be a well-looking child. He has Sarah's blue eyes and your Lordship's dark hair.' She pulled back the covering from the child's head, revealing a luxuriant growth of hair. ''Tis unusual for a babe to have hair at birth, but your child is well-endowed. I hope his fortune will be so too.'

'I shall see that he is well provided for.' John looked at the sleeping scrap of humanity in his arms. He was glad that Sarah had been safely delivered, and that the child was healthy, but again he felt somehow detached from the events in which he found himself. No overwhelming sense of pride in paternity possessed him. It had been the joy and pleasure of Sarah's fair body that had attracted him. The engendering of a child had no doubt been the natural consequence of their coming together, but this small bundle seemed irrelevant to their relationship, and its raising would cause him unwelcome expense.

'Sarah is absolutely besotted with him,' said Mrs Cooke. 'The only thing which worries her is that he does not suck well. She has to express her milk, which puts her in some pain.'

212

'I am grieved to hear it,' said John. He was vaguely irritated with Mrs Cooke's volubility. 'Can I see Sarah now?' He handed his son back to her. 'Is the cradle I had delivered proving suitable?' Mrs Cooke nodded as they mounted the stairs to Sarah's bedroom.

'Well, here is your young Lord, come to see you,' she announced on entering the room. 'Better late than never, I suppose.'

John gave her a cold look before turning to Sarah. Her face was flushed, and he could see that she had been crying. He bent to kiss her, and took her hands in his. They were hot and clammy, although the room was cold.

'My dear, you do not look well, and should you not have a fire? The month is December, and the weather uncommonly severe.'

Mrs Cooke sniffed. 'The coals your Lordship ordered in October have been used. I have no money to buy more.'

Sarah burst into tears. 'Oh Aunt, do not spoil my Lord's visit with complaints. I wish to talk to him alone.'

John looked up. 'Pray tell Will, who is waiting below, to go to a coalman and order fresh supplies. Sarah and I have much to say to each other.'

Sarah looked at John gratefully and reached out her arms for the babe. Mrs Cooke looked doubtful, but decided to indulge Sarah's wish. 'Here he is, but he would be better off in his cradle. We don't want him waking, do we?' She patted Sarah's shoulder, gave John a cold look, and closed the door firmly behind her.

The two young people smiled at each other with relief. They looked down at the child sheltered in Sarah's arms. 'He is just like you,' Sarah said. John failed to see the resemblance, but said that he heard the babe had Sarah's blue eyes. 'The most beautiful eyes in the world,' he flattered.

Sarah acknowledged the compliment, but said she dare not wake the child in case he cried.

'Does he cry a great deal?'

'Oh, endlessly. He fails to get sufficient nourishment, because he will not suck readily. The midwife says that although my breasts are full they are not well shaped for feeding, and I am in such pain with the milk that I could wish to die.'

213

John felt embarrassed. 'Cannot a wet-nurse be obtained for the child, and medicines and bindings be obtained for you?'

'Oh, yes – if you have the money to pay for them. I should be so glad if that could be arranged. I do not wish my shape to become spoiled. I shall need all my attractions – to charm an audience when on stage.'

John laughed, 'And to please a protector after the performance!'

'I shall be in no mood to put myself in the way of bearing another child.'

'But is not that the hazard of love?'

'Aye, and one that the woman must endure.'

'I hear there are ways of avoiding conception. I shall find them out for you.'

'Find a way to make me well first.'

'I shall make arrangements for the Queen's physician to call upon you. You shall have the best of care.'

Sarah's eyes were filled with tears. 'Oh John, it is so good to have you near. Nothing feels so bad now, and you give me hope that all will be well in the future.'

John wondered uneasily what her words implied. Did she imagine that their affair would continue? She was of course unaware of his new commitment to Elizabeth. She would have to be told, but not yet. She was ill and tearful, and needed reassurance. Let her reconsider her future when she had regained her strength, and when the babe was off her hands.

John put his arms around her and the babe. 'Let me assure you that I shall do all in my power for your welfare and that of the child. Do not worry. You will be a great success on stage, and my son will be well educated and maintained until he can support himself. I shall not be able to visit you during the next few weeks, but do not lose your faith in my friendship.'

'I shall not lose my faith in you, but I wish you would come more often, to cheer me, and to make me laugh.'

John smiled. 'I must follow my fortunes at court, or we shall both suffer.' He took her face between his hands and kissed her, knowing it would be the last time he would do so. 'I shall write and will send presents to cheer you. Remember you will have more company when you return to town.'

Sarah wept at his going, but had to be satisfied with his answer.

* * *

A Song

1

To this Moment a Rebel, I throw down my Arms,
Great Love, at first sight of Olinda's bright Charms:
Made proud, and secure by such Forces as these,
You may now play the Tyrant as soon as you please.

2

When Innocence, Beauty, and Wit do conspire
To betray, and engage, and inflame my Desire;
Why should I decline what I cannot avoid?
And let pleasing Hope by base Fear be destroy'd?

3

Her innocence cannot contrive to undo me,
Her Beauty's inclin'd, or why shou'd it pursue me?
And Wit has to Pleasure been ever a Friend,
Then what room for Despair, since Delight is Love's End?

4

There can be no Danger in sweetness and youth,
Where Love is secur'd by Good Nature and Truth;
On her Beauty I'le gaze, and of Pleasure complain;
While ev'ry kind look adds a link to my Chain.

5

'Tis more to maintain, than it was to surprise;
But her Wit leads in Triumph the Slave of her Eyes;
I beheld, with the loss of my Freedom before,
But hearing, for ever must serve and adore.

6

Too bright is my Goddess, her Temple too weak:
Retire, Divine Image! I feel my Heart break,
Help, Love, I dissolve in a Rapture of Charms;
At the thought of those Joys I shou'd meet in her Arms.

215

John laid down his pen and gave a sigh of satisfaction. The poem he had been composing for Elizabeth was finished. It gave voice to his admiration and his appreciation of her understanding. Their thoughts and views blended admirably. She had been remarkably reasonable when told that he had been to see Sarah, who had borne him a child. Elizabeth had taken the news of his earlier association very coolly, saying she thought it inevitable that men of passion and feeling would have early love encounters. She agreed that the child would have to be suitably maintained and educated, but not in their own home. All that she asked of him was that he should cease communication with the mother. Surely, she had said, the matter of the child's maintenance could be dealt with by third parties? Besides it would be unseemly to visit, now that he was about to take a wife.

John and Elizabeth met every evening in Frances Stewart's apartments and enjoyed lengthy conversations about their future. He had told her of the King's kindness and promises of help. She would be informed of the marriage arrangements only hours before the ceremony. Elizabeth realised that she would have to forego the excitement of purchasing wedding garments. She would need to slip out of her mother's house unobtrusively and in the plainest of attire. Frances had agreed to be her bridesmaid and had promised to purchase blue ribbands to deck her dress. The Queen had promised that once the ceremony had taken place, the usual marriage revels would be celebrated in the royal apartments.

It was probable that the wedding ceremony would be performed as early as eight in the morning. The King's daily commitments needed to be considered, and the marriage would have to take place during canonical hours, no earlier than eight and no later than three. Elizabeth would therefore have to leave her home at a very early hour.

'I fear I shall come to you in little more than my night shift,' she had said to John.

'Then I shall think you well dressed,' he replied. 'You know I would take you upon any terms.'

'I fear my guardians will seek to deprive me of my property. Will you think then that your bargain was worthwhile?'

'Yes, of course. I am marrying you for love, not your fortune.'

'How will you maintain yourself and fulfil your commitments if you have not the use of my money?'

'I shall live on my pension and the salary obtained from my court appointments. The King has promised me several posts about his person. Adderbury will come to me eventually, provided I do not offend my mother, and even when your estates are secured, I swear I shall use them only for your welfare and the interests of our children.'

'I do not think we shall quarrel about money. I hope we shall live in Somerset, and that you will be my good steward and companion. I weary of this life at court.'

'We will live in the country if you wish it, but I shall need to be in town at the beginning of every quarter, to fulfil my duties to his Majesty.'

'You wish to come to town four times a year?'

'I shall need to. You may stay in the country if you choose. It would perhaps prove more economical. A man alone can take reasonably priced lodgings. Hiring a large house in town would be expensive.'

'I hear you are leaving your lodgings in Drury Lane.'

'Aye, the quarters are too cramped, and Harry and I do not share the same domestic expectations. I move to Chelsea next week and intend to hire two servants and a cook-maid. I have no doubt that my mother will agree to our living there, once she has recovered from the initial shock of our wedding.'

'I fear we wrong our mothers sorely, but there is no choice. If your mother refuses to receive us we will journey to my father's house in Somerset. I wish to administer the estates as I think fit. They have been sorely neglected, but with care they should yield a good income.'

'Cannot a steward do that for you?'

'Yes, but I wish to know how to care for my own.'

John smiled. 'You sound like my mother. May God spare me another such instructor!'

'You fear I shall have the maistry?'

'I know you will have the maistry,' teased John, 'but I shall disappear if you act the tyrant.'

'I should not like you to disappear.'

'Then you will be always my sweet mistress?'

'Always,' pledged Elizabeth, with the confidence and blissful ignorance of youth.

* * *

During the week before Christmas there was much activity in Mistress Stewart's chamber. The King became an assiduous visitor. The Queen had miscarried for the fourth time, and there was much talk that she could be divorced by Act of Parliament, and the King left free to marry a healthy young woman who would bear him an heir.

Lord Arlington advised Frances to admit the King to her bedchamber and allow him the liberties he desired. If she became pregnant it would provide evidence of her fertility. Had not Nan Bullen done as much in the reign of King Harry? Frances reacted indignantly, saying she had no intention of bringing a bastard child into the world, half-royal or not.

The King continued visiting her apartments, putting her under constant pressure with his lovemaking. One day he brought with him the artist Roettier. He told Frances that he wished her to sit as a model for Britannia. The design was to be used for a proposed peace medal.

The French were persuading the Dutch to make peace with England. Both sides were short of money and it was doubted if new fleets could be manned and equipped before the next fighting season commenced. Negotiations were in train to settle upon a place for the conciliation meeting. Places proposed by the English failed to please the French; those put forward by the Dutch failed to please the English.

Frances laughed. 'Roettier will have plenty of time to design his medal!'

Savile came to visit John at Chelsea and told him the news. Most of the wits in London were laughing at the new satire on the war – *Third Advice to a Painter to draw the Duke by*. Albemarle and Rupert were furiously seeking to find out the author. Savile told John that it was written by Andrew Marvell, but no-one had proof, and Marvell's friends wished to protect him from the retribution of the great.

Buckingham was raising questions in the House of Lords about the non-payment of the seamen's wages. Members of Parliament were asking why the money they had voted for the Navy had disappeared. The King was angry with Buckingham for making difficulties with his ministers. Buckingham had also quarrelled with Lord Dorchester in the House of Lords, and had exchanged punches with him within those solemn precincts. The King ordered their arrest and they were now imprisoned in the Tower.

'What is the trouble with Dorchester?' asked John. 'He is always losing his temper.'

'Dorchester's daughter, the Lady Ann Roos, has been accused of adultery and her husband is determined to divorce her. He is obtaining an Act of Parliament to do so. Buckingham is a relation of Roos, and Dorchester is supporting his daughter. They are both at enmity, and fall out on the least provocation. Bucks said Dorchester was leaning upon his elbow when they sat next each other in the Lords. Dorchester denied it and pulled Bucks' hair. Bucks punched him. Things went from bad to worse.'

'And are they like to spend Christmas in the Tower?'

'Yes, unless the King relents.'

'I fear 'twill be a dull Christmas with Bucks absent from court.'

'No hazard of a dull Christmas, when we know that your Lordship is to be present. How goes your disguise?'

'Well enough,' John laughed. 'You must call and see me wear it. My mother will be in attendance at court so we shall be undisturbed.

'I am glad to hear that you and your mother are now well agreed.'

'Aye, I saw her yesterday at St James's. She was about to visit Lady Denham, and deliver a present from the Duchess of York.'

'I hear Lady Denham is still indisposed.'

'Yes, her malady is something of a mystery. Doubtless ennui is at the root of her trouble: she has an old fellow for a husband, and the Duke of York for a lover!'

'A terrible fate for a bright young woman.'

'Limbo would scarcely be a place of greater dread,' laughed John.

* * *

On the twenty-fourth of December Sarah received a parcel of goods. It contained a fine silk gown, two pairs of best leather shoes, and a warm cloak and hood. There was also a brief note from John saying that he was in attendance at court over the Christmas season, and would be unable to visit. He was, however, arranging for Dr Shorter to call and advise on Sarah's health. A hamper of food would be delivered later that day. Mrs Cooke declared the hamper would be welcome. She was running out of money, although she tried to be as economical as possible. Thank heaven the babe was now beginning to suck vigorously, and the expense of a wet-nurse avoided. Sarah, too, was in better health, although bitterly disappointed at the absence of her lover.

Mrs Joyner arrived on Christmas morning to share their dinner. She had news from Mr Killigrew, who was proving a good customer. He was a merry fellow to be sure, she announced. Lord Rochester had moved to Chelsea and was now reconciled with his mother. Mr Killigrew was to visit Putney in a week or so and hear Sarah as Roxalana. His father, Sir Thomas, had agreed to see Sarah in the New Year. If she spoke her part well, there was a chance of her appearing in the next production of *Suleyman the Great*.

Mrs Joyner looked at Sarah hesitantly. She took a deep breath and continued in a determined tone. 'So child, you must learn your lines, and pull yourself together. Put the babe out to nurse, and get this doctor who is coming to bind up your breasts.'

Sarah, astonished at the sudden ordering of her life by other people, declared emphatically that she did not like Mr Killigrew and did not care to train for the stage under his direction. In any case, she could not leave her babe before he was properly weaned.

'You may not like it, but if you wish to become an actress

you must learn that you cannot pick and choose amongst the powerful, or name your own time. Sir Thomas is manager at the King's Theatre, and he is considering you for a part as a favour to my Lord Rochester.'

'Then why does not my Lord visit me and tell me of it himself?' Sarah cried indignantly. 'Surely he would not have me leave our child prematurely?'

Mrs Cooke and Mrs Joyner stared at each other sadly. They both turned to Sarah and started speaking at once.

'Theatre business takes time to arrange,' said Mrs Joyner briskly. 'The play is to be produced in March, and must be cast and rehearsed at least two months in advance.'

'You know,' said Mrs Cooke fretfully, 'that the lease of this cottage is up in April, and that you must have some means of supporting yourself by then. My income from dress-making will not keep us all.'

'But my Lord will help me,' said Sarah, bewildered.

'Aye, no doubt of that ... if he remembers,' said Mrs Joyner darkly. 'Any help we get from that quarter will be a bonus, but do not depend on it.'

'How can you say such things?' snapped Sarah angrily. 'You are always carping, and doubting him.'

'Well, 'tis but my nature, child' soothed Mrs Joyner, softening her tone. 'Put it down to that. I have seen too much of the ways of this hard world.'

Mrs Cooke changed the subject. 'We must remember it is Christmas, and enjoy the good things which have been sent to us. I have made mince pies with the nuts and raisins, and there is a fine ham for our dinner. Let us welcome the New Year and hope for better things to come.'

* * *

Two weeks passed before Harry Killigrew made his visit to Putney. He came with high hopes of gaining Sarah as a mistress. He anticipated that the wench would be more welcoming now. Of course, she was still hankering after Jack, but it was obvious that the affair was over. Rochester was much in the company of the heiress of late, and was exerting all his charm in that direction. It was understandable, Harry thought, when one considered the fortune the haughty minx would bring a husband. Jack had told him that Sarah would need a new protector, and had asked him to use his good offices with his father to obtain a part for her on stage. Killigrew was happy to do so, because he liked little Sarah. It might well prove to his advantage if she were to be indebted to his family. It would be pleasant to have a pliant young actress at his call...

Killigrew's young wife had died some two years ago. He had no wish to re-enter the married state, but a man had needs, and whores were proving expensive. Furthermore, it would suit admirably to have Sarah resident, next to the playhouse.

For the past three months Killigrew had been paying court to Lady Shrewsbury. De Grammont, the gambler and gossip, had implied that a man could get fine entertainment at Shrewsbury's house, but it was becoming obvious that the Frenchman was a trickster. After his last visit Harry had given up hope that Lady Shrewsbury would admit him to her bed-chamber. She was an arrant flirt and jilt, but seemed disinclined to betray her husband. She had put on a fine display of indignation when he had ventured a little liberty, but Killigrew sensed that he had been hoaxed.

There was some talk that Lord Shrewsbury suspected Bucks of paying too much attention to his wife, but Killigrew doubted if his Grace had much time to woo a woman of the calibre of her Ladyship. She demanded a great deal in the way of presents, verses, and languishing looks, yet had always a ready excuse when a man suggested a private meeting. In any event, Bucks was out of the way now. Although he had obtained his release from the Tower two days before Christmas, he had re-offended the King by appearing at court on Christmas day without tendering apologies for his misdemeanour. Charles had lost his temper and had banished him to his country estates. If it had not been for Jack's appearance as the Armenian astrologer, it would have been a very dull Christmas.

Killigrew reminisced on the change in his fortunes. The King had lifted his banishment, thanks to Jack's persuasions. Of

222

course, Lady Castlemaine had given him a sour look, but Charles was paying little attention to her of late. The Scots virgin was the ascendant star at the present time, and was putting a high price upon her maidenhead. There was even talk of Charles divorcing dull Catherine so that he might marry Mistress Stewart.

Mrs Cooke wanted to hear of events at court during the Christmas season. Killigrew happily obliged. The King had been delighted with Lord Rochester's impersonation of a mysterious astrologer. His Majesty had been completely hoaxed at first, but began to doubt the astrologer's answers when he had declared himself affianced to the daughter of the Great Cham of Tartary. Jack often referred to this imaginary ruler when fooling, and Charles remembered it. He looked about the company and demanded 'Where is the Earl of Rochester? I think he would welcome meeting this foreign sage.'

Of course, Progers declared that the Earl could not be found. Everyone laughed when the astrologer announced that if the candles were snuffed he would, by magical means known only to himself, produce the Earl in a trice. 'But it must be done in complete darkness, and the Earl, when he appears, must be offered a crystal glass of freshly-opened champagne.'

Charles had chuckled and had announced that once the magical delivery had been effected, all present would enjoy several bottles of the wine. It had turned into a very merry evening.

Mrs Cooke expressed herself pleased to hear the court news, but Sarah was cool. 'It would appear that my Lord is fully occupied as the King's jester. Pray tell me, what is his business today?'

'He is having a busy time of it, I can tell you. He is attending an autopsy at the Royal Society.'

'An autopsy?' said Sarah unbelievingly. 'Whatever next am I to be told!'

'Aye,' said Killigrew rattling on, quite unaware of the cynicism implicit in Sarah's remark. 'My Lady Denham died on the sixth of January, and the Earl's mother has been accused of poisoning her with chocolate.'

'Good heavens!' cried Mrs Cooke incredulously. 'Whoever

has brought such a charge?'

'The enemies of the Duchess of York,' Killigrew replied. 'They say Lady Rochester acted on the Duchess's behalf.'

'What nonsense!' Mrs Cooke spluttered indignantly. 'I know both ladies can be severe, but they are moral women and take Christian values seriously.'

Harry laughed. 'Well no-one really believes the rumour, but the town likes to see the mighty fall. Lady Rochester is secluded in her rooms at St James's, until the autopsy has been performed. Of course Jack, as his mother's representative, insisted on being present at the opening of the body. The lady's husband, who is the more likely suspect, insists that several of his Royal Society friends should attend. The autopsy is being held today, in the King's presence.'

'Good gracious, what terrible news you bring us, Mr Killigrew!' Mrs Cooke exclaimed. 'So his Lordship is reconciled with his mother?'

'Oh yes, some time ago.'

'He is certainly much occupied,' said Sarah. 'I am sorry to hear of his trouble.'

'Aye, and that is not his only concern. He has been endeavouring to get the court musicians paid. They are five years in arrears with their wages, and now, as an economy measure, the Court of Green Cloth has made a rule that they are no longer to eat with the King's servants, as their calling allows them to supplement their income with employment elsewhere.'

'How cruel,' said Mrs Cooke. 'No-one can be calling for entertainment in this bitter weather.'

'I agree – the poor wights are starving. Jack and I treated a party of them to dinner at a tavern last evening, but of course they need proper maintenance. The King's Welsh harper died last night. Jack says he will raise the matter with the Steward, Sir Winston Churchill, and if he fails to obtain relief for them, he will take the matter to the King himself. Of course, he will need to choose his time carefully. The King is damned tetchy, with this hullaballoo about the seamen. They marched up Whitehall last week, saying that they had lost their advocate, and would seek to free the Duke of Buckingham from the

Tower.'

'We heard that my Lord Albemarle was sent out with guards to disperse them.'

'Aye, he told them that the Duke had been released, and had gone into the country. They broke up, after some sharp encouragement from the guards. Dammit, we can't have such roughnecks invading the court!' Killigrew turned to Sarah.

'And how are you faring, my dear? Have you learned your part?'

'I have memorised some of it, but I do not wish to journey to London until my babe is weaned.'

'That will take some time, will it not?'

'Yes. I am hoping your father will agree to see me later in the summer.'

'Perhaps, if I ask him.'

'I am chary of asking favours of you, Mr Killigrew.'

'Why is that? Surely we are friends?'

'Friendship betwixt men and women is rare. The relationship is usually that of protector and servant.'

'I would wish to be both protector and servant to you.'

'You are kind, but it is too early to talk of my return to London.' She smiled at him, but her eyes were cold. 'Visit me again in April. We will talk of my future then.'

Killigrew tried to engage her in further conversation, but she said that her child needed attention, and left the room. Mrs Cooke tried to smooth matters, asking for more news of the town. She said she was shocked to hear that Prince Rupert was ill, and would have to be trepanned. Killigrew said that the Prince's suppurating wound had been caused by a blow to the head during the last battle with the Dutch. The scandal-mongers, however, considered that he was suffering from the pox. The only other news of note was that the young Duchess of Richmond had died.

Mrs Cooke sensed that her visitor was no longer interested in conversing, now that Sarah was gone. She therefore expressed herself much obliged to him for his visit, and said that she hoped he would excuse Sarah's coldness. It was obvious that Sarah was worried about her babe, but as soon as the child was off her hands she had no doubt that they would see a return of Sarah's old sprightliness.

Killigrew took his dismissal philosophically. Women were creatures of mood, he knew, and he had no doubt that time would bring the wench round to his way of thinking. With a child to care for, she had spoilt her chances of marriage with a fellow of her own station. She would need a succession of protectors – and he intended to be the next.

15

A wedding

By the third week in January the bitter weather had ceased, and bright sunlight was making the month unseasonably warm. John was at Chelsea in company with his mother when he received a message from Lord Clifford. His marriage was to take place in the Chapel Royal at Whitehall, early in the morning of the twenty-ninth. The King had consented to give the bride away, and the Duchess of Buckingham, who was one of the Queen's Ladies of the Bedchamber, had arranged to receive Mistress Mallet at Wallingford House. Although the Duke of Buckingham was in disgrace, his wife retained the confidence of the Queen, and she had been entrusted with arranging the details of the marriage. Thomas Sprat, the Duke of Buckingham's chaplain, had agreed to conduct the ceremony. His discretion could be relied upon. The bride would need to be informed of the time, and be told to contact the Duchess about the final arrangements.

John was full of these thoughts when his valet entered the parlour with word that a rough seaman was at the back gate, demanding to see his Lordship. The unwelcome interruption made him wonder at his ill fate: he was pursued by business when all his thoughts were diverted to getting his important message to Elizabeth. He had just evaded his mother's probing enquiries with a brusque reply that Lord Clifford had informed him that his attendance was required at court on the twenty-ninth of the month. Lady Rochester sighed, expressed herself pleased to hear that her son was so much in favour with the King, and said she would leave him to his business.

John, thankful that his mother had recovered from the shock of two weeks ago, was nevertheless finding it a strain to live in the same house with her. His respect for her was deep, and he had been outraged when she had been slandered and persecuted, but the Lady Denham drama was now passed. The Duchess of York had suggested that his mother should take a rest from her court duties for a month or so. The ordeal had brought them together, but he and his mother were falling into their old ways again. They both cared for each other, yet resented each other's disinclination towards real communication. The autopsy on Lady Denham had acquitted his mother of all involvement in the death. It appeared that Lady Denham had died of a growth in her stomach; no trace of poison had been found in the intestines. Strangely enough, the autopsy had also revealed that the lady was *virgo intacta*. It was evident that neither her husband, nor the Duke of York, had known her carnally. So much then for the gossip of the town!

The valet returned to the room. 'My Lord, the man says his name is Frank Jones, and that he wishes to see you on a matter of great importance.'

John raised his brow. 'I know the old fellow, but I cannot think what he wants with me. Pray bring him into the parlour.'

What had Frank Jones to tell him? He had surely not come to repay his debt? That would hardly rank as a matter of "great importance".

The old seaman was shown into the room. John's supercilious valet regarded him suspiciously. Frank Jones glanced at the valet with unconcealed contempt. The servant turned to John.

'Remember, my Lord, that your tailor is to call. I informed this fellow that he would have to be brief.'

John nodded to his man. 'Please leave us.'

He greeted the old sailor. 'Well, Frank, how are you, and what is this matter of importance?'

'I am well enough, my Lord, thanks to you. I have a comfortable lodge at Wapping, but it is not so well for others, especially Mr Heydon.'

'Heydon? Heydon the astrologer?' John laughed. 'What is the matter with him? Your friends have not kidnapped his boy again?'

'No, my Lord. The King's men came and took him away to the Tower two days ago.'

'Did they indeed?' John frowned. 'How surprising ... Upon what charge?'

'Treason, my Lord. They stripped his lodgings of papers and took those away. Some of our leaders have been arrested too, and are being questioned in the Tower. The Duke's enemies are looking for grounds to ruin him, and thought Mr Heydon would have incriminating letters.'

'Heydon!' scoffed John incredulously. 'Do they know the poor fool? He could not conduct a plot to save his life!'

'Mebbe not, but I have been sent here to ask you to convey a message to the Duke. He must not trust Richard Braithwaite – he is working for Lord Arlington. One of our number has discovered 'twas he who gave Lord Arlington the evidence to have Mr Heydon arrested – something about casting the King's horoscope, or similar such mumbo-jumbo.'

'The plot thickens... And where is Braithwaite now?'

'Employed by my Lord Arlington. I fear 'tis an ill time for my Lord Duke, or for any who fight for our cause.'

John frowned. 'Do any of your friends know that you have come to me?'

'No, my Lord, 'tis of my own will and judgement. You are a friend of the Duke's, and you have been a friend to me, so I thought you might wish to warn him, if you know of his whereabouts.'

'I thank you for your kind action. I am to see the Duchess of Buckingham today, and will tell her of your warning.' John took Frank's hand and pressed a crown into the palm. 'I am in some haste today, so our interview must end. Do not tell anyone of your visit here. Where do you lodge at Wapping?'

Frank gave him directions. 'If your Lordship intends to visit that way, wear plain clothes, and bring a strong man with you.'

John thanked him for his visit and dismissed him. As he looked through the window and watched the old man make his way towards the river, he reflected on the strange business of Heydon's arrest. The seamen's riots and high politics were becoming confusedly mixed. Lord Arlington was a dangerous man to offend. He would pass the warning to Buckingham, but he had no intention of taking up Heydon's cause. He was to be married in two days' time.

* * *

Elizabeth dressed herself carefully by the dim light of a lantern. Little had she thought on her arrival in London some four years ago that she would prepare for her wedding with so little ceremony! She had slept only fitfully during the night, sitting up and replenishing her fire with coals so that it would not go out. She had stolen a lantern from the kitchen on the previous evening. She lit it with a spill from the fire and prepared for her secret departure. It was a little before six in the morning, and she would have to hurry before the maids rose and went about their business.

She put on a fine silk shift, and then a petticoat and dress of grey satin. The shift was newly-purchased, and her mother had questioned her extravagance. 'Why do you need best French silk? You have been well content with linen until now.'

Elizabeth said she found the unseasonable warm weather trying and considered that silk would be cooler and lighter. Lady de Warr proved curious when she heard that her maid was altering Elizabeth's grey satin gown. 'You told me you did not care for it and were about to discard it.'

'Frances tells me grey is all the mode this season.'

Elizabeth hated deceiving her mother, but knew it would be fatal to her plan should it be discovered that she was preparing for her wedding. She moved silently about her room, finally donning a fur-lined cloak and hood. She had purchased it when the weather was cold. It was heavy to wear, but she would need a covering once she entered the dark street below. She picked up the lantern and gently lifted the latch of her chamber door.

She hesitated at the top of the stairs, listening for the porter's movements. She was hoping that she could slip out of the front door before the porter roused the servants for their day's work. If he saw her, he would be astonished, so she was hoping to slip out when his back was turned. She heard the watchman calling out six of the clock, so she grew anxious to be gone.

She peered over the balusters, shielding the lantern with her cloak. Luck was on her side! The porter had taken down the cross-bar from the front door and had placed the key in the lock. Elizabeth watched him yawn and scratch himself. He was stiff with dozing in his hooded chair. She watched him stagger towards the kitchen; once he had broken his fast he would be off to his bed. She moved silently down the stairs. She must escape before the major-domo came on duty. Holding her breath she turned the front door key, and blessed the servants for keeping it well oiled. She stepped onto the cobbles of Henrietta Street, easing the heavy door into place behind her. The household would be surprised to find the key turned, but she hoped the porter would not be blamed.

She looked up and down the street. Lady Buckingham had said she would be sending two of her servants with a chair. Pray heaven they were the figures standing on the other side of the road. It was dangerous for a young woman to stand alone in the street in the dark. Dawn would not break for another two hours. She held up her lantern and crossed the street boldly; it was best not to show fear. She discerned three figures standing in the shadows and saw that they had a chair. It bore the arms of the Duke of Buckingham. Thank heaven all was working out as arranged. She addressed the man at the fore.

'You are to take me to Wallingford House. The Duchess is expecting me.' The man nodded and assisted her into the chair. The journey was soon accomplished, and Elizabeth was greatly relieved to find the Duchess ready to receive her as she entered the Hall. She had dreaded encountering strange servants at such an early hour.

The Duchess hurried over to greet her. 'My dear child, I am so glad to see you here safely. It was a brave act to venture out into the darkness. Pray God grant that this marriage will prove a happy one. You have taken great risks to bring it about.'

'As long as my bridegroom loves me, all will be well.'

The Duchess smiled indulgently. 'He loves you well, and sends you this message on your wedding morn.' She handed her a note. 'Read this while I call my maid to provide us with hot chocolate. You will need to break your fast before venturing to Whitehall.'

Elizabeth opened the paper, and a second sheet fell to the ground. It was a set of verses. The accompanying note was brief;

Dear Mistress, I send you Dr Donne's Epithalamium. I hope you will share in its sentiments, as does your humble servant. Till we meet in better sheets than these, may the gods protect you. Your devoted servant, Rochester.

Elizabeth smiled fondly. It was so like him – clear, and to the point. She picked up the verses and started to read:

O Light of Heaven, today rise thou hot, bright and early, here shine, and this Bride to the Temple bring. Each verse bore the refrain – *Today put on perfection, and a woman's name.*

When the Duchess returned with her maid, they drank chocolate. The Duchess was obviously on edge.

'Wear this vizard mask until we reach my apartments at Whitehall. We must enter the Palace before daylight. No-one must see you before you are married. Did you tell your maid you were not to be disturbed before eight?'

'Yes, I acted as you advised.'

'I shall be more at ease when we arrive at the Queen's apartments.' The Duchess gave a sigh of relief when told that her coach was ready at the door. 'Frances Stewart will deck you for your wedding.'

'I rejoice that John and I have so many friends.'

'It is the King's will that this marriage should take place, but we love you and wish to see you happy for your own sake.'

When they reached Frances Stewart's apartments, the Duchess left to wait upon the Queen. Frances greeted Elizabeth with affection. They had been friends for four years, having arrived at the court during the same season.

Frances gossiped as she sewed blue ribbons to the shoulders and sleeves of Elizabeth's dress. 'The King has suggested that Lord Clifford and his Grace of Richmond should be Lord Rochester's groomsmen.'

'I hear that the Duke is a widower.'

'Yes, he has been in low spirits, and drinking deeply. The King thought today's activities might cheer him.'

Elizabeth looked concerned. 'But I thought my marriage was to be a well-kept secret?'

'The secret of your wedding is safe, have no fear. The Duke is a man of great discretion.' Frances changed the subject. 'The grey of your gown suits well with blue ribbands, and all is as it should be: something old – your grey dress, something new – your fine silk shift, something borrowed – my diamond neck-lace, and something blue – these ribbands given with my love.'

The maid threaded pearls through Elizabeth's hair, and tied her curls in bunches on either side of her face. She assured Elizabeth that this was the height of fashion at the French court. At eight o'clock they were ready for the marriage. When they reached the chapel door they found that the King, the Queen, and the Duchess of Buckingham were already there. The bridegroom and Lord Clifford were standing at the altar. Thomas Sprat met bride and bridesmaid at the door and ushered them to the King's side. After the necessary obeisances had been made, Charles smiled at Elizabeth and took her hand. They moved to the altar and he signalled to the chaplain to begin.

'Dearly beloved, we are gathered together here in the sight of God and in the face of this congregation, to join together this man and this woman in holy matrimony...'

Elizabeth raised her eyes to John's and was reassured as she met his admiring gaze.

By half past eight the ceremony had been completed, attended by witnesses of such consequence that the marriage could never be disputed.

'The bride must be bedded,' declared the King. 'The Duchess of Buckingham has agreed to put her lodgings at our disposal until the dinner hour of three. We will make our way there without delay.' He laughed and put his hand into his pocket, drawing out a great handful of rice. He handed some to the Queen, and laughing they threw it at the bridal couple before leading them back to the Queen's apartments. Wine and sweetmeats had been laid out for the bridal party, and the Queen's Maids of Honour were told that the Earl and Countess of Rochester had just been married.

There was now no need for secrecy. 'In fact,' said the King, 'the more people who are told of this morning's work, the better.'

He turned to John. ''Tis but a light repast, but no doubt you have other feasts in mind. He took John's arm. 'To your work, boy. This marriage, to be indissoluble, must be consummated without delay.'

John and Elizabeth looked at each other dumbfoundedly. John turned to the King. 'You would hurry me to my bridal bed, Sire?'

'And so I should. Once the bride has been bedded, her step-father will have no grounds upon which to dispute the marriage.'

John and Elizabeth turned to each other and laughed.

'I had not bargained for a public coupling' said Elizabeth blushing.

John turned to the King. 'Sire, I once saw a performing bear at Oxford. We students had obtained a female bear to pleasure him, but whilst they were observed, the bear would not approach his mate.'

The King laughed. 'The point of your story has been taken, but we will see you installed in the bridal bed before we take our departure. The stockings must be thrown. I hope that Frances, who is the only unmarried person present, will find a lover before the year is out.'

Frances refused to meet the King's eyes, preferring instead to pelt the bridal couple with comfits. She turned to the Queen.

'With your permission, your Majesty, I will accompany the bride to the Duchess's apartments and will prepare her for the marriage bed.'

The Queen nodded, saying she and the Duchess would join them when all was ready. There was much gaiety and cheering.

The Maids of Honour threw ribbons around John and bound him tightly. They delivered the reins to the King saying, 'Here is a prisoner. He can be released only by love. Take him to the Temple of the Goddess, and prepare him well for his duties.'

John was led away by the King, Lord Clifford and the Duke of Richmond. He was undressed in an antechamber, where all had been prepared for his reception. After cracking many ribald jokes, the King wrapped a fine silk gown about John's body saying it was a bridal gift, and remarking that it would be the last time he would seek to cover the nakedness of his fortune. He would now be well provided for. When they received the message that the bride was ready, the groomsmen conducted John to the bridal chamber. His hands were placed in Elizabeth's and they were settled into the bridal bed. The attendant ladies sat on Elizabeth's side, the King and the groomsmen on the other. The Queen snatched Elizabeth's stocking from Frances and threw it over her shoulder; it hit the King. The King threw John's stocking and it hit his wife.

Queen Catherine gave a rueful smile. 'It seems I am beloved of my husband – a happy state for any wife, and especially so for a Queen.'

The King smiled indulgently, but looked across the bed at Frances. 'No lover for you during the coming year, unless you attend another wedding.'

Frances cried out, 'It is time for the love posset! I will fetch it from the antechamber.'

The potion was duly brought, and the company watched the bridal pair self-consciously drink it. Then Frances drew the bed curtains, and the merry party took their leave.

'You have six hours, boy,' called the King as he closed the door. 'Do your work thoroughly.'

John turned to Elizabeth. They were alone at last. It was by now half-past nine in the morning and the brilliant winter sun was beginning to stream through the bed-curtains.

John took his bride into his arms. 'Do you know Dr Donne's poem *To the Sun Rising*?'

'No,' said Elizabeth, 'but your ancient poet is a powerful advocate of the joys of love. He has convinced me that today I shall attain perfection.'

'And gain a woman's name,' murmured John as he kissed her long and tenderly, and loosened the silken ribbons of her shift.

* * *

An age in her embraces passed
Would seem a winter's day
Where life and light, with envious haste
Are torn and snatched away.

Six hours passed all too swiftly and at three o'clock there came a knock upon the door. The sweet sound of flutes and viols invaded the ears of the newly married couple. John put on his robe and opened the door. The King was standing on the threshold with a fine silver cup in his hand.

'Refreshment for the lovers!' he announced heartily as he strode into the room. He parted the bed curtains. 'Has the young cub pleased you, Bess?'

Elizabeth, disconcerted and embarrassed, pulled a sheet over her head.

'The bride seeks to hide her blushes,' laughed the King. Frances, who had followed the King closely, ran in and knelt by the side of the bed. She gently pulled at the sheet. 'Pass off this intrusion with a joke,' she whispered. 'I have a wrap here to put about your shoulders.'

Elizabeth, hearing her friend's voice and realising she would be shielded from onlookers, quickly recovered her worldly assurance. She smiled at the King and reached for the proffered drink.

'He has pleased me so well that I rejoice to see a cooling draught. I am afire with love and contentment.'

'You hear that, John? You have a fine wife!' declared the King. 'Has she proved herself bonny in bed?'

'Delectably so,' murmured John, smiling reassuringly at his wife. He returned to the bed and took her hand.

The King was in jovial mood. 'Then let us observe her conduct at board. We hope that it will equal her other attractions. Cheerfulness at meals is essential for good digestion.' The King beckoned his attendants and a host of ladies and courtiers entered the room bearing trays of food and wine.

The King turned to the company. 'Lord and Lady Rochester were married this morning and we have come to congratulate them upon their nuptials. You have heard the bride declare herself well contented. Let us therefore offer them refreshment, for they have had much exercise!'

John decided it would be politic to put a good face upon this public invasion of his bedchamber. The King meant well and his action had a genuine purpose: that no-one might later be able deny the validity of the marriage which had taken place in the royal presence.

When he reflected upon his circumstances, a flood of happiness invaded his being. John smiled at his beautiful wife. He was indeed the most fortunate of men.

THE END

EPILOGUE

Five days after the wedding, Mr Samuel Pepys of the Navy Office attended a performance of *Heraclius* at the Duke's Theatre. He thought it a fine play and well done. His wife enjoyed viewing the company and noting the new fashions amongst the ladies of quality. He wrote an account of the evening in his diary:

The house was very full, with great company. Here I saw my Lord Rochester and his lady Mistress Mallet, who hath after all this ado married him; and, as I hear some say in the pit, it is a great act of charity for he hath no estate.

A month later, the dowager Countess of Rochester requested her old friend Sir Ralph Verney to act as one of the negotiators in the settlement of the Mallet estates. 'The King, I thank God, is very well satisfied with the marriage, and they had his consent when they did it, but now we are in some care to get the estate. The de Warrs are come to desire parties with friends, but I want a knowing friend in the business, such a one as Sir Ralph Verney.'

Sir Ralph did his work well. Elizabeth and John were reconciled with her family a year later.

In due course Elizabeth produced an heir to inherit the family estates. She also gave birth to three daughters, all famed for their beauty in their own time. In spite of many stresses and tribulations the marriage remained strong, but ended in early death.

Elizabeth lived in the country, John in the town. He joined

his wife during the summer months, but became notorious for his drunken exploits at court. He died of syphilis thirteen years after the marriage, at the early age of thirty-three. Bishop Burnet effected the Earl's death-bed conversion and later wrote an account of his life, which included a detailed account of their discussions of religion. His Grace stated that the Earl's wife expressed a most passionate concern for her husband when he lay dying. She herself died a year later.

Many years afterwards, the Comte de Grammont recalled life at the court of King Charles the Second, and dictated his memoirs to his brother-in-law, Count Anthony Hamilton. He described Elizabeth as *une triste héritière*. Whether he considered her unhappy in that it was her fate to marry Rochester, or whether he shared the dowager Lady Rochester's opinion that her daughter-in-law had a naturally melancholy disposition, is not altogether clear.

De Grammont comments on Rochester's interest in actresses and the theatre. He states that Sarah Cooke became 'the prettiest but worst actress in the kingdom'. It is recorded that she read the Epilogue to Rochester's play *Valentinian* when it was produced at the Duke's Theatre four years after his death.

Rochester became noted for his satiric wit and his poetry. Drunkenness and sexual excess darkened his later life and reputation, but he had many friends. Even John Dryden, who is said to have suffered at his hands, would pass no opinion upon his varied and scandalous career. King Charles's poet laureate, on hearing of the Earl's death, said 'My Lord Rochester was a nobleman whose ashes I will not disturb.'

Perhaps a fitting statement with which to end this story of the brilliant beginnings of Lord Rochester's career.